Silver's Threads

Book 1

Silver's Threads

Book 1

Spinning Colours Darkly

Penny Reilly

ISBN 13: 978-0-9924759-0-1

Silver's Threads
© 2012 by Penny Reilly

Cover and interior design by Penny Reilly
Cover Art 'I Think I Saw a Fairy', by Josephine Wall
Self-Published by Penny Reilly, 'the readers' Pty Limited
Project Editor Penny Reilly

Printed in Australia

Revised 29/05/2014

Acknowledgements

My gratitude and my thanks go to my beloved husband David for his patience through the long process of creating this book and in advance for those to come. To all my close friends who have supported the pre-birthing stages Rhys, Sonya, Errol, Leigh and Cathy, who read some of these pages as they grew and to my wonderful friends at 'The Reading/Writing Coven.' especially Kim Faulks, Carole Lane, Aynia Breeze, Stacey Macintosh, Joanne Stucken and Luke West, all talented writers in their own right. A special thanks to the quiet followers of my Facebook and blog pages. Last but not least, to Alison Kenney for all her help in the process of making a transaction with Josephine possible.

Special Acknowledgement

The extraordinary artwork on the cover of this book, 'I Think I Saw a Fairy,' is by the very talented, Josephine Wall …her work has inspired me and thanks to this, I feel I could write a story for each of her paintings.

Please visit Josephine Wall on …her Facebook page…

www.facebook.com/TheOfficialJosephineWall

…support the artist, visit her Gallery and buy her beautiful art at www.josephinewall.co.uk

My thanks go to Wordzworth for their technical help and to the team at Ingram Sparks for their continued support.

Dedication

*I dedicate this book to my ever-present
...but never silent muse ...Silver*

Contents

Spinning Colours Darkly

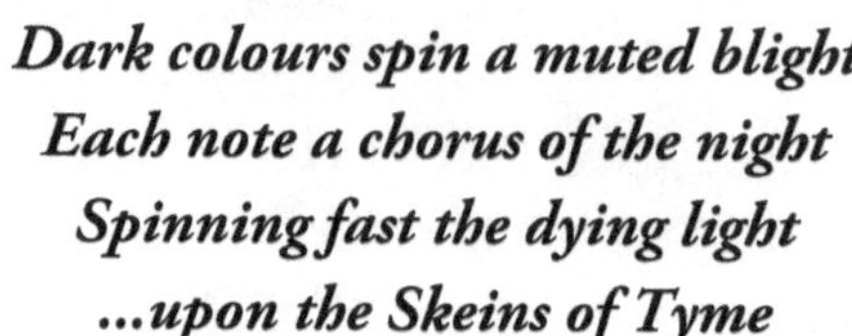

Dark colours spin a muted blight
Each note a chorus of the night
Spinning fast the dying light
...upon the Skeins of Tyme

We did not fall descent was slow
On gossamer wings in ebb and flow
We came, a planet's seeds to sow
...upon the Skeins of Tyme

But then in sleep we tumbled 'til
The darkness every thread did fill
Humanity birthed, forsook Her will
...upon the Skeins of Tyme

Webs are woven by intent
Spiraling out the weave is bent
Earthly tides are almost spent
...upon the Skeins of Tyme

Arianwen Isil'Lindir & Aithlin Farandir
From Skeins of Tyme

Prologue

Merry Meet, I am the one known as Silver. I am the one who will be whispering in your ear as I share a story of mystery and magicks of which you may be unaware. I will be there as you turn these pages, leaning over your shoulder as you read. You may not know I am there but then you may feel my breath upon your cheek, although told this is very rude.

I observe your body language change; your facial expressions give so much away. Mirth ...scorn ...doubt ...fear! It's really all the same to me for after all you're the one choosing to read this book - which indeed, has been long in the cauldron of creation. I have coaxed and cajoled Sybille into putting pen to paper or fingers to keyboard but here 'tis and together we will tell you our story of discovery for we are one in truth.

So let us begin in the beginning; for that is where I assume we must in order not to confuse, as I am often wont to do in my ramblings!

I am my humankin Sybille' Trueshape. I am her continuing self after the Littleshapes fall away into physical decay - like feathers falling from a bird's wing or petals from a flower. I say physical with good reason for the Littleshapes journey on unless they doubt and then, I too shall diminish a little.'

Chapter 1
Sybille

The wheel turns on. Trees whisper secrets and birds leave messages on the wind. Nothing remains the same and yet in change we find renewal.
Extract Sybille's Book of Shadows.

Pulling her journal from its little hidden cavity in her desk, Sybille sat down to write brooding as she did on the changes she sensed were afoot. Little things that for others perhaps might go unnoticed she knew through experience were the prelude to significant shifts. She dreamed of flying to other realms where flickering figures who threw no shadow, stalked her. At times, she felt overwhelmed by the feeling of wobbling off course. This in itself gave her the sense that she would not have enough energy to create space or physical time to complete unfinished things or to share the knowledge gained in a lifetime ...yet alone five or six.

A great urgency overcame her; with a weary sigh, she began to write yet paused as she considered the four women who embraced the Mother's Way, albeit hard for Maeve, who struggled with the oldest fear that Magick might indeed be real. Flora and Bethan she had no fears for other than their both being sensitives, empathetic to everyone else's pain. Then there was Sam! Well, that must unfold as she worked through what she thought were fair or unfair advantages in life. They would all need to consider what it truly meant to be a Wytch. For what is a Wytch anyway? Picking up her pen, she continued writing...

So now, my affairs are in order. The Wytchwheel turns and I know I will be moving on soon. I never know when, only my Trueshape Silver does and I inevitably, will be the last to know. I have not yet found the words to share with my girls why but at least they have come far enough along the Way to follow in part ...the rest I must leave in the Mother's hands.

Stretching, she put her journal aside and reaching over gave her cat Morgana a scratch behind the ear, which was greeted with a deep rumbling purr of contentment. Morgana opened her eyes; she looked into Sybille's face and 'knew,' her human friend would be leaving her behind. How long would it be this time?

'Mmmm, not long now,' Sybille said to her. 'I can feel a stirring in the ethers I've not felt before.' She gripped the arms of the chair, willing herself to stay present and reached for pen and parchment to write a letter to each of her friends before the energies pulling at her had their way.

My dear Flora, you are the one I sense will learn to understand what I am about to tell you. I must go and I do not know when I will be back yet...

...she continued to write for a few minutes and then finished with...

I leave a small note for each of you along with further instructions until my return, if that is to be, with the hope that this won't be too big a burden for you all...

...she trailed off unable to continue, feeling the earth shift beneath her a breeze touched her cheek; she smiled. With a fondness, she thought again of the three young women she had trained in the Mysteries of the Way. She had always been clear about her methods of training, which underscored the experiential over the documented and had taught them to work on the emotional levels to balance their weaknesses and strengths, perfecting their skills through self-understanding and responsibility.

Becoming a true Wytch took courage. The world of the Wytch is a constant circle of change requiring discipline and trust, no two cycles ever being the same. Stepping out of the broom closet can become a trap; with the need to wear the right clothes, an enigmatic smile and a patchouli perfumed air of mystery.

A letting go and emptying out of old agendas was imperative in order to fill themselves anew with the concepts of what True Magick is. She, well- schooled in all the Traditions of the Craft, knew the pitfalls of coming to the Way with illusions of grandeur and the belief that Wands were all in a flick of the wrist and the right incantation spoken, rather than the science that Magick was in part.

There had been many promising students through the years but none as gifted as these.

Recovering herself, she sat to write in her new Book of Shadows and Light. Her old book filled to bursting with all the information she used in her teachings, which was a living, organic testimonial to a Wytch's life. She was particular about her writing, so that there could be no doubt as to what she was imparting, there being no room for error in Magickal workings. Too much of the Wytchways had already been lost from the past, through poor translations or worse, a deliberate need by some to control others. The latter had created a hierarchical order to the Way, which was now becoming its own downfall. She sighed, bringing herself back to her task; she reached for a piece of paper for a first draft, before entering in the Book itself...

A year for the Wytch begins at Samhain, pronounced Soween or Sowan ...30th April to May 2nd in modern day reckoning, here in the Southern Hemisphere of this beautiful planet. The last Harvest, root vegetables, Pumpkins and Squash.

The feelings in the air are of deep relief after the hard work of the active seasons. The following months are for introspection tempered with grief as the Lord and Lady leave to take the hands of all the souls who have passed beyond or of those who may have been lost in the 'Between.' They will accompany them through the gates of the Summer-country ...the lands of peace and beauty, only imagined and for some onwards still, to discover their Trueshape.

The real reasons for the gathering at Samhain has nothing to do with 'trick or treat' or dressing up as ghosts and vampires. This is the miss-information passed around through superstition. It is a result of fear of the unknown.

In truth, the three-day festival of Samhain is Celtic New Year and All Hallows Eve, when all over the planet we honour the spirit of our ancestors and ancestry. We make offerings, give thanks for the year given and ask for blessings for those who have died to this world that they may be renewed. The origins of the Pumpkin carvings were to ward away the spirits that were lost or were of negative intent, that they might follow the light from the Altar candles and through the gateway to the world of spirit, the Otherworld.

What does all this mean I hear you say? What is this talk of Wytches and Magickal lands? What is a Wytch in truth? So I'll tell you as simply as I may because just as we are approaching Samhain, so is this a new beginning for all who are tired of the tick tock world of illusion and hierarchical ordering.

Eons ago, long before there was the written word, there was knowledge free to all those who asked the right questions. There were no elite; only those who had listened to the inner voice of the Mother longer. This was a time long before there were names and titles, a time when all who knew of the Lady's Way were known as the Wise Ones, the Wytchwise, male and female alike, all Her priests and priestesses, all Her people and Her tribes.

Pausing, she felt Silver's presence close and knew her journey would be changing soon as she whispered to her in the strange language of the spirit...

She felt Silver withdraw again, restlessly now. She looked down in wonder at the page filled in Silver's hand, so unlike her own. She wondered what the girls would make of it when they saw the writing in two entirely different styles. She smiled wryly and continued...

Therefore, at Samhain I honour the ancestors. As a modern day Wytch, I honour the energy that lives within my cells and of every being that has ever lived and is still living on this planet. As I was taught, all who have been, are and will be, are still here sharing space with me, breathing with me ...everything is here ...now...

...and then the world suddenly shifted sideways and spun. She felt herself falling, drifting, afloat in depths of wonder; no pain or physical sensations just peace, ultimate peace and the sound of bell like voices calling ...*'Gela en'ardai, gela en'ardai.'*

Then she was falling further still, a small pinpoint of life, a tiny being of light with fragile wings closed behind her ...arrowing down toward a faintly glowing, molten mass. As she flew and dived, many others accompanied her. Small, winged entities screamed with sheer, childlike glee, *'We've come to sow the seeds of a planet!'*

She was flying with her kin through the ethers, seeing for the first time the glowing orb that would become the earth covered in tiny lightening bugs, little Makersouls with split wings; iridescent beings, clinging limpet-like to the cooling, solidifying mass that they might begin the planet's greening.

Then there was absolute silence and she fell inward.

Chapter 2
Samantha

Falling leaves gather like floating gold,
...soft scents of wood smoke recall times of old.
Where will you be, when the winds set you free?
...safe in your bed or outside in the cold
From Season's Change by Arianwen Isil'Lindir

Samantha woke to a strong foreboding of change, of something not quite right. The memory of her dreams still fresh and she needed to record them, while they remained vibrant.

All her life, dreaming, had been a rich tapestry of colour and movement. Lingering sounds of crystal-clear voices and aromas of something sweet and warm, like vanilla bean or violets, filling her senses.

Now, suddenly her dream memory was crowded with rasping sounds, clicks and guttural voices; her senses filled with the pungent aroma of damp, loamy leaves and woody lichen. Stretching, Sam rolled onto her back; something crunched beneath her, something crisp and dry. Sitting up, she ran her fingers across the sheets to find the cause of the scratchy, discomfort ...leaves, dead, amber leaves; in fact oak leaves ...how on earth?

The thought trailed off, her attentions caught by the state of her desk, in her writing room directly across the way and shoot the mess! Articles, books, OH NO, her journals, scattered everywhere; her desk a chaotic, disorder that was not of her making. Who would ...who, had done this? Her fresh ink sketches, which had so delighted her yesterday, were gone. They'd come from her dreams and were different to anything she'd created before, as were the new notes for the never discussed and carefully hidden away fantasy novel.

Leaping out of bed, she raced across the hall, leaves crunching underfoot, 'Wait a minute ...leaves?' she shrieked as she saw yet more, strewn in a trail, from bed to desk. 'What in the name of...'

From where had they come? Sam tried to remember whether she'd left some on her desk in a vase and if she'd left the window open. She often brought bits and pieces home, found on her walks, bits of bark, dried leaves or lovely stones, anything that took her eye. Quickly scanning the closed windows; no entry made that way!

'Mmmm what's going on?' she huffed, scrubbing her face with her hands, 'I can't make any sense of this?'

Taking a closer look, she saw that her article for work was sitting untouched on the desk amidst the other chaos. She had a deadline for the paper she worked for and at least, heaving a sigh of relief, that was intact.

'Ok, Sam don't panic,' she said aloud, 'first you need a potent brew before you can even think of sorting this out'; so saying she went to the kitchen.

Her head buzzed with thoughts. What, on earth, had happened? Had someone broken in while she slept?

Her hands worked automatically as she set up the coffee machine for the brew, craving the caffeine to clear her head.

Drawn back to the chaos again, taking a cup with her, she reviewed the damage. Carefully putting the cup down out of reach of her papers, she stood looking at what had been her notes and what remained of her journals. On one page, there was a doodle; a small Fae figure pulled together from fragments of her dreams. It had changed, had taken on a life of its own in fact, the facial structure clearer; the intricate drapery resembling clothing was more detailed, consisting of almost web-like, gossamer threads. The finely traced silver and russet leaves of organic fibres had previously escaped her pen; nevertheless, here they were on paper. Had she drawn this and forgotten? No! She couldn't possibly have done it and not remembered, surely? The angle of the head and the candid gaze, frozen in an expression of surprise and fear, gave her pause to think it was somehow familiar. How had anyone been able to get in and do this without her hearing, her sleep had been so light of late?

Shaking herself, she replaced the sketch on the desk and looked around in utter frustration. Automatically she reached for the phone to call Sybille, her Aunt. Stopping herself, she remembered again with deep sadness; her Aunt had disappeared without a trace, leaving only a note of instruction as to what to do with her property and possessions. Her going, so unexpectedly had left Sam bereft and with no understanding of why or where she may have gone. Her note hadn't even been addressed to her but rather to one of her students, Flora, who'd always been the one to look after Sybille's home when she was away giving her talks and signing books for eager fans. Her insightful writings, on Wytchcraft and the Occult, were enormously successful.

Sam consciously pulled back from the edge of despair. She thought about the loss of a woman who had cared for her and kept her steady, after her parents unexpected death. They had died on one of their many spiritual pilgrimages, when she was not quite 18; Sam realised that her thoughts had led her back to this, probably decisive, moment. Today she may find out where her Aunt had gone and why. Today was the year and a day since her disappearance. Sybille had prescribed this be the day, when Sam would meet with Flora and the two other women Bethan and Maeve, who had been Sybille's top students and closest friends, should she not return in that time.

Sam still felt somewhat resentful the note, wasn't addressed to her. That it had not been her, entrusted with the key to the amazing restored barn, where she had spent so many intriguing hours with her Aunt over the years. Sybille had been her anchor, when as a misunderstood and moody child, her parents had sent her to stay with her during their long, (and boring) journeys, searching for their own personal grail, whatever that may have been, for eventually it had killed them.

Her frustration at not being able to express herself fully to her parents, for they brooked no argument, led Sam to start writing a journal from an early age, describing all her deep and intimate beliefs. Her love and understanding of words had her dreaming of becoming a writer. Children's books she'd thought as she was also clever with fantasy art but as always she talked herself out of her own dream.

Even as a child, she'd had a way with words; it had brought her trouble, more than once. She'd had an enquiring mind and always posed questions, sometimes with great frustration when adults, teachers especially, whom she in childlike naivety presumed to have all the answers, couldn't or wouldn't, answer all her deeply searching question.

Her very strict and rigidly dogmatic parents had never allowed her room to debate her views that deity was not a far removed or judgemental patriarch, angry and unforgiving as their scriptures depicted. Samantha knew that her version was a smiling and benevolent being who watched over her and the planet with tolerance and patience.

Sybille had been the guiding light, supporting her in her understandings and encouraging her to be strong and direct. To never settle for someone else's ideas for her and had also given her, ever so subtly and gently, a whole new viewing point of the world as an amazing, evolving being and the Goddess as well as the God, approachable, rather than a separate or distant entity. Tentatively Sam had listened and in part begun to understand why her Aunt Sybille had always been so different to her sister, Sam's mother, Anne.

'Sybille,' she remembered, her parents had spoken in whispers, 'is a Pagan, a Wytch!' and yet they had given the guardianship of their own daughter in her care.

The deeply ingrained conditioning by her parents had seriously limited her ability to believe in herself, so off she went to Uni as a 'good girl' should, with her parent's intention that she studied law.

Her intellect, strong enough to achieve high marks, only left her with a sense of outrage when she discovered that the laws were only about the person who could manipulate them to the highest advantage. It was purely about winning ...whether the accused was actually guilty or innocent did not count much in the equation apparently!

The first two years were torture, so she had somehow, plucked up the courage to change stream midway. She started a course in journalism and entered a different world. She'd told her parents it would lead to writing and analysing court cases and the wheeling and dealing behind the scenes. Again, what she found, behind the masks of bargaining for the good of the victim of any crime, rested in the hands of the cleverest person who could twist the law to suit.

She'd felt guilty about her subterfuge; still her love of the written word and her drawing drove her. She completed her journalism courses together with creative writing, and an illustrating course, which she'd told herself was just for fun. She'd continued to send articles to the more progressive, magazines and papers and had finally landed on her feet, due to the excellence of her word style, in a small, edgy newspaper. Now, at 25 and three years on the job, she was their youngest, lead author.

Today, now, she realised, glancing at the clock, it was time to get ready for that long awaited meeting with Flora, Bethan and Maeve, her Aunt's one time students of philosophy and closest friends, despite the difference in age.

Washed and tidied, she stuck her tongue out as she caught her slender, reflection in the hall mirror, black choppy hair sticking out every, which way, due to her constant habit of grabbing handfuls, whenever she was thinking deeply. Leaving the mess behind her, she grabbed keys and bag on the way out, then hesitated, hearing a rustle of leaves and the faint haunting sound of words on the wind,

'Gela en'ardai, gela en'ardai,' as soft and as fragile as a wraith caught in the wind as musical as a glass wind chime,

'No,' she said. 'No, I'm not listening. Go away!'

Shrugging off the chill as the sun disappeared behind the scudding clouds, she almost ran to her car, her thoughts whirling; there was that feeling again that she should know something, understand something forgotten.

Chapter 3
Flora

Bend gently, do not weep,
Dig your roots in deep
Learn to dance and sway
Then the higher you can reach
Without floating away
From Grounding by Arianwen Isil'Lindir

In Sybille's home in the hills, Flora awoke electrified, her already wild, brown hair on end as if full of static. Rain beat a tattoo on the roof and her heart, thumping erratically, returned her in a rush to a waking state. Woozy, flesh goose bumped stomach churning; she sat up and starting to roll out of bed hit her head on the corner of the night table. This took her rapidly to full consciousness and to the words that were repeating, a litany, in her mind,

'Hmm, birds?' She said, aloud to the room.

As she sat on the edge of the bed, her mind still reeling with the remnants of a dream; a single black feather floated down in front of her eyes to land on her bare toes.

'Birds?' she repeated, picking up the feather gingerly as if it were something hot... 'What the?'

With this, she recalled strange-feathered beings, the sounds of wild, untamed music that had filled her ...haunting and evocative. There was a quiet presence a lady, tall and seemingly sedate yet she smiled gently at the antics of the strange beings, then turning had looked at her and she had felt the gaze penetrate to her very soul. Something was sliding into the dark recesses of her mind, unreachable. No images were available to explain her churning emotions in visual form.

For weeks now, she'd been experiencing disturbing dreams and the sensation of flying to other places, other worlds. It hadn't happened since childhood, at least, not with this intensity.

As a child, Flora's parents and teachers would often chide her for being a dreamer and so, when the pressures of school and when finally the adult world had taken over, she'd somehow managed to suppress her tendency to daydream and in so doing her nightly forays, into strange and colourful lands diminished, eventually to disappear.

Just recently, she'd mourned the loss of this intense dreaming state, but now she felt so unsettled she almost regretted having had the thought, in case it had somehow manifested her present state of disorientation.

Putting the sleek feather aside, she looked toward the window, where the pale light suggested it was just dawn. She was awake, edgy. What better time to start looking at her latest projects to take her mind from the disturbing sense of a nameless something, lurking, ready to jump out of the shadows at any moment. Walking to the window, she looked out at the soft glow of autumn's morning mist, the rain had ceased as the sun rose. She raised her arms as if to embrace the day and whispered a chant... 'Blessed Sun I greet you, Lord of heat and flame, may this day be spent in joy, worthy of Your Name.

Lady I greet You through the Veils of Tyme, in gratitude I honour You for this life Divine.'

Breathing in the fresh air and allowing the Sun to kiss her skin for a moment, she smiled. A perfect start to the day she thought to collect her herbs with the dew still fresh on them and then, to experiment with some new coloured dyes for her friend Bethan's fine, homespun thread. Looking again at the inky blue-black feather, she wondered if the oils that had such a wonderful musky odour and that kept its owner dry, would somehow translate into a usable commodity for waterproofing and the colour itself into a dye. Then, she thought aloud,

'But where did it come from?'

Looking up, she considered that perhaps it had been stuck on the rafters after blowing in through her, habitually, open window.

Mentally shaking herself from her reverie, she stretched her small, strong, frame, preparing to go downstairs to the kitchen and a potent brew of fresh coffee. She knew that later it would probably add to her edginess but felt that, the simple task of doing something mundane, would aid her in banishing the haunted feelings that lingered. Perhaps some food would be a good idea too as she struggled to recall the last time she'd actually sat down to a cooked meal, rather than on the run, or worse, not at all. Although she was an excellent cook; she loved to feed others and be creative in the kitchen; she simply and too often, forgot to feed herself!

With this, a pitiful miaow sounded from outside the open window, as if agreeing with her, a small, sleek, burnished brown cat leaped into the room and wound herself around Flora's legs, purring deeply. Teddy, short for Theodora, was a new addition to Flora's life. She had appeared unannounced, scrawny and half-starved, with the visible signs of a cat that had recently given birth and an air of tangible sadness. Flora had related to her instantly due to her own feelings of the recent loss and so her arrival had been a joy.

Since the very messy ending of her seven-year relationship with Dan, shortly after Sybille's disappearance, there had been no one to share her thoughts on a regular basis. Now, Teddy filled the empty space with her warmth and gently comforting presence. She may not be able to converse with words but her communication was by no means without clarity, particularly when it came to making demands for food and the ability to turn up whenever Flora even thought about it. Chuckling to herself at that realisation, she headed for the pantry to find something to satisfy both their needs.

She collected what she needed and as her hands were busy, Flora considered her life. She'd started out, after studying herbal medicine, as a florist to earn her daily bread. As skilled as she was with creating beautiful arrangements, she knew that her calling was to as a herbalist and midwife, especially to women who claimed their right to home birthing. This was a journey she needed for personal happiness and fulfilment. It was, after all, a woman's right to choose herbals and natural birth over drugs. Birth in itself was a natural process. The majority of women who chose the natural way were sensible enough to know that, should anything go wrong, they would not leave it too late for intervention if it became necessary. They certainly didn't need anyone to dictate to them what they should do with their bodies and the birthing of their children. Women just know.

Bringing herself back with a start to the moment, Flora looked down at her hands and saw that she'd been carving and hacking at her loaf of bread until it no longer resembled the pretty high-top she'd extracted from the oven yesterday. Glaring at Teddy, who was once more, weaving her undulating dance around her ankles as if it was her fault that she'd 'vagued out' again, she saved what she could of it for her toast, crumbling the rest for the chickens to enjoy later.

Breakfast finished, she went out to the garden; the early autumn mists were clearing and it promised to be a beautiful crisp, sunny day, so typical of the highland region where she lived. Going about her morning chores, she fed the fat birds their scraps, thanking them for their beautiful brown eggs then, letting the goats out of the night shedding she and Dan had helped Sybille build, she wandered with them into the area she'd had fenced off for them to forage in.

The fence was covered with auburn-leaved grape vines. She'd shared and enjoyed fruits only recently with a neighbour. There was nothing like fresh grapes on a platter of goat cheese and a good bottle of last year's blackberry wine. The old woody vines would be just right for a project she had in mind for an intricate and unusual wreath that kept appearing in her mind's eye, like a web but with subtle differences that escaped her at the moment.

She noticed that the umbels of juicy berries, on the ancient Elder trees that shaded the area, were ready to harvest; they were for cough tinctures and herbal teas, Elderberry tonic wine and for the rich, dark burgundy dye, obtained from what remained of the pressings.

As she went about her practical tasks, she thought again of the strange experience of the earlier, rude awakening from sleep, 'gela en'ardai, gela en'ardai,' echoed again in her mind combined with another image of a bag of herbs and a woven vine wreath but still couldn't find the link somehow.

Shaking it off with unusual impatience, she took sturdy gloves from a basket by the shed door and went about her tasks; moving on to harvest the stinging nettles that grew like weeds. Far from being a pest, they would produce an amazing emerald green dye for Bethan to use in her magnificent woven wraps, cloaks and throws. Each piece as unique as the person who would, eventually wear, drape or hang, her works of art.

She worked, feeling more like her usual peaceful self and remembered, with some excitement, the lunch date she had today with her two friends Bethan and Maeve and with a little trepidation, Samantha, Sybille's niece.

Bethan and Maeve, she'd known for years, having spent student days sharing an old house in a leafy Melbourne suburb. None of them could possibly have afforded it alone or without some help from family or from student loans. They had been there for each other, sharing life's pain and pleasure in equal amounts through heartbreak and celebration until life spilled them out into the world, each to stake a claim in their chosen fields of expertise. They had remained in contact with each other, however, no matter where their travels had taken them and finally, they were all back home in Australia and all, living in the same state.

They had reunited a few years ago when Flora had heard about a course scheduled to be run in her local town, Springsmeet. It had been a weekend intensive in psychic and creative awareness. The flyer she'd seen had piqued her interest. It had described, the tools developed, could help to answer questions that the participants had been asking all their lives.

Her friends had the same visions, to learn and grow through their chosen fields of creativity. They'd all had the same need to identify their spiritual path, to enable a clearer understanding of their earthly journey; so they'd met again in the beautiful highland town, close to where Flora and Bethan lived, at a little esoteric bookshop and teaching centre, to begin the journey to make sense of their lives.

Sybille, their extraordinary, enigmatic teacher had taken them, not just on a weekend journey, but had invited them as promising students to continue with her in a weekly group, which was designed to teach and discuss, all that she had to offer.

Although Maeve had to travel from Melbourne every week for the evening gatherings, she would stay at Flora and her lover Dan or Bethan's cottage overnight. It meant an early morning start for her to return to the city and work, but it would be at times as if the years between had not passed at all. Over shared food and wine, after their two hours with Sybille, they were all worldlier, somewhat wearier, but no less eager to share all that her teachings gave them. As they practised, all she taught they became more aware of their personal journeys, where their own goals were concerned ...all thanks to Sybille.

Two years, into Sybille's training, with one kicking and screaming and two embracing their gifts with awe, they discovered that their journey had given them the acknowledgement that they were all of the same persuasions. They had all studied the same methods and texts, looking at every possible philosophy and religion under Sybille's guidance and vast knowledge and all had asked themselves, each other and their teacher, 'What was before that?' They'd searched and researched back in time through history, myths and legends to find one day, almost with one breath as they read a piece of text from a book on earth magick and ritual,

'Oh my God, we're Witches!'

Flora had said, 'Yessss, of course!'

Bethany, 'Oh that explains so much!'

Maeve had gurgled hysterically, 'No way!'

Sybille had laughed; she shared the story of her self-same journey to this discovery and how she'd felt as the truth emerged from within. She explained her training to High Priestess in the oldest and fastest growing religion on the planet. Embraced by women and men alike, all reclaimed their identity in the Goddess and God as well as their connection to the Old Ones and the Fae Folk. There had followed heated debates on the right and wrongs of the now, more commonly known, Wicca path but as Sybille had said, Wicca was an old Saxon word that meant the same as Wytch ...namely Wise One and that the much maligned, Craft of the Wise, or Wytchcraft, formerly Wiccaecraeft, was now a legalised religious practice and that,

'There's nothing wrong with the word Wytch anyway!' she'd laughed.

Now, nearly three years down the track, each of the three women had embraced their own, 'Wytchyness,' more or less and each saw their creative work and the quality of their lives strengthened; enriched by their discoveries as they continued their exploration of the Way.

Sybille had taught them that there is never need to harm another, in thought or deed because all returned to the doer and thinker, threefold. Self-responsibility was the name of the game and when each of them realised this, it was empowering to be out of the continual trap of blaming others, or playing the victim of circumstances and that, if they couldn't manifest their own needs, they just didn't need it enough. The key was always there and had been the very first time their teacher had said these words,

'Where your mind goes, energy flows.'

Her words had created a time when Flora and each of her very, uniquely gifted friends, had realised, were the link that had opened their awareness to all things mystical and Magickal. Each brought something different to their craft and each found inspiration in their daily discipline and continuing studies into the Way itself.

Close to a year ago, just before Lammas, however, tragedy struck. Sybille had disappeared without a trace. Her house neat and clean, her clothes all hung or folded away. Her beautiful Book of Shadows was where she'd always put it, wrapped and hidden in the false bottom of the chest, with her tools of the craft and her ritual robes. The beautiful chest doubled as a small altar; always decked with flowers or the foliage of the season; a shrine, where a candle had always burned for the Old Ones.

One inconsistency was a note Sybille had left for, 'her girls,' as she called them, leaving her house and everything in it, in their care and for Flora, who would she'd said; need it to move into, one day soon. At the time, Flora hadn't understood the implications but after her recent and messy, separation from Dan, her long-term lover, she knew that Sybille had foreseen this eventuality.

Everything, she instructed must be left as was, for a year and a day in their hands. They'd shared the duties of upkeep and basic garden maintenance. All the current bills were paid and Sybille had opened a bank account in Flora's name for any emergency repairs. Although the house appeared to stay, surprisingly, untouched and the garden Sybille had loved and nurtured had gone into, what could only be described as, some sort of stasis. Nothing had died exactly but neither had it truly thrived. Then Flora moved in and the seasonal, autumn changes, manifested rapidly under her nurturance. Her friends too had benefited from that move, with fresh produce and eggs. It had given Flora a place to heal her heavy heart and for that, she was most grateful to Sybille, whom she missed dreadfully as, she was sure, did her cat.

Morgana, with fur as silver as Sybille's hair, had refused to be moved and would only appear, with a disdainful tail twitch, when food was presented. She came and went through the cat flap in the back door and spent most of her time in the old apple tree that overhung the veranda, unless wet weather drove her inside.

Flora's moving in and the arrival of Teddy had put the proverbial, cat amongst the pigeons and Morgana's nose had been put further out of joint, when Teddy refused to even deign to notice her as if she were invisible. Flora would laugh at this, but none of her attempts to draw the two together, worked.

The three friends had grieved Sybille's sudden disappearance and had struggled to work out what had led Sybille to just up and go. After nearly a year, they had ceased trying to make sense of it all and just decided to settle down to wait. It was as if the house remained in a time warp until her return.

Unexpectedly, a week ago, a letter arrived in Sybille's handwriting, addressed to Flora, together with a large package, addressed to all of them. She'd found it on the doorstep, on her return from assisting at a birthing. It was for that reason she'd contacted the others, nearly a year and a day since Sybille's abrupt departure and so they would meet to discuss the baffling turn of events the letter had revealed.

With a jolt, Flora came back to her senses as a Raven with an unusual silver streak on one wing croaked from a fencepost close by. Realising her thoughts had made her forget the time, Flora hurried to finish her chores. Bunching and tying the herbs and hanging them in the dark, cool drying room before going to shower and change in time to drive into town to meet the others.

Ready to leave, she was almost to her car, when she remembered the package that had arrived so mysteriously. She went back inside to Sybille's cosy den, which doubled as her library, to the desk where she'd left the parcel. Grabbing it and turning to go, she saw the chest, where Sybille kept her sacred things was thrown open; the Book of Shadows lay uncovered in the bottom of the chest and she certainly hadn't been anywhere near it, since her disappearance.

'What the hell is going on?' She yelled to the universe in general as she approached the open chest.

The book lay open. She held her outrage in check, when she saw her mentors' writing and another's, strange hand as well on a sheet of fine parchment. There was a drawing of some sort too, that tugged at her memory. Underneath were a series of symbols, writing, which she also thought she recognised. Plucking up the courage, she picked it up and stuffed it into a leather binder, propped up against the back of the chest as if in wait for the seeker.

Slamming the lid to the chest shut, she ran from the room and out the front door, at a loss to make sense of anything herself, she needed to see her friends. Starting the car, she failed to see Morgana's expression of horror as she leapt, un-Morgana like, doused with water from the puddle by the gate by Flora's undignified exit.

Chapter 4
Bethan

Not far away from Flora's early morning musings, another woman sat at her spinning wheel contemplating the same agendas that Flora had discussed with her the previous evening. What right had anyone to tell a woman what she could or could not do with her own and her child's life? Bethan had supported her friend one hundred percent when she had shared her feelings of outrage in regards to the attempt by the medical bodies to ban natural birthing and no longer give accreditation to natural birth midwives.

As Bethan worked, she found herself slipping into a trance like state as she spun, teasing the silky wool to watch it unfurl into the thread she used, to create her weavings. Working with Flora to obtain the knowledge for the colourful dyes fresh from nature's harvest, was one of the best things she had ever done. The colours for the yarns were clean and pure and the work before her would continue to spin fast and free from her loom in a complexity of rainbow fragments, geometry forgotten in the weaving of an intricate web, gossamer fine. Automatically blowing away a curl of silvery hair that continually fell in her eyes and often, spun into her weaving, she tried to recall the dream she'd awoken from that morning. The memory, slipping through her fingers like the yarn she spun had been as bright and rich in colour as the dyes she would later use on the newly spun thread.

'Gela en'ardai, gela en'ardai,' she heard echoing in her head. What was that strange language she knew she should know it, understand it. She remembered only that she'd travelled again to the lands she always visited in her dreams, remembering the first time as if it were yesterday, when she found herself walking through a grove of trees, feeling she was intruding in someone else's space. It had been Summer Solstice, Litha; the air had been fragrant and balmy with all that grew amidst the trees. Laughter carried on the breeze from the people milling around, children and dogs running, shouting and barking with sheer joy ...in fact bedlam reigned. Then suddenly, as if a siren had sounded all fell still.

Two robed figures appeared, dressed in hooded black, heads bowed. She'd known somehow that the High Priestess and Priest had come, followed by their acolytes, each carrying a lit candle. The wind, she recalled, had become brisk and choppy yet the candle flames had not even flickered as they were carried forward into a circle, where all faced inward. She'd felt conscious and active in the dream and remembered looking down that she wore a robe of the deepest blue edged with silver and that she'd glowed with an unearthly light. All faces had turned suddenly towards her as if by silent order and the High Priestess had smiled and said, 'There She is; She's come to us. Welcome Arwen, you honour us with your presence.'

The dream repeated often over the years, up to that point, but this time, although not truly afraid, she had the urge to turn and run. She flew out of the grove and into the woods. Ahead, the trees formed a corridor lit by the rising sun. It became narrower as she ran. Beth recognized other states of consciousness when she moved towards a portal of light. Sybille had told her it was a dream of 'dying to the outgrown'; an out-of-body experience of some kind. Reading up on 'near death experiences,' she found description of similar occurrences; of walking in other dimensions, fully aware.

This time everything had passed again through her mind as she ran in the dream and the corridor of trees had opened into a field of brightly coloured flowers; as bright as the dyes her friend Flora brought to her for her thread. No fear here - no ill-timed death awaited - she thought, sanity returning, only the fast and bone-jarring return to her physical reality and the strange words, *gela en'ardai, gela en'ardai,* repeatedly ringing in her mind. Sounds, wind chimes, finely tuned voices mocked her inability to keep the dream alive in her awareness. With a shake, she brought herself back to the moment and put the now finished skein of thread aside in order to go prepare for the meeting with her friends.

As she got ready, combing out and braiding her ash blond hair, she thought sadly of the events of the last year and her friend and mentor Sybille, with whom she shared such a close bond. Where had she gone and why? What had driven her to disappear so unexpectedly? She had picked up her energy from time to time as if her friend was standing by watching her at her work or walking with her in her meditations.

Gathering the rest of her things she went, still pondering this, to her car. As she drove a snatch of melody, words eluding her, wrapped around her senses. 'What was that?' she hummed to herself.

'Drifting mm hmm the warp and weft... 'Gela en'ardai, gela en'ardai, mm hmm, mm hmm, mm hmm ...upon the mm hmm time?' What did those words mean she wondered ...what language, so familiar yet strange. She knew she'd heard it before ...and that wisp of haunting music. She'd talk to her music teacher, Bran about it. She had a good ear for music and was proficient on the small lap harp she'd found at the back of a junk shop, covered in dust. She'd claimed it for her own before she could even coax a note from it and had found a local class that taught, harp making and playing. She'd been ecstatic when her tutor said she was a natural.

She brought herself out of her reverie as she pulled up outside, 'The Providores' the restaurant they'd agreed to meet at, putting the puzzle of her dreams aside for now to tackle the greater mystery of Sybille's disappearance, with her friends.

Chapter 5
Maeve

You dance your own dance; you sing your own song but never forget to smile at a stranger.
A note from Sybille to her student Maeve

Maeve pushed back the small shield protecting her face from heat and droplets of molten metal from the forge and in so doing, snagged her hair in the buckle. She yelped as it pulled at strands, not unlike the copper wire she used in her work.

Already more than a little frustrated at how her work was shaping, or rather not, she flung the face guard down on the bench. Scooping up the mangled piece of metal, she tossed it into the recycle bin. Somehow, in her haste to get the project from the mind to hand, it had twisted out of the shape intended, warping the design into something other. She stepped back from the bench stretching her spine and flexing her hands while peeling off the gloves she only sometimes remembered to wear. Looking at her hands in the growing sunlight, she could see the fine network, a delicate web of scars, covering them the result of that forgetting.

Walking to the cooler she kept by the door, she grabbed, opened and downed half the contents of a bottle of water in one, thirsty swallow, then ran the cold surface over forehead, cheeks and neck, to speed up the cooling process after an hour at her forge.

With a scowl at the offending piece of twisted metal, she went to find some breakfast for her growling stomach. When her work consumed her, there was nothing and no one, that could break her focus and with a new project in mind, she had been eager to get to her studio before daylight, to begin the process of making, which had gone so wrong. She considered going back to see if the piece was redeemable or to work on another project, barely begun but which held great promise. Her frustration however was not the best fuel to work with, no - first a cooling shower and nourishment.

With hair still dripping, her body cooled but her mind still furious, she walked past her studio door on the way to the kitchen. Halting, she thought she glimpsed something moving in her peripheral vision; there was a strange sound ...but what?

Something triggered inside her as she realised that the dream last night had been of precisely this moment. She paused, but there was nothing there, only a vague feeling of being watched, which created an all-pervading sense of déjà vu. The dream moment escaped her and, pushing it uneasily to the back of her mind, Maeve continued to the kitchen for that promised nourishment, remembering that she also had a meeting with her friends that day. Perhaps they would be able to help her make sense of this strangeness. She knew she should be used to it after all Sybille had taught her, but this was really trying her patience beyond measure.

Buttering toast, topping it with avocado; silently thanking Flora for the fresh tomato the result of her work in Sybille's once more luscious and productive garden, she paused, remembering,

'Gela en'ardai, gela en'ardai'

With an immediate sense of falling forward and a wave of nausea, she grabbed the doorframe. It was as if the world had clicked out and back into focus, in a split second of memory. She remembered moving through her house in just the same manner as she had before, pausing at the doorway to her studio with a sense that she was not alone ...but what had she seen?

'Aaaaaaaagh!' she screamed aloud, knowing it was there in the corner of her mind and if she could let it go it would surface but patience was not her strongest point, particularly this morning.

Abandoning breakfast, she went back to the studio. To her horror the other piece, she had been working on lay split; shattered on the bench, where she'd left it to cool. Shrieking with frustration, she raced in, tenderly picking up the now totally broken and fragmented crystal shard, she'd cut and shaped for a particular order. Not able to believe the beautiful crystal was completely, destroyed. How had this happened, she'd been so careful, been sure it was the right piece to embed in the shaft of the copper wire wrapped, oak wand. How could she ever find another crystal with just that form and depth of colour?

Turning to grab a cloth, to mop up spontaneous tears at the loss of this brilliant specimen, her eye caught droplets of water on the floor. Random markings, speckled droplets in uniquely patterned, web-like imprints, symbols or writing but nothing she'd seen before, hearing echoing again, 'gela en'ardai ...gela en'ardai...

From deep within the large cauldron of spring water she used to cool and set the metalwork of her pieces, there came a deep gurgling; a column of water shot upward to remain frozen for a moment in her mind's eye, before cascading back into the cauldron, which made it shake on its stand before settling into silence.

She stood in stunned silence, unable to begin to understand what had just happened. Sybille, I must speak with Sybille she thought but with a groan remembered, Sybille was gone! I must speak with Flora and Bethan. Thank the Goddess I'm meeting them today. I don't know what's going on, but this is too weird for me. Grabbing bag and keys, she fled without a backward glance to her car and drove.

Chapter 6
The Meet

In your daily life, lift up your gaze and look around.
You never know what you may be missing,
If your eyes are only on the ground.
A note from Sybille to her students.

As Flora turned into Springsmeet, she admired the first signs of change in the Ash trees on the way. A long corridor of ancient trees planted when the first settlers came to the region, turned the broad road into a glorious boulevard; a tunnel of green and gold branches formed an archway of living colour.

Lights seemed to flicker in them as the late morning sun shone through and her mind went back to the dream of this morning. There had been trees, no wait, a tree so vast that had hummed and sung with chiming voices. Faces of unknown origin looked down at her from above and a huge blue-black Raven had flown from under the canopy screaming in its Raven tongue the words, 'gela en'ardai, gela en'ardai,' as a warning.

Shaking herself free from her daydream, she found a parking spot outside the lovely Providores, where excellent organic foods from the local area, were lovingly prepared. She parked and getting out of the car, couldn't resist pausing outside the local nursery, situated next door to the Providores. She promised herself that she'd take a good look another day when she had more time, for plants and seeds for the winter vegie garden.

As she turned to walk to the restaurant, Maeve and Bethan drove up simultaneously and all else was forgotten in greeting and hugging the friends who were more like sisters to her. Ash-blond, red and chestnut haired, the 3 women were striking and uniquely individual. All had a particular something that turned heads wherever they went.

'Shall we wait for Sam, do you think,' said Bethan, 'or shall we go on in and find a seat before it gets too busy?'

In one voice, laughing aloud, Maeve and Flora said, 'Let's go in, I'm starving!'

Like teenagers on an outing, they pushed and shoved each other to find a seat and get comfortable, their laughter ringing. Their enthusiasm sparked laughter from the table next to them, where another group was contemplating the menu and loosening up over a delicious glass of local wine.

They browsed the menu, not mentioning Sam, who was yet to make an appearance. All three of them were vegetarians but the choices, although a little more limited were nevertheless stunning to say the least.

'Mmmm, what to have, what to have?' crooned Flora.

'We could share a few smaller dishes then we can have a little of everything vego,' suggested Maeve.

'I'm not particularly hungry,' said Bethan. 'I'm too nervous about seeing Sam and also about finding out where the hell Sybille's gone.'

Flora and Maeve immediately sobered. It was easy to forget why they were here at the simple joy of being together. As customary, it was Bethan, who reminded them of the purpose for their meeting. Just at that moment, the door opened and in flew Sam. She hesitated looking around and then spotting them, waved, pushing her way between the now crowded tables to fling herself down on the bench next to Flora.

'Sorry, I'm late but there was a rather unusual occurrence that made me forget the time.' She was as forthright as ever. In that forthrightness, she suddenly seemed so much more like Sybille than they'd realised until then. The three shared a glance, all thinking the same thing, causing Sam to stop to ask,

'What is it? What's wrong? Have I got toothpaste on my chin or something?'

This broke the ice.

'Just for a moment,' said Maeve, usually the most guarded of the three, 'you really reminded us of your Aunt.'

'Have you any news of her?' Sam asked. 'I miss her so much I'm desperate. Don't you think we should go to the police, in spite of what she said in that letter?' She addressed Flora directly.

'No! I know it's hard for you; it's hard for all of us but her directions must be followed. If she thought she was in any danger, she wouldn't have given such a clear message and her affairs in the order she did. She covered all bases and at least we haven't had to worry about that,' Flora replied. 'Now before we eat let's look at the package that came. She included a note for me,' and at Sam's sharp glance said, 'Sorry, I didn't ask for this you know, it was Sybille's choice!'

Reaching into her bag, she pulled out the note attached to the package. Opening it, she read it carefully, her big eyes growing even bigger as she read.

Impatiently Sam said, 'What? Get on with it, the suspense is killing me!'

With a deep breath, Flora read aloud, her voice catching as she read the words from their friend and teacher, *Merry meet my dear Flora,*

You are the one who I sense, will learn to understand what I am about to tell you.' Flora glanced quickly at Sam's flushed face. *'I must leave and I don't know when I will be back as yet. You will find this difficult I know and all sorts of questions will remain unanswered, but I am relying on you, Maeve and Bethan to keep our little circle alive.'*

'What circle? What does she mean,' interjected Sam again.

Holding up her hand to stem her questions, Flora continued, while Bethan reached out across the table to touch her hand in empathy, which Sam shook off distractedly.

'There is so much I have yet to show you, so much left to do and yet I must go. There is no choice for me in this matter and this you will understand, one day

If you remember at the last Full Moon, I began a new Book of Shadows, which I leave for you all to use. It contains much to help you continue deciphering the questions that will arise very soon for you all, much of which I can't speak of here. Years of embracing being a Wytch has shown me so much about how the world operates, including my place in it, but that's not a straightforward matter to teach in this short note. There is so much to share. I am right now at a loss to know where to start, but you will understand soon enough.

I leave a little note for each of you along with further instructions until my return, with the hope that this won't be too big a burden for you all to manage…'

With that, the letter simply trailed off, unsigned; the ink left an unsteady trail down the page.

Sam snatched the letter from Flora's fingers, turning it over to see if anything else was written on the other side. Fingers shaking, her one need was to find out any information to suggest that her Aunt was all right as tears welled and ran unchecked down her face to fall in fat drops onto the note. Astonished, they watched as Sam, throwing the letter onto the table, buried her face in her hands and sobbed. The group at the next table turned in concern and Maeve, who had been watching open mouthed at Sam's uninhibited outburst, gathered her wits and said to them,

'It's, okay she's just had a shock, she'll be okay,' and turning, put her body between the tables, blocking their concerned gaze.

Meanwhile, Flora quietly gathered Sam to her in a warm embrace and Bethan; slipping round to join them did the same. They let the grieving girl sob, crying with her until there were no tears left between them.

Finally, Sam straightened, recoiling from Flora and Bethan's touch as if burnt. Embarrassed beyond belief at her outburst, she blew her nose on a handy paper napkin and attempted to get up. In that instant, her head spun and she sat down quickly, feeling something shift.

'I have to get out of here,' said Sam, 'I can't stand this. Something's wrong, I have to go.'

'Sam,' said Flora, 'wait, there's more. I have more information here that came last week. A package came with that note attached to it. The note may have been for me, but the package is addressed to all of us. So please,' she said, reaching out again to Sam, 'sit down and let's look at what this is. It might give us more insight into what's going on. Your Aunt must have had her reasons and I for one am not giving up on her!'

'I'm not giving up!' Exclaimed Sam, in a manner they were all more accustomed to, 'I want no, need to know where she is. In truth, she's all I have in the world and we haven't spoken in a while!'

'Ah,' said Maeve, 'now I understand what this is all about! You're just feeling guilty, it's not really about your Aunt, it's all about you!'

Sam stood up, ready to leave in anger.

As one, Flora and Bethan stopped her. Turning to Maeve, Bethan said, 'Now that's not fair Maeve,' with unaccustomed sharpness, 'particularly under the circumstances. Put yourself in Sam's place. Sybille is her Aunt. Although she's our best friend, she's still Sam's Aunt!' As usual, the voice of Bethan's reason made the difference. 'What say we all head back to my place and open this there, away from the public eye? You never know what may be in there and I have a feeling we've made enough of a spectacle for one day!'

'You're right Beth,' said Flora, 'but let's go back to Sybille's. After all, it's where this all began. Perhaps we can get a different slant on it if we actually look through her things to see if there's something, we've missed. We haven't exactly searched for anything that could explain her leaving like this, have we? We've just allowed her to state what we're supposed to do and we've done it but now it's just on a year and a day since she left; it's Lammas,' ...she trailed off, looking round at the others.

'I agree,' said Maeve. 'After all she could have been in trouble of some sort. She'd been getting nasty notes a while ago and the locals were always a bit funny about her openly being a Wytch!'

'Ok,' said Sam, recovering herself again, 'let's have a look! Are you all right with that Flora? Sybille did leave the place in your care?'

They all looked at her in surprise at the apparent change in attitude.

'I know,' said Sam, eyeing them all; embarrassed, 'I haven't been the easiest to get along with since Auntie left, but I can't go on like this and I don't want to be alone anymore.'

Fearing another emotional outburst, Maeve stood; grabbing the package, she said, 'That's settled; let's go!'

Her usual composure returning, Sam laughed. 'Yeah, let's go, before I embarrass myself more!'

With that, the energy restored a little; they gathered their things. They apologised to the group at the next table for all the drama. 'You know, how it is! Man trouble!' They waved to the girl waiting to take their order, apologised again and went.

'Humph,' said Maeve. 'I don't think they'll let us back in there again too soon!'

'You go ahead,' said Sam, 'I'll go get us something yummy to take back to the farm for later. It's my fault you all missed out on lunch so, my shout!'

'No, that's okay, I'll come with you,' said Bethan, 'I need some fresh air and to stretch my legs anyway.'

About to refuse, Sam changed her mind, 'Thanks,' she said with a wry grin, 'thanks a lot.'

Chapter 7
The Birthing Tree

As above so below
As within so without
Listen to the whispering trees,
They will dispel all doubt
Notes from Tree Talk by Sybille Madison

Deep within Nature's Heart, in Her rich, moist, fertile cradle, something awoke. Not in a slow, stirring, stretching, awakening but in a 'snap to' moment. The Spirit of the Forest of Secrets heard the call and turned the focus inwards to the place of greening, burgeoning life.

The tiny seed, offshoot of the Birthing Tree, was sending down its own first tentative roots that reverberated through all the realms on the Skeins of Tyme. Down it went, through the plant and mineral kingdoms, to the earth elemental realm and deeper still, into the molten heart of Terra. Reflecting off an enormous, multifaceted crystal shard, a remnant of the original planetary core, it sent out a pure signal; a sound so sweet, for an instant it was felt by humankin as a time to hold the breath and listen, enchanted. Further, out it went through the Elven, the Fae race's realms of light. Out to the center of creation where the Makers, gleaming like crystalline stars, pulsed even brighter in their tending of the

Trueshapers stirring in their gossamer cocoons. Ever spreading, like a net of fine silken threads, each thread a colour; notes sounding in joy and triumph announcing the imminent birth of a new immortal ...an awakened one, heralded.

In that same instant the radar screens and tracking systems of every government security in all of Terra stopped ...strange signs appeared on the screen for a moment and a small, shining, split-winged being of pearlescent light, was briefly seen, accompanying one clear note, heard throughout all the realms before it fell, corrupted, withered and blackened as it felt the fear, the war and the carnage that had been created by humans on the planet. In a brief moment of life its light winked out and was gone

The Trueshapers, renewing themselves stirred as they felt the fall, a ripple of terror like a sullen wave swept through their realm. At the same moment, stillness, darkness came for the first time in the realms of light. As one seedling of the Birthing tree died, one small Maker fell, catapulting into the cocoon where the Trueshaper Silver and her renewing Littleshape, Sybille, slumbered. Torn from the cocoon, the Trueshaper flew to the Birthing Tree. She called the Makers to assist in creating another cocoon, while cradling the comatose Littleshape, attempting to bring back her spark of life from the void, where it had fallen with the tainted Maker.

Chapter 8
Legacy

Love binds us close when dark threatens to smother us. We grieve we mourn, but the light will prevail. Always remember; without the darkest night, we cannot see the stars.

From Sybille's notes to her students

An hour later the four women sat down together for a little feast Samantha had bought for them, of fresh crusty bread, a selection of salads, fruit and cheeses and a good bottle of crisp white wine. Over food and wine, they let their thoughts on the contents of the package go for a while. Chatting about their lives, they found there was a strong bond with Sam, through her fondness for her Aunt and as she shared a little about herself and her childhood. She spoke of the accident that had taken her parents unexpectedly. Sybille, her guardian, had truly understood; she was the one person she trusted in the entire world.

'Now she's gone,' she said, her voice drained of all emotion.

'Now,' said Maeve quickly to avoid another emotional outburst from Sam. 'Let's look now.' Picking up the parcel and handing it to Sam, she said, 'Here Sam, you do the honours!'

At a loss, Sam took it with a little smile, saying simply, 'Thanks Maeve.' She had trouble with the string so, with her more characteristic impatience, Maeve gave her a small knife. Opening the package; all craning their necks to see the content, she uncovered five notes addressed to each of them in Sybille's hand together with a cloth wrapped package, a fat document file attached.

With a deep breath Flora said, 'Okay, what first?'

'Our letters!' said Maeve.

Flora handed them out, realising there were actually five, one addressed to, 'Tara.'

'Who's Tara,' they chorused? A seed-thought sowed itself in the quiet that followed. Exchanging glances they realised the situation was more than anything they could imagine. None knew quite what to do with their individual opinions, let alone another mystery by the name of Tara.

Breaking the silence Bethan said, 'Okay, let's leave figuring that out for now! Who's going first?'

With a deep breath, Sam said, 'I will if you like, but I don't know what this all means so I hope you will!'

Written on the paper in Sybille's hand was a rhyme, a riddle... *Earth you are, from earth you came, your intellect from Air you gain. Your Fire should burn, with flaming ire, yet Water has put out your fire.* What the!' she stuttered, 'is this some sort of sick joke,' ready to explode again in frustration.

Bethan interjected. 'No wait!' I have one too.

'Yeah, me too,' said Maeve.

Flora nodded ascent.

Bethan read aloud... *'Spirit sings within your frame, on your loom and through your pain. Water washes all things clean; Air brings truth to you again. Fire is needed, Earth to ground when the web you weave, all things abound.'*

Again they shared a puzzled glance as Maeve spoke up... *'Fire is harsh and anger sings, don't go too close you'll burn your wings/ Earth yourself go deep within; let Water again become your kin. Let Air breath you, let laughter ring.'*

Then Flora, shaking her head at a loss to understand... *'Earth you are, compassion grown, Fire and Water becoming known. Air will sing when Fire alights and Water washes all things bright.* Well,' she said, 'as ever the practical one, 'I don't know what all this means but surely Sybille taught us enough about Magick and rhyme to work out what this means!'

'It looks to me as if the four elements are being used to describe us and our characteristics,' said Bethan.

'Why yes of course,' replied Flora.

'Can't we just wait and see if Sybille returns; she said she would,' said Maeve. 'Surely she'll be back for Bethan's birthday on the 1st of May? It's her 29th so her Saturn return occurs. Surely you can't think she won't be back for that, can you Flora?'

'Well, I would have thought so but this parcel arriving rather made me think differently. Why would she send this to us now, she left at Lammas, which it is again and there's still Mabon before we can even think of Samhain, her formerly predicted return date? I just don't get it!'

'There are still the parcel's contents,' said Sam, 'Let's see if that makes any more sense of things.'

'Right,' said Maeve, 'here you go Sam. Open it, the suspense is killing me!' she exclaimed.

With jerky movements revealing her nervousness, Sam took the package and tore the paper off. Inside was a heavy silk covered shape. On opening it, it revealed Sybille's newly begun Book of Shadows. Opening it, she saw that it was blank!

'How strange,' said Bethan, 'I remember Sybille starting this. Didn't she say in her note she'd left it for us to use while she was away; which was Lammas? Hmmm, why would she give us a blank book on her predicted return, which was supposed to be a year and a day after her leaving? Something's really not right here. Whatever Sybille planned with all of this, wherever she had to go, something's changed since then. Something's gone wrong, I can sense it.'

Always aware of Bethan's sensitivities and premonitions Maeve shut her mouth quickly, not prepared to voice what she'd been thinking. Exchanging glances with Sam, she said, 'Is there anything else in there Sam, any other clues?'

'Wait,' yelped Flora, 'I have something else!' She related the incident from earlier, when she'd found Sybille's chest and her Book of Shadows open, with the parchment resting inside, just before she was leaving.

'And you're only just sharing this now?' said Maeve irritably.

'Yes, sorry I just remembered. I was in a hurry to leave so I simply stuffed it in my bag.' So saying she pulled her bag onto her lap and brought out a leather bound folder, containing the parchment she'd found. Opening it quickly, she saw, what looked like an excerpt from Sybille's Book of Shadows.

A year for a Wytch begins at Samhain, pronounced Soween or Sowan ...30th April-2nd May in modern day reckoning in the Southern Hemisphere of this beautiful planet. The feeling in the air is one of deep relief for the coming months of introspection, combined with grief as the Lord and Lady leave to take the hands of all the souls who have passed beyond and of those who may have been lost in the between. They accompany them through the gates of the Summerlands ...the lands of peace and beauty only imagined and for some onwards still, to discover their Trueshape.

What does all this mean, I hear you say ...what is this talk of Wytches and Magickal lands? What is a Wytch in truth? I will tell you as simply as I may because just as Samhain is a beginning, so is this a new beginning for all who are tired of the tick tock world of illusion and hierarchical ordering.

Eons ago, long before written languages, there was knowledge free to all who asked the right questions. There was no elite only those whose studies allowed them to hear the inner voice of the Mother clearly. This was a time long before there were names and titles ...a time when all who knew of the Lady's Way were known as the Noldo'er or Kurinimen' the Wise Ones the Wytches, male and female alike. All Her priests and priestesses, all Her people; Her tribes.

Flora paused again, 'Just a moment!' she said, 'This bit isn't your Aunt's writing Sam! I wonder who wrote this.' She showed the others the parchment with the two distinct handwritings.

'What next!' said Sam, 'What had Sybille got herself into? This doesn't make any sense.'

'Keep reading anyway, Flora,' said Bethan, 'perhaps there's more to explain it.'

Flora continued reading the now different spidery script... *'This is what I would share with you ...this is what I know as truth ...my truth, yes ...my version ...yes. Somewhere in the depths of your unconscious, if I can move you ...stir you just to look a little ...then there may be a few of you who will awaken and remember...remember the role you chose to play in the changes afoot on the planet today which through your thoughts and dreams must now manifest.*

She is awakening the Mother. Remember! Remember the place you need to be is right where you are standing. You created this time, so that you could read these words and yes, you have it ...remember! There is nowhere to go ...just here ...only here ...if you were somewhere else how can you remember this now and all the 'nows' that have led you here?

I know you all love this planet with a love that is at times so great it overwhelms you. That you long for a world without the wars, the cruelty to the Mother's children, the bullying, the 'better than,' attitudes...need I say more?

Where are you, kinfolk ...who are still asleep! Our Humankin have created a world of fear and lack, through their belief in false tales, designed to trick and to lead you astray from the Mother's teachings.'

Then in Sybille's hand it continued. *Therefore, at Samhain I honour the ancestors. As a modern day Wytch, I honour the power that lives within my cells and of every being that has ever lived and is still living on this planet.*

As I have learned, all who have been are and will be, are still here, sharing space with me, breathing with me ...everything is here ...now

...and with that, the writing trailed off again, unfinished just as the note to Flora had.

They exchanged a puzzled glance, each contemplating what was happening and why. Where was Sybille? Why had she had to leave? They all spoke at once.

Maeve picked up the Book of Shadows.

'Why is she speaking of Samhain,' she queried aloud. 'It just doesn't make sense; she disappeared a year and a day ago today, at Lammas?'

She looked around at the others; flicking through the pages distractedly, an envelope, tucked in a pocket at the back, fell out. Addressed to all of them, it appeared to be a legal document.

'Hang on, look. What's this?' she said.

They all fell silent.

'What now,' Bethan exclaimed, 'What is it?

Snatching the envelope impatiently, Sam ripped it open. She had an idea of the law and so saw that it was indeed a legal deed and a large ornate key that they all recognised immediately. With mouth dropped open in surprise, she stared at them all, completely dumbfounded.

'What!' they all chorused.

'I don't know if we were to find this before now but,' she gasped for breath astonished; she continued, 'Sybille has left us the house in town.'

Turning to Flora, she said, 'for you to open a herbalist's practice and natural health shop even a wytchy shop.' Silence fell. 'For you Maeve to open a studio and shop for your art and jewellery but you must move to Springsmeet.'

'NO!' yelped Maeve, 'she couldn't have!'

'Maeve,' said Bethan, 'Let Sam finish! Please!'

'But,' replied Maeve, 'I,' she trailed off.

Sam continued, 'For you Bethan, to set up your shop for spinning and weaving and for your music too and for me to open the book shop I've always dreamed of and I have to move here too,' she breathed, 'but there's one proviso…'

'I thought there would be a catch,' said Maeve, cynically.

Holding up her hand to quieten her, Sam continued, '…that we do this together with a focus on running the Circle, whatever that means,' She looked to Flora questioningly, 'and courses as she used to, to train others in the Way.'

'But we don't have her experience and knowledge,' said Flora. 'I know that the three of us have studied with her for a few years but for us to teach it and what about you Sam? What has Sybille taught you of the Craft?'

'I grew up with very Christian parents as I'm sure you all know but Sybille has shown me a few rudimentary bits and pieces like Circle Casting, basic ritual and, of course, the Lore and the laws of the Way.

I have celebrated all the Rites with her over the years. Although my parents would be turning in their graves if they knew that,' said Sam ironically. 'More than that I have only gleaned from books she put under my nose every now and again. For my writing, my book,' she added shyly in explanation...

'A book! You're writing a book!' exclaimed Maeve, 'We didn't know that!'

'It's a novel,' said Sam, ' urban fantasy. If things continue like this, I'm going to have a lot more information too,' she laughed, lightening the mood a little.

'Well,' said Bethan finally. 'What more can happen? I can't believe she won't be back. That she won't just walk in that door unannounced and tell us it's all just been a joke and she's back.'

'I know,' said Sam. 'It's amazing that she's left us that beautiful house and you Flora,' she said turning to her, holding out the paper for her to see, 'she's left the farm to you because you are the only one of us that doesn't have their own home and because you have always loved the land. She says that you must bond with it now as she did.'

'Ah Goddess, she hasn't, has she? That means she knew she wouldn't be back then,' said Flora tears welling again.

None of them knew what to say; they fell silent as they shared a moment. Looking into each other's eyes, knew that this was it. They had work to do and somehow would pull themselves together to do it well Sybille, but she would not be back anytime soon. She'd put this final legacy into their hands.

Without a word Flora, Bethan and Maeve stood as one pulling Sam to her feet with them. They reached out to each other to hug, to comfort then, in the lovely room where Sybille had taught them all so much, Bethan started to chant. Maeve and Flora followed her lead; Sam joined in haltingly.

'Lady aid us on The Way, guide us all to heal this day by Earth, Air, Fire and Water's foam guide your Priestess Sybille home,' ...trailing off they paused to look at each other questioningly.

In that instant, they felt something strange. There was a pause; a breath held in the silence, just like before an earthquake and then a sound of such sweetness filled the air; each knew they had discovered bliss at that moment. As fast as they heard it, felt it as an energy coursing through their minds and hearts, it was gone replaced by a feeling of utter grief and loss.

A feline howl of anguish came from the Apple tree by the window as Morgana leapt down from her usual perch and crashed through the cat flap. A large cat; she threw herself at Bethan, knocking her backwards onto the couch, burying her face under her jacket.

Everything was at that moment just too much for Bethan, who simply fainted away. Maeve felt as she had earlier; the world shifted sideways. Putting a hand to her mouth, she raced to the bathroom to be violently sick. Sam and Flora looked at each other speechless in horror at what they felt.

'Sybille!' they said with one voice.

'I can hardly feel her,' said Flora.

'She's gone,' howled a distraught Sam, 'Oh Lady, where's she gone!'

Flora, for the second time that day, held the sobbing Sam in her arms and rocked. There was a space that Sybille had always filled. The training in ritual and Magickal workings had formed an amazing bond between them all and now there was just a gaping void where Sybille had been.

They held each other, trying to give and receive mutual support. All the resentment Sam had previously known simply falling away, leaving her spent.

Finally, gathering her wits, Flora looked around for Maeve and Bethan.

'Oh Bethy,' she called out, 'are you all right?' Leaving Sam, she raced to help her friend who had fainted, dead away. She saw that there was blood coming from her ears and that tears of a pinkish colour were rolling down Beth's face, unchecked. 'Beth, Beth, can you hear me? BETH!' A spitting Morgana, fled once more, heading for Sybille's special room; she disappeared under the couch.

Bethan stirred, 'Oooh, my head,' she groaned, stirring.

Maeve, returning from the bathroom, pale and drawn, ran back in and after grabbing a towel, went to the freezer. She pulled out trays, scattering ice in her haste to wrap them in the towel. With, unaccustomed gentleness, she lifted Bethan's head, slipping the improvised ice pack under her neck. Bethan's eyes fluttered open.

'What happened?' she whispered, then, remembering, 'Oh that beautiful music and then, that terrible, terrible sound, like the sound of something lovely dying.' She raised shaking hands to her ears as she felt the cooling trickle of blood.

Passing her a tissue from the table, Flora said, 'I'd say, that sound was at such a dissonant pitch, your ears just couldn't handle it, I think you should get yourself checked out Beth, just in case.'

'No!' said Bethan, 'No need. I just need a warm bath and sleep if that's at all possible. I don't want to be alone though!'

She looked searchingly first at Sam and then at Maeve, 'Are you two okay she said,' then looking at Maeve's ghastly pallor she said, 'I'll get you some Raspberry leaf for the nausea ...and you Sam ...Hmm, Fringed Violet essence for you.'

'No!' they said together with watery grins, at the fact that they kept saying the same thing at the same time.

'Sybille,' said Sam, 'She can't be gone, there has to be something we can do.'

'We will Sam but first we all need to rest and take time to calm down. I'm going to make us a brew for later to help us relax and hopefully, reason will prevail in the morning.' She went to the kitchen, leaving them to sit in stunned silence.

'She's so together,' said Sam, How does she stay so cool, calm and collected after all this? I envy her that.'

'Don't be fooled Sam,' said Bethan, 'that's just our Flo's act for our benefit. When she's alone she'll let it all go, trust me. We need to keep an eye on her when she's, Miss Super-cool though or she'll forget to look after herself while looking after everyone else.'

'I think I need a walk,' said Maeve, I have to clear my head.'

'Want some company Maeve?' asked Sam.

About to refuse, Maeve glanced again at Sam; seeing how suddenly slight and fragile she looked, said, 'Yeah, come on then, I'll just let Flora know so she doesn't play mother hen with us.'

She headed to the kitchen, leaving Sam alone with Bethan.

Searching Bethan's face and seeing the utter grief written there, Sam sat down next to her, taking her hand gently. This sudden and unusual overture of compassion brought on fresh tears. When Maeve walked back in to see if she was ready to go, Sam stood up quickly, giving Bethan a quick hug before heading out the door.

Flora came back with a tray of homemade biscuits and a pot of heavenly scented herbal tea. Putting the tray down, she sat next to Bethan, gazing searchingly into her friends face,

'Are you all right Bethy,' she said gently, taking her friend's hand and feeling her pulse, still a little ragged from the shock. 'Do you want to tell me what happened yet?'

'No,' said Bethan, 'I need time to find words for the rush of images I returned with me. Somehow it's tied in with a dream I had last night too but I can't quite grasp the threads of it all yet. Mmmm yes, threads, tapestry.' She remembered the song that had come to her that morning. 'Agh it just won't come to me.'

'Stop trying Bethan, you've had a shock. I know how sensitive you are to changes in energy, particularly where Sybille and the planet are concerned. Let it go for now, just as Sybille,' she broke off her voice trembling, 'taught us, let it go and it must return to you.' then, 'Come on, drink some tea and try to eat something, you haven't had much today and I have a feeling we are all going to need our strength for what's to come.'

They sat in the companionable silence that only close friends shared, listening to the cottage, once so full of Sybille's energy, shift on its foundations as if in protest at the loss of her presence.

A small sound drew Flora's attention to the window, where an unusually timid Teddy cried to come in. On entry, she allowed Flora to stroke her only briefly before she shot off in the direction that Morgana had disappeared.

'Oh no, there'll be a fight. I have to stop her.' Running into Sybille's den, Flora stopped; silence. 'Teddy' she called softly, 'Morgana, where are you both?' She turned and there to her surprise, were Morgana and Teddy curled together in Sybille's favourite chair. Teddy, lovingly washing Morgana's ears, looked at her smugly as if to say, 'See I told you I'd bring her round eventually!'

with the closest a cat could get to a smirk Flora had ever seen. Smiling and shaking her head, she left them to their own version of consolation.

Chuckling to herself, she walked back to the lounge to tell Bethan, only to find her curled up sound asleep. Sitting, she ran her hand over her friend's silvery braid and breathing a small sigh of relief, leaned back. Closing her eyes in utter weariness, she slept.

Chapter 9
Sybille

Falling, hurtling into the deep, feather-soft floating into the folds of sweet sleep. By Sybille Madison

Sybille stirred from a space of deep peace, enveloped in gossamer threads interwoven with little chiming bells reminiscent of calling birds. Somewhere, there was the sound of a gently throbbing drum. A heartbeat; drummed her body, vibrating her senses. What had she been doing before she slept and had within that sleep been collapsing, falling and drifting inwards, downwards. Stretching she tried to recall ...why in bed asleep, of course! Bed; there was no bed. A cocoon of finely spun silken threads held her. It seemed to move and sway in an unseen breeze.

Where was she? Why wasn't she in bed at home, where she'd fallen asleep? Where was Morgana? Was she still dreaming? Then why was she so lucid, so aware? If only she could remember ...aah yes of course, it came in a tide of emotion. She'd been at her desk writing and known that it was her time again to renew. How she became aware of this was always a mystery and in between, forgotten, until the time approached again. Then she would remember, not the details, she would simply disappear and then as suddenly reappear where she had been as if falling asleep. Why did this happen? To replenish the mortal body so that the awful feelings of stretching thinly like wet parchment would abate for another hundred years. Each time she returned to renew, it became more difficult to separate herself from the physical life she lived and the freedom found, in knowledge of her real immortal self 'Kanto'noldo,' her Trueshape, Silver. Afterward all was lost again in the ties and tides of natural lives.

So many people thought it would be wonderful for things to stay forever unchanging, forever young of face, but if only they knew the pain of seeing loved ones move on to transition and having to fill the days with what was still to do, to experience, in order to continue to help others to wake up and remember.

In truth no one really died, only the character, created for a short leg of a long journey, sloughed off like a discarded overcoat. Life continued with a different body, a different face. Few realised that it was not just one life at a time but also multiple lives, all in the continuum of eternal now ...then she was drifting again. This time Sybille sensed something was very different though ...before she plunged deeper, into the sleep of renewal.

Chapter 10
Silver

Awaken humankin awaken ... it's time. Silver

Each time it felt as if there was more to do for the preparation and more to do after waking from the renewal process; harder to remember in which aspect she'd been and what she'd been doing in space and time, which layer of her being she'd travelled to or from. She remembered clearly she'd been focused strongly in the personality of Sybille, which was one of her favourites as this one was a true wildwytch and more aware than most on the Skeins of Tyme.

Stretching, she turned and twitched aside the cocoon of silk to better gauge what stage she was at, in her renewal. Looking out she saw she was at the very top of the Birthing Tree, hanging suspended from a huge branch and around her were many others of her siblings, all at different stages of return or renewal.

She looked, almost with envy at the veiled and swathed bud of silk closest to her. It showed the signs of completion as the Makers of Light flew and fluttered around, preparing the inhabitants for their final journey. Not back to the world of man but onwards to the Lands of the Lady.

Falling back into her silky nest, she relaxed again into its embrace. It moved to accommodate her change of position and mood the musical chimes growing sweeter, purer.

Still caught in part in the Littleshape of Sybille, Silver felt her stirring again within. She needed to remove the clutter of the mundane human thought patterns in order to renew. Silver drifted into Truedreaming listening to Sybille's dreams, to extract the data she needed as she remembered her first experiences through her, whose thoughts and emotions she felt deep within, awaiting renewal.

Chapter 11
Sybille Dreams ...Remembrance

Become a child again, not to be childish but rather to be childlike, for in that innocence we are complete and free from doubt.

Extract from the personal journal of Sybille Madison.

It all began for me so long ago when as a child, I would 'see' what others could not ...touch a gravestone, a book or any object to have them reveal the story of the person and their journey through life.

My grandmother called me Fae; said she thought the fairies had left me here. Sometimes that is exactly how it felt and still feels today as I contemplate this from deep within my Trueshape Silver's vast being, which is indeed Fae.

I was, so connected to nature it hurt ...a butterfly with a broken wing and no hope of repair ...a squashed beetle not quite dead ...anything lame, injured and dying brought up empathetic pain within me.

Today that pain is still there ...as an empath it now encompasses the entire human race with all their continuing pain and fear. It sometimes seems I hear the whole planet screaming for help and of course, on many levels, she is ...but it is not as much the planet as the human race, held in their own ignorance about the greater scheme of things of which they are all a forgotten part.

As a Wildwytch, a walker between the worlds of the Old Ways ...so much is becoming clear ...not separation no ...all is one.'

I was a wild child, not a delinquent, but I knew I was very different. Open to the forces of nature that it seemed only very few children remembered. My first aware interaction with Spirit was when I was barely eight, although there were many meetings and games with the Fae folk, this was with a human 'ghost.'

I remember waking from a deep sleep, lying facing the door to the bedroom. It opened and a fine-featured lady with wild silver hair walked in, looked at me and smiled, then turning, walked out again. She was totally transparent and dressed in what looked to me like old-fashioned flowing nightwear.

I always knew before these events occurred; even a bad dream was and is to this day, preceded by cold chills that cover the top of my head, sending goose bumps down my arms and spine.

The following morning I told my grandmother of the experience and she asked me to describe this person in as much detail as I could recall. Having done so, looking at me with one eyebrow raised, she asked me if I had ever seen a photo of my great, great grandmother. I hadn't, so she showed me one. It was the woman I had seen to the last detail. She had been a medium as I became, 'Fae.' So many more events of this kind occurred through the years, but this one in particular stayed in my memory.'

As Silver reached deep within to her own Truedreaming space, Sybille stirred again, battling to come to the fore. The Makers watched, stroking their senses gently, that they might both be soothed in the rememberings.

Chapter 12
Silver

Stretching out with her awareness, Silver sensed the many threads unravelling ...becoming a frayed fabric of memories lost in the Skeins of Tyme. How long could she hold the threads of this tapestry together, how long would it take to weave them into some semblance of their Trueshape again? Would it happen or would she drift further and further into the outer-reaches of the cosmos, forever floating into forgetfulness, no longer aware of the turning wheel of human lives and loves that she'd experienced, through all her myriad Littleshapes.

Something was amiss, she'd never felt this weak, this fragmented. She re-surfaced, sensing the now agitated movements of the Makers as something cast a shadow across the soft nest. A Maker hovered at the entrance to the yet unfinished cocoon, but something was wrong; it appeared to be in some distress, its brilliant light was flickering erratically. With something akin to human horror, Silver felt her Littleshape Sybille, stir from her dreaming to surface again. This had never happened before; Littleshapes were privy to a little information at a time at this stage of renewal or their psyches could go on overload ...too late, Sybille emerged fully clothed in her human Littleshape, gazing with awe at the silken cocoon and through it to the huge Tree of Birthing from which they were suspended.

The movement of the Makers became frantic. They rushed from the struggling Maker to support the now faltering Littleshape and her Trueshape Silver as they confronted each other across the narrow space of the cocoon; the impossible happened. With the attention of the Makers diverted the distressed Maker's wings simply folded, crumpled and it dove, cannoning into the gossamer veiled cocoon and tearing the delicate threads that anchored it to the Tree, fell with it into the void.

Silver reacted instantly; unfurling dragonfly wings behind her she grabbed the now shocked and struggling Sybille. Tearing through the veil with an audible ripping sound, she flew with her to the Birthing Tree, alighting on a bough. This was just too much for the rudely awakened Sybille and she fainted cold away; hardly a trace of her remained, only a feeble flicker of her life force pulsing, somewhere beyond her small, frail, human body.

The Makers hovered not knowing how to help, having never experienced anything like this; it just could not happen to their dear Littleshape. This precious one had been making such advancement in understanding; teaching about real human condition and their origins of first coming to green, beloved Terra. What would Terra do? Why had one of Her Makers suddenly sickened and dare they say it died. This was impossible; the Mother's sparks of life could never die for this was Her promise to all life. Their singing, chiming voices rose in hope that they may heal the fallen Maker and revive the unconscious

Littleshape Sybille. Suddenly among the sweet, vibrant sounds, one note, thin and harsh rang out as the fallen Maker rose from the void with a flutter of tattered, darkened wings and a mutated, impure form. They rushed to assist, but the fallen one raised a spiky discordant energy field and simply vanished.

The fallen Maker saw for a brief moment a tiny spark of light. A strange being, a wingless Maker, was falling through the ethers, tearing through the Skeins of Tyme into the realms of man. With a shriek, it dived after the falling Littleshape, following the only light it could see, it fell through the veil into darkness.

Nursing her Littleshape, cradling her in strong arms, enfolding her in bright wings, Silver, with a few fluid, liquid notes, called the Makers to once again, begin the weaving of a cocoon for her to renew in. She was at a loss to know what would happen to Sybille, her light had fallen. Therefore, as the Makers wove, she fled within to call out to the Mother to come to their aid, but it was as if a shadow was dimming even Her light from being reached...

Chapter 13
Finding Their Way

In the mellow autumn evening sunshine, Maeve and Sam walked in silence drinking in the quietude and the liquid warbles of Magpie. Giant Pine mushrooms flourish along the track amongst the moist roots of the huge Pine trees and tiny wrens flitted in the leaf litter. Stirring up loamy aromas, they caught little winged bugs for their supper, mid-flight.

They had both managed to find companionship through the loss of their mentor. Although blood related to Sybille, Sam felt that the others all had a unique and special bond with her, similar to her own. She had not attended many of the group meetings but, having lived with Sybille from the age of, not quite 18, she'd been, exposed to Sybille's unique relationship with the planet; how she had lived her life as a Wytch and how compassionate a person she truly was. Sybille was her saving grace, having patience for the raw, fractious girl who gave no thought to the fact that Sybille too was grieving the loss of a sister and who had had her life turned around when the guardianship papers were presented after the will was read. Sam often wondered how Sybille had truly felt at that moment, to find an awkward teenager foisted on her whether she liked it or not.

Silently considering this, Sam realised Maeve had stopped and was staring at something intently. She stopped; turning round, she wandered back to Maeve.

'What's wrong? You look as if you've seen a ghost or something.'

Maeve just stood staring so following her gaze; Sam saw a transparent figure hovering just above the ground among the trees. The figure looked lost and weak and Sam realised that it wore her Aunt's face.

'No,' she screamed, 'Auntie!' The wraith-like figure turned and looking at her blankly, head on one side as if trying to remember something, smiled tremulously before disappearing into the grove of trees.

Sam made to follow, but Maeve, with the strength, born of determination grabbed her arm, dragging the now frantically struggling Sam, back the way they'd come.

'Come on,' Maeve snarled, 'that wasn't a ghost, I'm sure of it but somehow Sybille's in trouble, that I do know. If she were dead, she would visit us in the usual manner not be out here wandering, looking lost. Come ON Sam we have to tell the others. I think we need Bethan to trance to see what she can find on the ethers.'

Sam used all the strength she could muster and pulling Maeve to a halt stood dumbfounded. Her teeth began to chatter so Maeve slipped out of her jacket, wrapped it around Sam's shoulders and with a little shake, brought her back to her senses

'We need Bethan to whaaa?' said Sam.

'Come ON!' Maeve repeated pulling Sam with her back towards the cottage.

Meanwhile, Flora and Bethan slept on and in sleeping, found their way back to their dreams of the night before.

Bethan was running through the forest again. She didn't know why she was running; she'd had this dream so many times before and knew the usual outcome, yet something was different.

There was an acrid odour drifting on the air that smelt of burnt feathers and as she ran, looking up she saw birds were falling from the sky. Some were hanging inverted in the trees, where death had claimed them, trapped in black sticky threads and strange creatures were wrapping them up in more. Small, black, shiny winged beings, like beetles, were flitting through the trees.

The same sweet sound she'd heard earlier today trembled the leaves, vibrating the bodies of the dead birds. As the sound rang out the birds were changed, coming to life again with a cry and a flutter of wings, whilst more winged creatures arrived, white, iridescent and glowing with light, they tended the birds, dispersing the sticky threads with a harmonious note and the dark creatures disappeared.

Standing awestruck, Bethan saw a Tree so vast it defied all definition. She walked to the base; it was as big as a block of houses. Reaching out to touch it, something stopped her when she saw the sap running like blood from its bark. One of the tiny beings flitted closer looking deep into her eyes.

In a strange tongue it said, 'Tua lye, tua lye Arwen. Lye il' dagor 'tel morchiant ereb. Lye yele nan' 'tel aa' 'tul telwa. Tua lye fallanherim 'tel ornrin en' nostad.'

With a start, Bethan returned to the waking state. Groggily she hunted around for pen and paper to write the vision down before it escaped. Once more, the haunting music filled her and another snippet of the song recalled. What was that language and why is it so familiar? I understood it in that dream, but not on waking, she thought? What did that beautiful creature say to me, it seemed so distressed?

'Mmmm I need my harp.' She sang the line, 'Drifting through the warp and weft, fragile… Fragile what? Aaagh this is so frustrating.'

At that moment, Maeve and Sam returned from their walk talking animatedly to each other, they stopped seeing Bethan looking more like herself again.

'How are you feeling Beth?' said Maeve. 'We have something we need to talk to you and Flora about.'

'We have to let her sleep a while longer I think,' Bethan replied. 'It's a lovely evening; let's go sit on the veranda 'til she wakes up.'

They sat in the quiet listening to the call of the forest beyond the boundary, each wanting to share what

they had just experienced and impatient for Flora to wake
so they could.

Flora slumbered on oblivious to her friend's desire she
wake soon. She could somehow sense their impatience but
was deep in a dream state as if frozen in time.

She was a spark of life, of light and could hear and
understand a language that was ancient, primordial. It was
the language of the trees the plants and animals the
language of the planet Herself ...many voices speaking the
ancient tongue as one.

She was straining all her senses to hear, what
whispered to her. She felt the urgency and heard again,
'Listen...' then. 'Flora, wake up! FLORA! Come back now!'

She felt something sting her face and someone
shaking her, gently at first, but then more insistently. She
was floundering caught in heaviness her limbs leaden, but
something was pulling on her, shaking her. She struggled
to the surface as if from a deep muddy pool. Her eyes
wouldn't open; her body wouldn't obey her. 'Wake up
Flora, wake up,' said a voice insistently, followed by a
cold, wet cloth placed over her face ...she rose indignantly
to full awareness again gasping in shock.

She felt arms around her as she regained her
faculties, life returning to numb hands and feet, warmth to
cold lead weighted limbs. Struggling again to open her
eyes, she groaned,

'Oh, my head!' then coming rapidly to her senses, 'Quick I need paper and pen, I have to get this down before it goes away.'

'Wait!' said Bethan, 'you must drink this first.'

Gulping down some now cold tea, she revived a little.

Sam passed her the notebook she always carried with her and Flora wrote down fast and furiously as much as she could recall.

Once again, Maeve and Sam waited impatiently for Flora to finish writing. They needed desperately to share what they had seen in the lane and Maeve was ready to explode. Bethan looked at them, a silent query in her eyes and whispered, 'What in heaven's name has happened to you two, you look fit to burst.'

'We...' they began to speak at once but Bethan held up her hand to still them, peaceful energy washed over them and they fell silent again, waiting.

Finishing with a sigh, Flora realised that the trio were watching her intently; nervousness emanated from Sam and Maeve like smoke, concern from Bethan like cool silk.

'Okay, that was weird but I think I got most of it. I guess the rest will come when I'm not so shattered.' Looking round at her friend's faces, she said, 'What's happening? You all seem concerned, but I'm all right, really.'

'You were groaning and thrashing around,' said Maeve, 'We thought something was hurting you. We couldn't wake you!'

'I'm fine now really,' she said again, 'What's, been going on? I'm frankly on total overload, but I think it would be best if you all stayed the night and we thrash this out as best we can right now.'

'I agree,' said Bethan, 'we have to work out what we're going to do with Sybille's request. What Maeve and Sam will do about staying in Melbourne or moving here...?.'

'Whoa,' said Maeve. 'What do you mean moving here, I have my studio established and it will be an enormous task to even consider bringing it all here? It's ridiculous, expecting us just to drop everything because Sybille wants us to. What was she thinking?'

'If Sybille had organised all of this to be done before she disappeared, then she'll have sound reasons as well you know Maeve,' said Flora, 'she never acted on a whim. There has to be a deeper meaning behind it all, she obviously knew she was going away but I think it might have been planned for later perhaps Samhain because she used to take her 'sabbaticals' then. I for one am going to find out what's behind the sudden change in her plans.'

'You're right,' said Sam, 'she may have been eccentric to say the least but she never did anything without real purpose.' Then, with a pause and a glance at Maeve,' she said. 'We should tell them Maeve, you know, what we saw.'

'Yeah, I've been waiting for the opportunity.'

Between them, Sam and Maeve explained what they had seen. Bethan and Flora both agreed that Sybille would not be lost in the mists if she'd actually died to this world. She would visit them as any other spirit would in dreams or meditations and they knew her advanced knowledge would not have her drifting as some wraith in the woods. No, this was much more serious. Something had happened to her very spirit and she couldn't find her way back.

Recovering her composure, Bethan told them of her experience. ; how her recurring dream of years had changed, showing her that all was not well in other realms and that she'd now been asked to help.

'I sense this dream and the terrible images shown me of nature in trouble isn't just an analogy of what's wrong in our world in the physical sense. It's also what's going on in other realms too and I think that this may be the cause of Sybille's difficulty in returning to her body, wherever that may be right now.'

A stunned silence followed as they all took this in.

'And,' said Flora, 'it ties in with what I was just told in my dream. Here, listen to this,' waiting for their attention she read,

'I am that which is your bones, teeth, nails and hair; your skin dark or fair. No difference does it make to me ...for you are on, in all ...in me.

When the element air wafts through your hair it lifts my leaves and blesses them with coolness or rips at them with taloned fingers pulling them from their last clinging, to their near dormant tree ...until falling, falling they land on my skin and become in their rotting ...one with me again. Mould spoors and fungi are born from their dying. Small pelts of furry mosses cover my body and lift tiny star faces to their larger shining siblings above ...to bathe in starlight ...moonlight then closing, nestle deep within the fronds of ferns to hide from the face of the blinding one's glare.

When the element of water, pours its silver weight on the boughs of my trees or pools in earthy furrows, before breaking loose; gushes thrillingly, mindlessly joyful, in their rush to reach a larger blending of their sweet and salty siblings. Always moving ...never still unless; caught by the great Blinding One in a puddle of my muddiness; they too grow over with slimy algae and frog spawn. Water becomes earth while the rest seeping ...oozing down, down deep within my body, quenching my thirst for moisture and germinating seeds that have lain dormant beneath my skin ...like a minor itch to scratch they break the surface and are nurtured by the Blinding One until they stretch their new limbs to Him in supplication ...greening in His light.

When the element of fire ...an offshoot from the blinding one breaks loose upon the earth, all flee in fear of His heat ...and yet again deep within my hardened crust new life awaits the greening. Life force, within all things is akin to this fire, hungry to grow ...no fear of change, more fearful that they will not.

Yet, nothing remains stagnant or still for long, when even on the stillest day, my skin is rock hard and burning to your feet. A fresh breeze can lift the heaviest hair from sun drenched, sweat-salted skin ...there you have gushing from your pores, your kindred the ocean, of which you are a part; pooling in the furrows between your breasts or running down your face from soaking hair.

When you cut me, I bleed just as you do. I spill my guts to you in rich black oils, full of the fossilised bones of my many selves. My trees run red with gooey resins and sap runs in translucence through pliant stems, just as your skin runs red with blood when cut, no different to your lymph fluids, which lubricate your innards. All are the blood in my veins; the plasma deep within my seething molten core ...hot ...red ...pulsing, like the blood that rushes through your heart ...oxygenated by the element of air; pumping the fiery heat, animating your limbs, your brain, your nerve endings. Helping you breathe, to smell the aroma of your environment ...and the fluids of saliva run, to taste the sweetness of the bounty of my body or the bitterness of your own destructive ways...

...And so all is one, through all the bindings and blendings of these elements, no two operate in isolation ...so why would you think you are alone, separate or different to them in your being. All run through you as they do through me ...and then, Great Goddess animates us all ...yes, even I have come from her ...Primordial One ...listen, listen and awake!'

'Oh,' said Sam, 'that's beautiful. I didn't know you could write like that Flora!'

'No,' said Flora, 'that came through me but they're not my words. I'm just a vessel.'

'Well, I don't know about that,' Sam replied, 'this is all very new to me, despite my Aunt's teachings. I obviously have so much to learn. I guess I've been putting it off for years, but the opportunity that she's given us is amazing. I don't know how this all fits together with the building and our personal skills, but my intuition says this is just the beginning.'

'All this aside,' said Flora, 'we need a plan. I'm almost too tired to think, but I suggest we have something to eat and have a brainstorming session about everything. Firstly, working together and secondly, our individual needs and then of course we have some work to map out before Samhain.' Turning to Bethan, she said, 'We're going to need you to trance or scry to see if you can find out where Sybille is,' then added with a grin, 'not to mention a birthday coming up.'

'Never mind that,' replied Bethan, 'it's not a time to be thinking of celebrating. I don't feel in the least like having a party, I'm too concerned for Sybille right now.'

Maeve stood and walked over to squat at Bethan's feet. 'Sybille has been gone for just over a year and a day,' she said, 'nothing's changed about that, except now we have some inner realm work to do as well. I for one love a challenge and we have just over a couple of months to sort this out, but I also feel that Sybille would want you to have the celebration of your 29th anyway. It will do us all good and give Sam a chance to get to know us better and us, her. You're not at all what I expected Sam,' she said turning to her, 'you showed courage this afternoon when we saw Sybille in that state and I admire you for that.'

This, unaccustomed sentiment, from Maeve had Bethan and Flora exchanging a silent high five behind her back as Sam said quietly, 'Thank you, Maeve,' then, 'All right, let's get started!'

'Let's see what we can rustle up to eat,' said Flora, heading for the kitchen

'I'll help,' said Bethan.

A while later before they ate Flora broke a fresh loaf of bread with her hands, offering each a piece for the Lammas sacrifice and passing round Sybille's old chalice filled with rich, pungent herbed wine. Bethan blessed the food and raising the chalice in the gesture of old said, 'To the Triple Goddess,' the others replied, 'None greater.' Over cheesy omelette, green salad and more Lammas wine they shared their hopes for the future, what they needed to let go from the past and toasted Sybille wherever she may be. Then they went outside to scatter the remains of the Lammas bread and the Blessed wine onto the ground for the Spirit of Place before wearily exchanging brief hugs they headed upstairs, giving Sam her own bed while the others, being long-term friends, were happy to share for the night in surrender to the sleep of exhaustion.

Chapter 14
Sybille

Where will I be when this life sets me free?
…when this body is frail and bent
Will there be signs that shall guide me?
Who will be there at the top of the stair, to wipe away tears
and stroke my white hair?
Will I find my way through intent?
Musings from the personal journal of Sybille Madison

Drifting, floating, released from the pull of gravity and the weight of the physical body, Sybille saw two women coming towards her. It was like looking through a mist, a cloud. She thought she should know them. She wanted to cry out, but there were no words only images and a strange detachment. As if this were all she was, all she knew, this wraithlike creature; she knew it wasn't so but more she couldn't remember.

She had a life, a physical body somewhere. What had happened? She felt a tug as a gentle voice called to her, but she didn't even have the will to find out where the voice came from.

She drifted off again into the forest and there far away in the mists was an outline, the shadow of an immense tree. She floated towards it and saw little winged beings were working to stem the flow of sap oozing from its skin. She knew she should be worried, but the emotion barely registered. Instead, she drifted upwards looking for a resting place in its boughs. Tired, so tired. Finding a small hollow in its broad trunk she slipped inside ...sleep she thought, I just need to rest and then I'll remember.

Chapter 15
Silver

Was I once human? Did I sleep?
Was I cast out to drift in the deep?
Are humankin right …do we err and then fall
…and only in endings find Oneness in All. Silver

Silver too drifted, searching the ethers for the Littleshape known as Sybille. She could feel her, sense her distress but was powerless to find her until she could anchor the cocoon again to the Birthing Tree. The little Makers were frantically trying, but the sickened Maker had ripped the threads from the tree so direly that the Tree wept, oozing thick green-red tears and refusing to allow the Makers near to reattach the gossamer threads to begin a new weaving. The Birthing tree grieved all Her children.

The other nests hung suspended unaware of the drama enacted all around. The Trueshapes herded their Littleshapes into the sleep state of renewal that they may siphon their thoughts, extracting the experiences they needed to enable their journey home to the Land of the Lady.

Chapter 16
Morning Dawns

Side by side in the other realms are we Fae who left long
ago. Side by side in the other worlds are the elves
…the nymphs and the gnomes
So if our planet was sick and gone
…where would we be when that, is done?
Floating through ether, flying the wind
…what would happen to all our kin?
Therefore, when you imagine you go somewhere else
…where is that place, alone by yourself?
…and do you consider the planet Herself?
So where will you be when that's done?

Dawn lifted Bethan from a deep dreamless state to see Sybille floating through the room although this Sybille was dressed in strange and ancient clothing. Morgana was sitting bolt upright on the desk yet strangely unperturbed by the wraithlike visitation of her mistress.

Holding her breath as if the very sound might scare Sybille away, she remained immobile, watching her friend and mentor who seemed to be searching the area around the chest that still stood open the Book of Shadows revealed. She seemed vague and distracted as if she didn't know why she was there. Bethan felt her anxiety as if it were her own. Slowly sitting up, she noticed that around

Sybille, tiny flashes of light like the little orbs seen often, captured by digital cameras. These seemed to have wings and were frantically trying to catch Sybille's attention, gesturing as if to show her something.

The movement surprised Sybille and peering at Bethan as if through a gauzy veil, she frowned in puzzlement and drifted away like smoke, the little beings winking out one by one in pursuit.

Bethan stood stretching. Glancing out the window at the new day, she saw several Ravens sat in a row on the roof outside and were looking into the next room that Flora had made her own. She had a flash of the dream from yesterday of the birds caught in some sticky black substance, dying and as if, as one, the Ravens turned to look at her. The same voices spoke in her head,

'Tua lye, tua lye Arwen. Lye il 'dagor 'tel morchiant ereb. Lye yele nan' 'tel aa' 'tul telwa. Tua lye fallanherim 'tel ornrin en' nostad,' but this time, astounded, she understood the words,

'Help us. You must help us Lady; we cannot keep back the darkmaker's blight alone. We have called, but the help that is coming may be too late to make the change complete. Help us heal Her.'

Four of the Ravens looked at her again and then flew, leaving one sitting watching her. She blinked as the outline shimmered and changed; the colour of its wings turning from blue-black to shining silver for a moment and its shape altered from bird to human and back again. To her shocked gaze it carefully winked at her and then with a ruffle of feathers, once more black with a flash of silver, it took flight with a cry like rippling laughter.

As she stood entranced, there came a gentle tap on the door and finding her voice, called out,

'Come in.'

Flora entered and saw her friend standing staring fixedly out the window. 'Are you all right,' she asked, 'I was woken by the cacophony of Ravens outside. Since my dream the other day, they were never far away. They plague poor Morgana something fierce,' she finished touching Bethan's arm gently.

'Oh, goodness, sorry,' she said distractedly, 'Sybille was here, she's just a shadow of herself and then the Ravens...' she paused to take a deep breath, 'One, of them was a shapeshifter.'

'Well, now that perhaps explains it. I've never seen it done, but Sybille said we all have the ability within us. Oh and then there was a feather that just manifested from nowhere - but who is that gifted?'

'Could be anyone Sybille knows from the past,' said Bethan, 'She had a regular number of rather curious characters passing through here at any given time. Sometimes I thought I'd stepped into an alternative time zone, which is probably why she always wanted us to let her know if we were dropping by.'

'Well,' replied Flora, 'I don't know how the others will take this. Maeve is still very sceptical and Sam is an enigma at the best of times. I don't know how she'll react at any time to this sort of thing. We can't baby her though; she'll have to learn the truth about Sybille one day I guess.'

'I don't think any of us really know though Flora,' said Bethan, 'If anyone is an enigma it would be her!'

'True,' laughed Flora, 'how true. Come on, I have to feed the chooks and cats or I'll never get ahead for the day. I have a feeling this is going to be a huge one for all of us. We have to sort out the building in town, look at the financial side of things and how we're going to handle everything. I for one probably have enough to get started, but it's not going to last forever.'

'Ever the practical one aren't you! At least you have this Flora,' as Bethan gestured to the room in general, 'and all thanks to our Sybille.'

'I'd rather she was here Bethy, I do miss her. Not that I'm ungrateful, 'cos she must have foreseen that my relationship with Dan was going nowhere fast.'

'She trained us well to be intuitive but she was ...is, amazingly accurate in her ability to see clearly.'

'You have that too though Beth. She always said you would be her natural replacement one day. Sadly, that day's come. Now we have to knuckle down and put things in place for the future so that all she built isn't in vain.'

'Speaking of which, I guess we should get started,' said Beth, 'I'm just not sure where though yet.'

'Egg collecting then breakfast,' stated Flora!

'Oh, you and food Flora, you should be the size of a bus!' Beth laughed.

Flora slipped outside, collected the eggs and let out the goats with unusual haste before heading back in to make breakfast

Sam was brewing a pot of coffee when she returned the stove, always ticking, leant warmth to the room that was welcoming.

'Hope you don't mind Flora,' she said, 'I needed my morning fix and I wasn't sure of your routine.'

'I'm usually up and around early,' she replied, 'but please, this is your place too, so don't stand on ceremony. I was going to ask if you wanted to move in here until you made your mind up about living arrangements here or in the village.'

'Thanks,' she replied pouring coffee and offering to Bethan and Flora, 'I haven't thought that far ahead yet. There's my job to consider too, although I do most of my articles from home and interviews on Skype so where I am isn't crucial to that. I don't know if I'll be able to afford to quit, at least not until the house in Melbourne sells or the centre takes off. I've got some cash stashed that my parents gave me which will help to get us started.'

'You'd sell your house Sam,' said Bethan, 'Your parents gave it to you, couldn't you rent it out?'

I thought of that,' Sam replied, 'it doesn't actually mean much to me as houses go. It's rather cold and clinical, a bit like my parents I suppose,' she laughed. 'It's not that I didn't love them or wish they hadn't died, but the house isn't me, it's just bricks and mortar and I already have it on the market. I've had a few nibbles too.

It's in an ideal possie and the real estate agent said there wouldn't be any problems selling it.

Sybille asked me years ago to come and live here, write my books and she'd give me some work in the centre. Things just didn't turn out that way. It was just never the right time. Now I feel as if I have little choice in the matter, which is a very strange feeling for me, I can tell you.'

'Now I feel as if I've taken away your alternative home Sam,' Flora exclaimed.

'No, not at all. Don't be silly; I didn't say that to make you feel guilty, although I was resentful when Sybille sent all the stuff to you about what she wanted done while she was away. Thinking about it now, I'm not really the alternative lifestyle type, at least not the daily manual labour part of it. I don't know how Sybille did it all. Come to that I don't know how you do it all and work too?'

'Well, the bigger jobs she and I used to do together and then there were always willing hands from her groups too. They were happy to put in a few hours helping if it meant they could take home some eggs or some incredible concoction she'd brewed up! Maeve used to do a lot and still does when she's here. She loves to help make the herb and fruit wines and tonics; well help sample them anyway,' she laughed, 'and Bethan's always round here helping out, particularly when we make dyes together.'

'What you make all those beautiful coloured thread yourselves?' said Sam, 'that's unbelievable!'

'All a labour of love,' laughed Bethan, drifting in silently, trailing off when she heard the clatter of boots on the stairs.

'Morning sisters all,' grinned Maeve, not usually so cheerful before her morning, heart starting, espresso, 'I had the most glorious night's sleep. A girl, who changed into a Raven and then changed back, again visited me. She said she would show me how to do it and I said but my feathers would be red,' pointing to her unruly mane of coppery curls, laughing, 'and this girl actually chuckled so loudly it woke me and there were the Ravens having a squabble right outside the window. Earlier, I was visited by this amazing looking hunk who said his name was Morgan and he ...well, never mind,' she grinned breaking off as she saw the look that passed between Flora and Bethan, 'What? What was that 'look' for?'

Bethan told her about the Ravens behaviour earlier. Instead of the usual, 'Yeah right,' from Maeve there was a stunned silence. 'Okay,' Maeve said, 'Now I'm really intrigued!' and when Bethan told her about Sybille, 'Well at least I wasn't too far out with the description then.'

Sam handed her a coffee. Flora made a pile of toast slathered with Sybille's special Raspberry Jam and they sat at the table, in the long, airy, dining room lost in their individual thoughts for a while.

Chapter 17
Maeve

Dance the dance of dragonfly
...silver trails across the sky
Transformation now and here
...grasp the movements of the year
Fly with Her, on soundless wings
...feel the joy that change can bring

Later that morning Maeve drove back to Melbourne to deliver some samples she'd promised to a lovely little shop in Eltham before returning to Springsmeet so they could visit the centre and have a good look in the parts of the huge building they were unfamiliar with.

She dropped in at home to check for emails and couldn't resist a look at the discarded work from the day before. It was definitely not redeemable. The beautiful shards of crystal she had left on the bench, she picked up and wrapped in a square of silk to take to show Flora, who had a deep affinity with crystals and stones.

The house was silent other than a few bubbles in the water tank again. Nothing like the day before though she thought relieved. As she turned the rumbles deepened and she had known even before she turned, something was about to happen again. Sure enough, a geyser of water erupted upwards and without a drop spilling splashed back down into the cauldron again.

'Hmm,' she said, 'If there's something I need to know could you be a bit more precise d'ya think!' Silence, then watery, gurgling chuckles, emitted from the depths of the cauldron before falling still again. Maeve waited, but all remained quiet.

Packing some clothes and a few other personal items, she locked up and left again. As she drove, she thought about the dilemma of where she would live when the centre was completed. She had the huge task of moving her forge and cauldron and all her tools, but that would be something maybe Sam and she could work out together, saving on transport costs if they could organise to share the load, assuming that would all fall into place for them.

She loved Springsmeet so it really wasn't a hardship to leave the city. The studio had been great, and she'd get good rent for it. Several people had said if she ever moved out, they'd love first option on it. She could look at a long-term lease as an income or she could give someone the option to buy. No hassles, either way it would meet her financial needs to set up in Springsmeet and then look for somewhere to live, maybe rent for a while until she knew what was what.

At that moment, her phone rang and taking a quick look at the display saw it was her Mother. 'Oh no,' she groaned, 'what more could she possibly want from me? I thought we were clear that I wasn't ever going back to Sydney.'

It bleeped again, showing a message left. Reaching over she simply deleted it, sighing deeply.

Springsmeet here I come, she crooned to herself as she turned into the beautiful town centre and headed to Floras' in streaming autumn sunshine.

Chapter 18
Samantha

What is passing from your life ...what is finished and done? Visualise symbols of these changes and imagine throwing them into the fire, a lake or the ocean or burying them in the ground, perhaps in the form of seeds or bulbs that will manifest into new 'ideas' in spring.

Extract from Sybille's notes to her students

Sam also drove back to Melbourne but in a daze. She was sad and happy all at the same time, which confused her more. Sure, she could share with Flora for a while until things were sorted out about moving but it meant she'd have to find somewhere to store her things. Alternatively, would she sell the old furniture too? Why not, she thought. It was still in mint condition because she really only used her office-studio and a bedroom. She rarely cooked and when she did eat in it was usually at her desk anyway.

She didn't have many friends and was a little wary of the men in her profession; journalists were a breed apart she thought.

Being a loner almost from birth, she was actually looking forward to getting to know the three talented women who interested but at the same time confused her with their lay back manner towards all the strange phenomena they'd been experiencing. Sybille's unseen presence was the decisive factor. She had to find out for herself what was going on.

Maeve rather daunted her but didn't seem as unfriendly as she'd previously assumed. Flora was very different, so down to earth and practical when it was needed and yet so sensitive too. Then there was Bethan. She really felt a kinship with her. There was something a little familiar about her, perhaps due to the mass of silvery blonde hair and a slight build that reminded her of Sybille. Then there were her uncanny seership abilities she shared with Sybille too. She'd never imagined there'd be another with such abilities as she'd witnessed with Sybille. What were the chances of meeting another such gifted seer? The idea of working alongside these three women was actually beginning to feel like a gift in itself somehow. She had no idea what was in store for them, but there would never be a dull moment.

Parking at the house she still thought of as 'her parent's house,' she saw the real estate agent Evelyn waiting for her on the doorstep.

'Oh, hello Ms Cartwright,' she said to Sam, 'I was going to leave these for you to look over,' showing the bulky yellow document envelope she held. 'We have a buyer for you; no haggling either and a straightforward, sixty-day settlement. Sooner, if you agree to their offer of course. These people don't have to wait for finances to be organised and are excited to be moving so close to the heart of the City. They both work there, so commuting's a snap.'

'Goodness,' said Sam, 'that was quick work! I'd expected it would sell reasonably quickly because of the location, but this is amazing. I don't know how I'll get everything done, but this is just what I need to motivate me. Thanks for your hard work.'

'Oh, this wasn't even from the listing,' Evelyn said, 'they haven't even seen inside. They were driving by and knew that it would be just the house for them. They have two youngsters that go to Scott's College so it's lovely and central for them too. So take a look at the contracts and when you're ready, we'll get everything signed and sealed for you.'

Sam truly amazed did a little happy dance on the doorstep as Evelyn walked away. She couldn't believe her luck. She had to tell someone or she'd burst. It would once have been Sybille she'd call with juicy news, now instead the number the same she called Flora. Flora answered straight away and was genuinely excited for Sam.

'Wow,' she said, 'talk about synchronicity; it's truly meant to be I think. Congratulations Sam, we'll have to toast this later today.'

'I'll be back in a few hours,' said Sam, 'I'm looking forward to seeing all of the building in town and having a look at possible properties too seeing as I'm about to become a local it seems. It will be great to live in the country again. I'm blabbering,' she laughed, 'see you later Flora'

'Yes, see you then Sam; bye now.'

Sam packed a few things to take and then went to her writing room to collect her Notepad and the article she had to finish. At least she could email it in by deadline. It just meant she'd have to take some time in the next couple of days to get it done. The trail of leaves crunched underfoot between bedroom and office. I'd better clear those up before I go she thought as she packed the rest of the things she needed. What a strange dream and these leaves appearing from nowhere. She still couldn't remember it all but hoped that it would come to her as she felt it had some bearing on the events of the last day or so.

After collecting everything she needed together and packed into the car, she did a quick circuit with the vacuum cleaner the autumn leaves now crisp and dried released a pungent odour of the woodlands near Sybille's farm and she wondered too at that connection. There were certainly no Oak trees around the inner city so where had they come from? In fact, where had she been in the dream?

She'd been walking Sam recalled. Yes, that's right, just like yesterday with Maeve. In fact, she'd had a sense of déjà vu then when they'd seen Auntie Sybille's; what had they called it? Ah yes, 'Wraith.' How odd.

Pondering still, she emptied the fridge of a few nice cheeses, some dips and olives and a couple of bottles of her favourite bubbly. She wouldn't go empty handed and yes, they'd celebrate the sale of her house.

As she was leaving, she caught a glimpse of herself in the hall mirror, just like the day before, caught in the same posture, hair on end in tufts from her habitual tugging at it and the same cocky expression on her face like an instant replay.

How strange she thought, she looked different somehow too: less stressed despite the experiences of the last days. Time to go she thought, looking forward to the drive home. Yep, that's it! I'm going home.

Chapter 19
Bethan

Every day is Her day ...every day is sacred. Don't wait for the Sabbats to come around, celebrate Her in every little thing you do. She is in those moments you miss while you're waiting for a 'special occasion.' Make each moment special; ...make every breath you take ...Hers.
Extract from the Book of Shadows

Bethan was the last to leave Flora's after helping her to make up the bed for Sam in the spare room. Last night they had all been so tired they had practically fallen where they stood. For tonight, they made up the beds with crisp, clean linen sheets and some of Bethan's soft throws for warmth.

Once the farm was, as Flora wanted it, Bethan left to go home. It was only a ten-minute drive away from Covenstead, behind the next village, Wells in the series of small villages between Groveham and Springsmeet.

She loved her old miners' cottage with its warm colours and polished wood boards. It had been her home since she graduated. Her parents had originally helped with the deposit, all of which she had paid back to them through her sheer hard work.

Parking in the driveway, she collected wood for the stove on the way in. It was beginning to get chilly now in the mornings and evenings with golden Indian summer days.

Bending to fill and light the stove, she paused to listen. Something was different. Yes, it was silent. Where were the birds this morning? Usually there would be a flock of noisy sparrows or the shrieks of cockatoo from the nut tree in the lane; she had to keep netted if she wanted any for herself. All was silent. Walking to the kitchen window, she looked out into the garden and beyond to the forest. It sprawled down the hillside to her back fence and over the hillside to the boundaries of the vineyard and cherry farm, which belonged to her closest neighbour. All was uncannily still.

As the crow flies, the forest would meet on the other side of the hill close to Sybille's, where Maeve and Sam had first seen her wraith. All things are connected after all and as the crow flies she could be at Sybille's in about twenty minutes via the connecting forest. She didn't know why she'd thought of it then, but the train of thought continued. She'd read somewhere that bracken, which grew prolifically through the region was probably, all one plant, spreading out underground and breaking surface in a chain of beautiful, coiled green fronds, separate yet same. So similar to what Sybille had taught her that all souls were sparks of the one; microcosms of the macrocosm no less and all were equal in the eyes of the Lady; plant, mineral, animal and human. All were part of the tides of life, individually unique and, therefore, special in that individuality.

Shaking herself from her reverie, she walked to her studio still aware of the uncanny silence for such a beautiful, sunny day. Too restless to weave, she reached for her lap harp, trying to remember the music and words that had come to her from the dreams. As she focused inward for recall, a single note fell from the harp before she could pluck a string. It resonated through the room and through her body; a tingle of electrical vibration as gentle as a first kiss.

She sighed and closed her eyes, her hands finding the strings naturally and intuitively, she sank into an outpouring of liquid sound. Words rose to the surface of the music like bubbles in a pool, each note a colour of such vibrancy she thought she would explode into a million fragments as each sound formed anew.

Slowly, a fragile melody immerged from the pool of sound and words rippled in the ethers just close enough for her to hear them if she stretched out her awareness. It was a symbiotic relationship; music, vibration and finally, words ...she sang...

'Perfect love and perfect trust are all that we should know; to rise above life's cut and thrust, we have a way to go. The darkness birthed within each soul its offspring known as fear and in our fearing we forgot the love that brought us here.

A greening globe a shining sphere that once knew only light; spun from orbit, falling deep into the veils of night but once we knew the silken threads that held us strong and tight, were not to bind us but to stretch, to help our soul's winged flight.

That guiding reign of pure intent forgotten in the deep is now ascending, pulling to awaken us from sleep. The web of light around this orb, our home away from home; birthed simply for Her Light to feel the darkness of alone.

So now, we feel the tug, a pull, as She reels us in. One by one, we must ascend re-joining with our kin. It's not that we must leave this realm; the reverse, in fact, is true, for there were also other kin, who left this Planet blue.

They were the Fae the conquered race who could not stand the dark, who then withdrew and humankind were left to make their mark ...but what a legacy we leave, now that we're almost done and who in truth remembers the one law, 'with harm to none.'

No guilt, no fears, no human tears can heal the rift we wrought but if that's so, has our descent been truly all for nought? The Mother knows She holds the threads; She guides us even here the depths of life's illusive paths, each step a mortal year.

Each birth anew upon the Wheel, together yet apart, we now as one ascend to heal Earth's frail and failing heart. On the edge as veils thin, to let us see beyond the Fae returning bring the light, once hidden ...almost gone.

These realms of beauty and of love cannot be as before; this turning sphere of spinning threads must change to be restored. As once again, life ascends and darkness fills with light, we see all that is mirrored as once day gave way to night.

No separation truly is, between each soul, each spark for She has never truly let us fall into the dark.'

...the music sobbed to a close the sound rippling out, extending into the ethers where deep in the heart of the Birthing Tree the one once known as Sybille in this human life, cried in her sleep and her Trueshape Silver reached out to sense where this melody had originated and sighed, hope renewing.

Coming to her senses, Bethan rose shakily, gently placing her lap harp down, she crossed again to the glass doors to her studio and stepped out into the garden.

Something stirred on the forest edge as birds flocked around a tall, slender shape, dressed in silver and green, carrying a small harp on his back. He stood watching her, head cocked to one side as if listening. He was a good distance away, but she could strangely see every detail of his face. Broad, high cheekbones, slanted violet eyes, long silvery streaked hair. Strange clothing in pale fine threads so like her weavings. He reached behind and plucked one note on the harp sending it rippling like a living thing towards her.

One note sent a few words in that strange language, 'A'maelamin tinu. Amin ilyanemie utu lle imya llie lindale.'

What is that language she thought? Who is that being, so strange yet so familiar? Are my eyes playing tricks on me! He moved forward; raising his hand in farewell turned and was gone leaving a burst of bubbling laughter behind and... 'The words mean my beloved daughter; I will always find you through your song.'

As he left, a ripple of energy coursed through her entire body and she saw a bright group of tiny beings rise up like a cloud to follow his path into the woods.

The meeting lifted her, music filled her and she knew that she was changed. Daughter? He had called her his beloved daughter.

Chapter 20
Flora

Now's the time for making preserves, from all that has been yielded, from your garden or from Wildcrafting as you turn the summer's fruits into jams, syrups, pickles and chutneys for winter; elderberries, blackberries and hawthorn, jam packed, (pardon the pun), with Vitamins for winter ailment's, will soon be ripe enough to harvest and so think about the fruits that you have harvested this year and how that sweetness can be preserved, in order for it to be ingested again in your produce as a reminder of all that you have to be grateful for.

A Lammas extract from Flora's Herbal Grimoire.

With a little time to herself, Flora went about her daily tasks in a daze. This house, the farm; hers ...home! She couldn't believe the possibility of it and yet there was the sadness of Sybille's absence warring with the joy. She knew what her mentor would have said; let me go Flora for I'm still here. That fact would have been well and good in normal circumstances she thought but how were they going to help Sybille, lost in the Mists of Tyme, where only the Lady could help her.

She thought about the Trueshape that Sybille had talked about often. Not a spirit guide but her true soul self with whom she was merging. Flora wondered where that being was now, if they were one and the same then was this being lost too?

'Silver,' she said aloud, 'that's what Sybille called you. Can you hear me now? Can you help her?' Only a Raven answered.

'Right,' she said to Teddy who came in through the open window to rub lovingly around her legs, 'work calls and then I'll be ready to go into town with the others to the shop.'

Heading out to the garden to pick some late Raspberries she saw the Raven following, chattering in its Raven tongue and felt the hands of the wee folk tugging at her skirts. She was often aware of them, especially when she worked with plants or harvested crops. There was always a joy felt in their presence as if things were all right with the world if they took the time to be with her. Today she sensed an agitation though and some of their little tweaks and pinches were less than their usual friendly play. They seemed to be herding her towards the orchard although she had intended to go to the Raspberry patch. Each attempt she made to change direction thwarted by a less than gentle pull on her hair.

'Oi,' she yelped, 'that's enough. All right I'm coming!' Immediately the assault ended and the little tugs and pulls became gentler as they shepherded her towards the orchard.

In amongst the old fruit trees the shade was cool and the colours muted. Apples and pears close to harvest ready, hung in juicy pairs from ancient, lichen-covered boughs. Something else hung there too; a leather bag, creased with age, soft and supple with use, its original colour no longer distinguishable.

'What's this,' she said to the gathering of tiny Fae she could feel around her, 'This isn't Sybille's so whose is it I wonder.'

"Ta 'ten lle 'tuulo 'tel Arwen, It's for you from the Lady,' came the prompt reply.

Spinning round to see where the voice came from she came face to face with a being of such beauty she almost cried. Feeling as if she would fall to her knees, she felt small hands supporting her as she looked into the eyes of the Lady, who visited her in dreams.

'It's for you,' she said again, 'Use it wisely, study the contents carefully, there will be no room for error in the times to come. Blessed Be child Blessed Be.'

The Lady smiled gently and was gone the little Fae let go of Flora so quickly she landed on the ground flat on her back as they hurriedly flew after Her.

Never before had Flora felt as small or humble as in that moment. She'd stood eyeball to eyeball with the Lady Herself. Airmhid Goddess of healing plants and midwifery had graced her with Her presence. Stunned, beyond measure, Flora took down the beautiful bag, carrying it clutched to her chest into the house.

Chapter 21
Grove Street

That afternoon they met at the doors to Sybille's huge house in town. She'd run her book shop, readings and training courses here for some years but with the success of her writing, finally decided to close the store through the week, only opening at the weekend when the busy tourist town was thriving and of course to continue teaching her groups. Over a year ago before her disappearance, Sybille had notified the people working for her that they would need to move on as she was going away. Her long-term receptionist Annie Savage had said she could still manage the desk for weekend bookings and organise the team of readers as before. Sybille was adamant that a new team would soon be taking over so her employee simply thought that Sybille had sold and was perhaps retiring. Despite her long-term employment, Sybille remained an enigma to her. Kind and caring, Sybille had always kept herself removed from all but her closest friends and did not share her personal decisions with many.

Packing up her books and other stock items into solid boxes she had closed the doors for what she thought would be a typical year and a day. When she returned she would as always pick up the threads of her life, her work to continue as if nothing had happened. This time she'd known would be somewhat different.

So now the four stood before the beautiful, solid doors to the building, Sam with key clutched tightly to her chest, her hands shaking so hard she couldn't bring herself to open the door. Gently Flora took the key from her with a small smile of understanding and together they fit key to lock. It opened smoothly and quietly; they stepped inside.

It was quiet as the doors shut behind them. Each walked the familiar rooms now empty of stock lost in their own thoughts; shelves and cabinets covered in sheets and a sad emptiness hovered, emptiness just waiting to refill.

As they wandered, calling out to each other from the less familiar depths of the beautiful, century old building, they discovered new delights; hanging oil lamps and chandeliers, polished wood boards and right at the top on the third floor, a bathroom that redecorated in the 1920's style, was complete with claw-foot bath and art deco fittings.

As Sam, Flora and Bethan met up there they heard a cry of surprise from Maeve,

'Hey,' she called, 'come and take a look at this.'

'Where are you?' yelled Sam.

'Up here,' came the muffled reply. 'There's another stairway I never realised was here.'

Calling out to each other and following Maeve's stamps on the floor above, they found a narrow spiral staircase leading up to the attic and a series of rooms that covered almost the entire roof area, previously unnoticed because there were no visible windows from the ground.

'I want first dibs on this space,' said Maeve excitedly. 'Look at the light through those skylights! This would make an amazing place to live and it would mean that the place would never be left empty for long.'

'How many rooms are there?' asked Sam. 'Would there be enough space for you up here and me on the next floor down where that small bathroom is Maeve? We could share the bathroom couldn't we? It'd save us both a lot of hassles and time spent looking and buying somewhere else and would mean we'd have more capital to put into any renovations and stock, perhaps even someone for the reception areas when we see how busy it gets.'

'It's an enormous space,' said Flora, 'and if you used the small room where the stairs come up as common ground, one of you could take the rooms to the right and one to the left. It would save you both some money although a kitchen would be an expense and you'd have to go up and downstairs to the loo.'

'The kitchen's not really a big issue, there's a kitchen downstairs we could use temporarily and we could put in a bench and kitchen cupboards easily enough after we have everything else sorted,' said Maeve.

'How would you want to divvy up the space Maeve,' said Sam, 'I only need a place for writing and a bed-sit type set up to live.'

'There's seven rooms,' interjected Bethan coming back after exploring the beautiful loft space. 'The front larger room would make a fabulous studio for you Maeve the lights great and there are two other rooms behind it. Then there're three rooms down the other end past the stairs, which is ample room for both of you if you share a kitchen and the bathroom below. There are two other loos downstairs…it just means you wouldn't want to be caught short in a black out,' she laughed

'Well, I'm fine with that,' said Sam.

There was a pause; all turned to look at Maeve, known for her unwillingness to capitulate too quickly yet surprisingly she grinned and said, 'Okay, done. We can work something out as long as I can have that front room for my studio.'

Bethan and Flora exchanged relieved glances as Sam and Maeve eyed each other speculatively. At that moment, there was a cawing from above as a Raven landed with a thump on the roof and looked down at them with a gleam of pure intelligence in its eyes. It wiped its beak noisily on the glass of the skylight and muttered to itself in the guttural language of its kind.

Watching in surprise, they noticed that along one wing was a bar of silver feathers standing out against the oily blue-black of the others.

'How many Ravens have you seen with a strip of light feathers like that?' said Bethan.

'Mmmm,' said Maeve, 'it's just like the one from my dream…'

'…and the one at the farm,' said Bethan and Flora as one.

'She visits me at home too,' said Bethan, 'That's quite a territory to cover.' Exchanging glances they went back downstairs.

The immediate need for somewhere to live taken care of for Maeve and Sam was a great relief, both being concerned at the time that might elapse before they could base themselves in Springsmeet. They each found the most suited spaces for their work. The shop area to be used as retail for books and all the other Wytchy paraphernalia and Bethan and Maeve's work, a few rooms being left as before for reading rooms. At the back was shared space for kitchen and bathroom facilities and wet room that had once been an old scullery when the house had been a family mansion, which suited Flora for her herb plant and floristry space.

On the second floor was the room Sybille had used for teaching; filled with book shelving, several other display units they could use, boxes of stock Sybille had packed up and stored and which would be restored to that usage again once they were settled. There was a lovely large sunny room for Flora's Herbal Medicine consultancy, which had an adjoining windowless room with a sink, ideal for mixing tinctures and the like and for storing herbs in the cool and dark. Off what could be a small waiting room was a bathroom for her clients. Above that were rooms for Bethan and Sam for studios, which would give Sam more living space upstairs in the loft.

A little dusty and tired, with the whole idea of the project a more tangible manifestation, they decided to stop for the day. Three hours had passed in their planning and dreaming.

The Raven followed them from room to room, uncannily interested in everything they said and just secretly, whispered Flora and Bethan to each other, their thoughts. The realisation dawning, this was one of the little magicks that Sybille had always talked about, that now with firsthand experience, was fast becoming a reality for them. Just one more thing to consider in all the unusual circumstances, constantly unfolding.

'I'm starving!' said Maeve as they gathered their bags to leave.

'Let's get some Indian take away,' said Bethan, 'there's a new place opened just across the way.'

'I feel like a spinach and pannier with Dahl. Oooh and some Roti,' said Sam, who was slowly beginning to relax in their company. Indisputable facts were manifesting, no matter how hard she tried to make them disappear, her reality was changed and it didn't look as if there would be any going back to how things had been before either.

Chattering like magpies about new concepts for the business, they strolled across the road to get their meal to take back to what they now agreed was Flora's home. As hard as the realisation was Sybille was gone and that with Mabon approaching, they'd need to come to terms, just as she had taught them, that death was not an ending but another path on the long Way.

Chapter 22
'Earthly Rites'

Nature is not tidy; let your garden grow wild.
Set aside your doubts and invite the Fae Folk in
Sybille Madison

With the sun sinking, fast they drove back to Flora's, to settle down for an evening of planning the next steps of their adventure. Pulling up outside they all stopped to revere the light of the autumn evening. The chill in the air indicated it would be a cold night.

Sam and Maeve helped Flora to put the goats away and check for late lain eggs, whilst Bethan took a moment to slip quietly to the edge of the forests to listen to the approach of night. She could hear the sounds of birds as they settled to roost for the night, light scurrying's of rabbits and saw a young female fox, the body of a small creature hanging from strong jaws, hurrying home to feed her kits. The fox barely paused in her steps, glancing sideways at Bethan she picked up speed. Bethan smiled at the sheer closeness of the contact and relaxed as she walked to just within the forest boundary.

She could hear as the birds fell silent, the haunting melody she'd heard before and standing still, the sun's last rays lit a pathway into the forest depths. Evocative, earthy odours pervaded her senses and she was sorely tempted to

go within to follow the calling of the haunting music...
'Gela en'ardai, gela en'ardai,' it called softly to her
...pulling her, drawing her in,

'Earthly rites, earthly rites,' she sang aloud. 'Of course;
that's the name for the store, 'Earthly rites.' I must suggest
it to the others.' All else forgotten in the moment, she ran
back to the house, not seeing the ghostly phantom that
followed behind her or the trail of Fae folk who watched
and longed for her to return to them, her kin. Aithlin,
raised a hand as if in benediction, calming them,

'Re tula a'lye. Re tule,' 'She'll come to us. She'll
come.'

At this, all the Fae melted back into the forest like
smoke, leaving Aithlin standing alone, except for one,
standing tall and proud in the shadows, watching Bethan
intently as she walked back the way she'd come as if
enchanted; a light in his eyes as he took in her brightness
and heard the music in her.

'Tenna tul're,' he whispered 'Until tomorrow then.'

'Is she for him then?' mused Aithlin, sighing. 'May it
be as the Mother wills for my little one.' and vanished
leaving the tall being alone to keep his night watch.

Bethan walked dreamily back inside to join the
others. A sudden thought crossed her mind. 'Tara Saark!'
she said aloud to the night. Who is Tara Saark?'

She repeated the question to the room, stopping
the noisy chatter instantaneously.

'We need to find her; she's a part of the legacy too. Here we are making all these plans and forgetting all about her. How can we find out who she is?'

'Well,' said Flora, 'Annie, Sybille's assistant might know where the records of students past might be. If she was a regular customer, surely she would know her or at least of her.'

'I'm surprised we've never heard of her,' said Maeve, with a somewhat disgruntled air.

'Yeah me too,' echoed Sam. 'You're making me feel like a kid caught with her hand in the lolly jar, Beth!' she exclaimed. 'How could we have been so stupid as to forget her?'

'Well in all the excitement and the weird events that have been occurring, I think we can be excused!' said Maeve.

'It was very wrong of us,' said Flora, 'but yes, there has just been so much happening', she trailed off, shrugging.' We'll just have to take the time to find out all we can and contact her as soon as possible,' she finished.

'This means, of course, that we may have to alter the room allocations we decided on,' said Bethan. 'I wonder what her skills are and if she will need a lot of space to set up in or whether she may be a reader, which means the reading rooms can be organised to suit her needs.'

'Well we can't know that until we find and meet her,' said Flora in her usual practical tone and with that, her composure returning, she headed to the kitchen to get plates and cutlery for the meal.

Later, around the old refectory table that Flora had lovingly restored, they sat to enjoy their meal. The long area, an extension of the old barn built specifically as a dining room, had windows on two sides for the entire length and double doors leading out to the deck, on each side of the hearth at one end.

On an autumn evening such as this, it was warm enough to sit with the windows open, allowing a breeze to blow through and the sound of birds to filter in from the surrounding garden. Roses merged their scents with the fragrance of the herbs clustered beneath them and the strong, earthy scent of the ripening elderberries was heady and delicious, Magpie and Currawong warbling and squabbling in their battle for the spoils. Everything seemed enhanced to their senses of late and appeared to be something they shared in common as had the dreams and visions, which were becoming more frequent.

They were relaxed after their afternoon of dreaming and planning and Bethan had shared with them her experience in the forest earlier, putting the suggestion to them for the name of their business and why. They all agreed without conjecture, feeling that it had the ring of something that described everything they planned to do and all of their skills combined.

They were all intrigued about the man that had appeared twice to her now and the ancient language that slowly but surely, she was remembering.

'What do you think he meant by calling you daughter do you think,' said Maeve, 'surely he wasn't literal was he?'

'I didn't know my parents,' said Bethan, 'and my father was never mentioned. According to my mother, who I might add will always be exactly that, my birth mother was always somewhat unstable and when she discovered she was pregnant didn't tell a soul. Except that when it became evident, my mother confronted her but she refused to admit it as if ignoring it would make it …'me' just go away.'

'How could you be like that about a child!' interjected Flora, 'another human being growing inside you, a part of you whether planned or not, another life.'

'I thought I had issues with my parents,' said Sam, but at least they wanted me, even if they didn't know how to cope with another individual more independent than they were,' she laughed. 'What happened, Bethan? Did your birth mother put you up for adoption? It must be dreadful to think you weren't wanted. You seem to be such a well-adjusted person, but it must hurt?'

'I have long since come to terms with it all Sam,' replied Bethan, 'My parents may not be blood, but I have truly been blessed by them, my brother Max too. My birth mother was my mother's best friend; they went to school together and were apparently, joined at the hip. Once she couldn't hide the pregnancy anymore she asked my parents to be godparents but then disappeared. Her body was found, three days later, on the edge of the lake in Springsmeet.

It was assumed that she had slipped; fallen in and had managed to crawl onto the shore but died from shock or exposure. The post mortem showed that she'd actually drowned and someone had fished her out but left her body there. It was obvious that she'd given birth just a day or so before, but there was no sign of a baby. The day her body was found, I was left on the doorstep of my parents with a last will and testament leaving what she had to me in trust and asking that her best friends be given custody of me.

The unknown person, who perhaps was the same one who found her body, was in all likelihood the same person who left me on the doorstep, but nothing has ever become known. It's funny though, my mother always said that my birth mother was very different but that we don't look anything alike and that there was no one on the scene that they knew of who might be my father.'

'What an extraordinary thing,' said Sam, 'it's all very intriguing, like out of a story. Have you ever tried to find out who he might be?'

'My parents did all of that but no one came forward and no one looked anything like me to even think they could be my father. There was something about the man I saw though, otherworldly, a Fae and definitely not of this world. I have to laugh, when I think my mother always said the faeries had taken me from my birth mother and left me for them to raise. I thought they were joking but seeing him, I'm not sure, he was so familiar. Sybille always said I was Fae too, come to think of it,' she laughed.

'You're not serious, are you? said Sam, 'You've got to be kidding me. I've heard some strange things that Aunt Sybille told me, but that's...,' she trailed off, unable to find an apt adjective.

'You know that there are other realms, other beings, outside but also alongside our own, don't you Sam?' said Flora 'You're going to need to stretch yourself now with everything that's going on, anything is possible and you have had those weird dreams and manifestations and what about seeing Sybille's wraith, you can't say there's nothing going on.'

'Yeah, I know but...' she hesitated again, losing track as she gazed out of the window to see the trees alive with dancing lights in the growing dusk. 'Holy shit, look ...look at them!' she exclaimed.

Following her gaze, they saw a host of small, winged beings swarming around the head of a tall silver-cloaked figure, who stood at the edge of the herb garden just outside. She was singing and as she sang, the wee folk were clustering around her. There was an air of sadness to the music and Bethan, muttering an oath, sprang to her feet and ran outside.

The being remained where she was, waiting; smiling gently, for Bethan to approach, while the others gathered by the window, straining to hear what, was said but it was all spoken in a soft sibilant tongue, they only knew from dreams.

With a gesture and a note the being, threw a veil of silence between the house and Bethan, to shield them from prying eyes and ears. She knew, of course that this Littleshape would share all with her friends but for now, it was important to communicate with her without her being distracted.

'Come closer little one,' she whispered, her very words a song to Bethan's ears.

'Who, what, are you,' she stammered, 'Are you one of the Fae?'

'I am the one known as Silver but hush now, just listen,' Silver commanded, the notes of the song strengthening their hold on the listener. Motioning at the ground for Bethan to sit, she folded elegant limbs to float in the lotus position, just above the ground.

Bethan collapsed, unable to stand, entirely overwhelmed as Silver began to sing Sybille's song, the notes becoming images for Bethan to see her story unfold and amongst them her own story too, in every detail, became apparent.

Chapter 23
Bethan, Silver and Aithlin Farandir

The wheel turns on; trees whisper secrets and birds leave messages on the wind. Nothing remains the same and yet in change, we find renewal. Her cycles are the key to a quiet joy and understanding of life as a simple, ongoing and natural process. It is only when we interfere with this process, we become unstuck. Find your joy in simple things and you will regenerate your spirit of innocence.

An extract from the Book of Shadows

It was a rare occurrence for a Trueshaper to make contact with anyone, even their own Littleshapes unless they had progressed enough to understand the implications. To Bethan, another of Silver's Littleshapes, she'd never shown herself except in dreams and even though Bethan had come a long way on the road to understanding, she hadn't recognised Silver as another part of herself, only sensing that the link with her teacher Sybille was a strong bond forged through eons.

Sybille had explained the passage of the three souls of humankin, to all her students, but not all had understood, as this in itself was the journey of the Way of the Wise, the experiential way of the Wytch.

The first part was what governed the physical manifestation, the body, housing the mental self that humankin called ego. In truth, this was a composite, in itself, of many Littleshape memories, gathered into one coherent moment on the time continuum. Tiny fragments of memory, written in the cells of a frail, yet so resilient, human frame. Any memory of where it had been and what it was now, watered down by the inability to maintain awareness as it descended deeper and deeper into the earth realm's torpid energy.

In its constant search for truth, it had fallen into the illusion of time as a straight line, past, to present, into a perceived future. This stretched the Skeins of Tyme so thinly, just one thread only remained, attaching each human life to the web; just one and now for Sybille, even that fine, umbilical thread to the Mother, had been torn adrift.

The second, Higher or Soul self as the humankin called it, the Trueshaper, was the one who gathered the threads of life experience needed, to weave the relevant memories into a tapestry, for the journey back to full awareness of Oversoul, of Goddess self. Silver was Sybille's Trueshaper and Bethan's too and so it was a rare occasion, indeed for Silver to give the Littleshape the nudge that she was about to.

Having Truedreamed, searching for her Littleshape, she had found only a remnant; a brief note in the soaring melodies that were Sybille, barely a tremble now on the Skeins of Tyme, Silver knew that she must act, risking everything achieved or still more would eventuate to twist and warp Ungwe, the web of the Mother.

So now, floating in the beautiful garden that Sybille had originally planted in honour of the Mother,

Silver waited while Bethan, hearing the sound of her music, tentatively walked outside. The others stood, their faces pressed to the window like children, eyes enormous in faces gone pale with a mixture of fear and excitement.

With a gesture and a subtle note, the little Makers floating around her, cast a fine silvery net between them and the house, veiling them from sight. Disappointed the three watching sat down again to talk excitedly amongst them.

'Who is that being, she looks like a Goddess,' said Maeve.

'She also seems a lot like Sybille and Bethan,' said Flora.

'Your right,' agreed Sam,' and she's strangely familiar, I'm sure I've seen that face before.'

They were straining to see what was happening outside, but the veil of gossamer energy hid the entity and Bethan from sight. Suddenly, briefly glimpsed through the veil strode a tall male figure who disappeared from view in a flurry as the mist parted.

'Ah,' sang Silver, 'I knew you would come, Aithlin Farandir! It was always wondered why you didn't step in earlier to claim your child.'

Breath held, Bethan turned, to see the tall being who had spoken to her in the forest, approaching through the veil.

'This is all too much, too soon,' she cried, 'tell me, what's going on and why did you...' she turned to Aithlin Farandir, '...call me daughter, or was it just a turn of phrase? I need to know.'

'Soon, daughter, soon,' soothed Aithlin, 'there is so much more at stake. First we must help your Trueshape Silver to find your sisterkin Sybille, for without her the world will change for all of us, in ways you cannot possibly imagine.'

So saying, with a wave of his hand, Bethan felt herself comforted by a single note as he bowed to Silver and stood, waiting with an air of respect for her to continue.

Frustrated, Bethan had no recourse but to wait and listen.

The story that unfolded, as Silver spoke of Sybille's disappearance being more than simply a physical one, left Bethan breathless. She had to understand, in terms of stark reality, that things could go wrong even in the higher realms of life and being. Sybille, separated from her Trueshape, whilst journeying to renew, caused the web of life, Ungwe, to break.

Every time Sybille disappeared, it was a conscious journey and her mentor had been ...was, Bethan thought, a person of extraordinary awareness, very near to becoming a true immortal. This time would have been the last time of renewal. This time she would have been back only to say goodbye and to work from then onwards from the world between worlds as an avatar and teacher, working in the beyond. The fact that this was now no longer a possibility, unless she could be found and renewed, was more than just the loss of one, mortal life, in fact, it was the loss of a human being returning to her true state, becoming her own Trueshape, answerable only to her Goddess self; the state known as, 'Becoming.'

Her personal involvement became evident when she thought about the connection she had always recognised between herself and Sybille and now the reality that she was in the presence of their shared Trueshaper, Silver and that there was work to do in finding Sybille, for all concerned.

The other astounding realisation was that here in front of her was her father. A Fae, an Elf Lord no less, apparently. Aithlin Farandir. How long had she waited and wondered? Now here he was, standing there as if it was the most normal thing in the world

Her own birth mother had fallen for the Fae Lord. It had been a mutual relationship and he had loved her as much as a Fae could. He was, however, unable to act in a manner her mother had demanded on finding out she was pregnant so, after giving birth to Bethan, it seemed that she had taken her own life.

He heard her calling on the ethers but was unable to save her from drowning. Bereft, he'd left Bethan on the doorstep of her foster parent's house. He couldn't take her as a Halfling to his realm because that was something she must, eventually decide for herself. So, not only was she a Halfling Fae but Silver was her own Trueshape, her Higher self as well as Sybille's.

Silver was not gentle in her telling, she was not inclined to spare the details or gloss over the events of

Bethan's birth and subsequent life. She was eager to share with Bethan what had become of Sybille and the need for her to ask; as she rarely did for help from her own Littleshape was an anathema to her.

Pulling her straying thoughts back to more important matters Bethan said,

'What do you expect that I can do in all this?' she exclaimed, 'I'm a mere mortal.'

'But no that's not true,' interjected Aithlin Farandir. 'Have you not heard what has just been revealed to you? Even the half of you that is Fae by blood makes you as close to being an immortal as your sisterkin who had to work so hard to achieve what you have through that blood.'

Turning to Silver Aithlin said, 'With all due respect Lady, why did not Sybille tell my daughter the truth?'

With a withering glance, Silver replied, 'Because that duty was yours and yours alone Aithlin Farandir and you have once again fallen short of your duty to your offspring.'

Bethan gasped. She would not have imagined that this gentle appearing entity, her own Trueshape she reminded herself, could be so scathing and yet. Silver's disgust was tangible as the tone of her melodious song became harsher; the trees around them shook with the change in energy, their amber leaves falling in a rustling shower around them.

To her surprise, Aithlin hung his head, tears forming in his eyes.

'You are right of course Lady; I have been most remiss and hope that you,' he said, turning to Bethan, 'can forgive me.'

Taken aback, Bethan hesitated a moment too long; opening her mouth to reply she realised that Aithlin had turned and stalked away. Was it arrogance, she thought? He didn't give me any right of reply after all this time. It can wait a while longer I suppose, she sighed. It's only been nearly 29 years after all!

She realised that Silver was carefully contemplating her and with an enigmatic smile at Bethan, said,

'You have a great and patient heart indeed. You have been given information that a lesser human would baulk at but here you are as stalwart as you have always been and it is for this reason that you hold the hope of millions in your hands right now. There will be help, as much as we can give you, but the work in the physical realms cannot be done by us and each of your sisterkin has a role to play, but right now, this time it is yours.'

'But what on earth can I do?' said Bethan.

'Work with what you have been naturally given from both of your parents. Your Fae gifts of sight and music are emerging, together with the natural gifts of the weaver, you chose for this personality aspect; this Littleshape that you govern,' replied Silver compassionately. 'Then there are your Mother's traits...' she trailed off, hesitating before continuing, 'Your Elven blood makes you very different to your friends, but it's those variances that temper the Fae indifference to human feelings and the human feelings that can totally overwhelm you.' With that, she turned, reaching out to Bethan with her essence and sang...

'Fea lindir yassene lle quenat, no' lle windele ar imya lle naikau. Alu nendar illya nat' poika; vilya cora anwar a' lle 'au. Nau 'ta anto, ardai a' talar; Iire 'I Ungwe lle vaira, illya nat' uuvar.'

Bethan understood, *'Spirit sings within your frame, on your loom and through your pain. Water washes all things clean; Air brings truth to you again. Fire is needed Earth to ground, when the web you weave, all things abound.'*

'That's what Sybille wrote,' said Bethan, emotion gripping her.

'Within this simple rhyme are the keys to the universe known as Bethan.' With that, Silver turned and drifted sedately into the mists, her little entourage of Makers, weaving their eternal dance around her.

Watching, Bethan realised that each of those little beings was a part of the whole that made up the Trueshaper Silver. Watching in awe she also realised that within Silver's body of light was a space, empty, darkening space. She watched aghast as this space darkened and deepened. Swirling galaxies of stars affected by the one that had winked out, leaving a small vortex to refill as nature always rushes to fill the void...

'But with what?' she said to herself, 'Oh Goddess, with what?'

'Nothing happens in isolation,' came the whispered reply, accompanied by the rustling of leaves as the Raven with the brilliant flash on her wing alighted above Bethan, looking down at her with a piercing blue-eyed gaze.

'Who are you?' questioned Bethan. 'What do you know?' she yelled at the Raven, 'and what about my Mother,' she called after Silver but with a caw, close to a human laugh the Raven took flight, causing a shower of leaves to fall.

Pausing for breath, to order her thoughts, she looked toward the house to see her friends standing as one at the window and then, turning, they ran out the door towards her, all speaking at once, eagerly.

'Wait!' cried Bethan, 'Just wait will you,' she said with an unaccustomed firmness to her tone. 'This is more than I can tell you in a few moments. I need to gather my wits, then I'll tell you everything,' and with that stalked off toward the house.

Giving her time to recover, Flora did what she always did and busied herself in the kitchen, making a soothing herbal tea and gathering her own thoughts before taking the tray into the dining room, where the others were patiently waiting for Bethan to share the events of the last few minutes. Only moments it had been, yet to Bethan it had been hours.

Chapter 24
Preparations

Layers of awareness are awakened by our dreams.
Our consciousness is hindered by the doing, plans and
schemes. If we could simply let the 'now', become our
journey's theme ...then soon we would discover
...not the 'how' ...but what living truly means
An extract from the Book of Shadows

The next couple of days passed for them all in a blur of activity. Maeve and Sam were working well together to get their move to Springsmeet underway, neither having to wait for the sale or rental of their properties. With Sam's already under contract, they were focusing on moving most of her things first, together with the heavier items from Maeve's studio, such as the cauldron, her solid workbench and forge.

Maeve was waiting to hear from another artist who had always said they would love to buy her studio, should she ever be ready to sell. That day had come sooner than either had expected, but the other party had been very keen, only waiting to hear for their financial advisor's okay to clear the monies and then would be ready to go.

They hoped to have it all finished and were planning to have an opening the week of Mabon. There was also the continuing search for Tara hitting roadblocks at every turn, the woman with an unusual name stubbornly remaining an enigma. On speaking to Annie the following morning, after their lapse in memory concerning the fifth name on the legacy, they had drawn a constant blank. It was not that Annie couldn't remember the name; it was just that she had suddenly become very vague about what she did know. Saying,

'Oh, she'll turn up no doubt, that's just typical of Tara.' before clamming up again and busying herself elsewhere.

They had decided to re-employ Annie Savage, as she was an organised and experienced woman after working for Sybille for so many years. They'd had to keep quiet, however, as to Sybille's whereabouts as they weren't sure how much, if indeed anything, Annie knew about Sybille's regular 'sabbaticals' as she used to call them, although they'd found it very strange that Annie hadn't commented on where they thought Sybille might be. She'd listened gravely to them when they'd approached her with their offer of employment but hadn't asked where Sybille was. They all had the feeling that she was far more aware than she was letting on about her previous employer.

Annie had however been a gem at helping them sort the stock that Sybille had stored away. Pointing them in the direction of suppliers that Sybille had used and introducing them to the sales reps as they turned up, to see if there was anything else they needed, showing them a plethora of new titles and other lines of new age and 'witchy' goods.

Annie's role was to be as before, handling the day-to-day running of the team of readers, taking forward bookings and organising their rosters. She was a whizz with all the administration, banking, billing, online orders and the like and she'd given them some really excellent tips on how Sybille had always run such a successful business. She had suggested a formal opening of the renewed 'earthly rites' centre and had surprised them by offering to contact some of the other people, who had been invited to gatherings in the past. These people had been in the main, Sybille's students. On asking Bethan if she was ready to start the calendar of events for the coming year of workshops and lectures,

'Oh!' Bethan had exclaimed aloud, 'I don't know if I'm ready for any of that yet. We thought that Flora might start the year with some talks on herbal medicines and even some ritual applications of herbs and Maeve might give a short course on crystals but that's as far as we got for now,' she finished.

'All right dear,' Annie had said, not without sympathy. 'I know you have big shoes to fill but Sybille would not have put you forward for this if she thought you were unable to do it, now would she?' With that, she'd bustled away again in her efficient manner, leaving Bethan staring after her, open-mouthed.

'Well, how about a little condescension perhaps,' she sniffed, with rare sarcasm.

Mabon was now fast approaching, but it was hard to focus on Equinox and the harvest when Flora and

Bethan were already working on the Rite for Samhain. This would be not only for honouring the turning year but also for all the information they could pull together to keep each of them safe, Samhain being the night when the veils were at their thinnest and there was no better time for an attempt to find out where Sybille was. It was their intention that Bethan trance, in order to glean the information they needed to find her and help her home.

They were all continuing to have dreams that went beyond that simple word. They repeated again and again, continuing on to linger with them through their days; little signs and symbols, constant reminders of the task ahead of them that still remained a mystery. They knew that the Rite of Samhain would be the point of no return and so they each struggled to maintain their composure by remaining as focused as they could on the physical task of setting up 'earthly rites.'

Sam had dreamed again of the rustling sounds of wind in dry leaves and the smell of the woods in her nose. She'd found her bed and the surrounding floor covered in leaves again and the scratchings and guttural chatter was repeatedly in her head all through the day. Her sketches, when she had time in the quietude of her temporary room at Flora's, had taken on a life of their own. The beings that flocked around Bethan, Silver and Aithlin, were predominant, as was a face she'd yet to put a name to until Bethan, visiting at Flora's one morning and seeing it had said, 'That's my brother Max. I didn't know you'd ever met him Sam?'

'Well, I haven't' replied Sam, 'He just keeps appearing in my dreams and his face takes shape on paper again and again, he's actually very attractive but I had no idea he was your brother. Why would I be drawing him do you think Beth?'

Bethan grinned and said, 'Well I'll just have to introduce you won't I. He's bound to appear at Samhain anyway, we've never missed one together that I can remember since I first discovered the Wytchways.

'Hmmm,' said Sam, 'yes …hot,' and then recovering herself blushed, saying, 'and then there's this being, which makes me feel very uneasy,' showing Bethan the sketch.

'Well, he looks like a Fae,' Bethan said, studying the picture carefully, 'but yes,' she continued, 'He isn't someone I'd want to meet alone on a dark night. He's very intense, almost broodingly dark in fact,' she finished, shuddering as she gave the sketch back to Sam.

'He has something to do with you Beth. When you tell me about your dreams he's always there in the picture watching and waiting, along with this rather stunning and curious fellow,' this time she said it with a cheeky grin. 'I wouldn't mind being watched by him!' and so saying she gave Bethan another sketch.

This time Bethan just stared, eyes widening, 'Oh,' she said and again, 'Oh!'

Sam found it impossible to read her friend's face at that moment. First, there was fear, then joy followed by, what she could only describe as, pure longing.

'Oh,' she said again, 'I'm sorry Sam,' as if to explain something, but then pausing, she drew in a sharp breath, 'He is the dream itself; He is the Spirit of Place, the Greenman, Herne. Lady, what could He possibly want with me?'

'What do you mean?' said Sam, 'He certainly looks like nothing I've ever seen before, but Herne, the Greenman? Surely they're just beings from myth and legend!'

'Ah Sam,' replied Bethan, 'Won't you learn to think beyond the norm, after all you've seen recently? Just think about it,' she continued with a touch of exasperation in her voice, 'If the Fae exist and the Lady Silver exists and my father Aithlin Farandir exists - wouldn't you say there's every chance that all the Gods are living beings too? Look at Flora's encounter with the Goddess Airmhid! You know how down to earth and practical Flora can be and yet, she has taken that visitation in her stride and has tangible proof too in that bag of herbs and paraphernalia the Lady gave her. What more can you want Sam. Wake up to yourself for goodness sake!'

Shocked at the frustration in Bethan's voice, Sam looked down at the sketch and muttered, 'Yeah, I know, I'm sorry. It's just all so new to me. I keep getting glimpses on the edge of my vision of these incredible little beings that look as if they're made from bits of flotsam and jetsam from Nature's recycling bin. When I turn my head, they disappear but I can still hear them. I don't understand what they're saying but I get the sense that they're trying to get me to do something'

'Well, sit with that Sam,' said Bethan, 'Let them talk to you. Honestly, listen and maybe just sit with pen and paper and see if you can get them to write through your hands. I'll help you. I'll teach you to find an altered state that you are comfortable and receptive in. It's not hard, but you have to trust yourself. You can obviously tell the difference in energy between these little beings you've drawn here,' she said indicating another drawing on the desk and the dark, brooding Fae, 'so it shouldn't be too difficult to let them come a little closer if you feel they are trying to communicate something to you. After all we need all the information we can get together before the Samhain Rite,' she finished, then with a brief pause, looking at Sam quizzically she said,

'Maeve told me that she'd been dreaming of a strange creature, she called a water horse. That it had no back legs only long merman-like scaly tail, front legs with cloven hooves and a horse's head with horns more like a goat's actually,' said Bethan.

'Flora's been dreaming of the nature spirits of all those strange herbs in the bag Airmhid gave her and I've been returning again and again to the Grove and running through the forest away from something that's chasing me but I haven't been able to see what that something is as yet. Therefore, we're all experiencing the otherworld in one way or another and each of us has to try to work out what this all means to us as individuals. Think about the rhyme that Sybille left each of us Sam. Perhaps we all need to sit and look through those again and even open Tara's letter, to see if she has one too. She may be the missing link that can help us work all of this out.' she stopped, 'what?' she said as she saw Sam's, shocked expression.

'Well,' faltered Sam, 'you don't suppose that dark Fae is the 'something' that's following you in your dreams, do you Beth?'

Bethan paused a moment before replying,

'All I can say is I hope not Sam. I really don't like the look of him at all. Perhaps I'll have to see if I can turn and confront him rather than mindlessly running though. At least then I'll know the source of my fears and face them.'

At that moment Flora came running in excitedly, 'We've found her,' she cried, 'Tara Saark, we've found her.'

'That's funny,' said Sam, 'Bethan was just suggesting we open her letter to see if there was anything in there that we could use to help us understand everything better.'

'No need,' said Flora, 'she's coming over tonight. We can give her the letter and hope that she has some insights into what's been happening and where Sybille might be.'

'Well,' said Bethan, 'I'm not going to hold my breath on the latter but here's hoping she'll have a different slant on things, where Sybille's concerned. I wonder what role she's played in Sybille's life prior to her disappearance and why we've never met her before, after all the years we've known Sybille and been her students. Ah well. I guess we'll find out soon enough now.'

They spent the rest of the day continuing to clean and in setting up the newly named centre 'earthly rites.' People were becoming more and more interested to know what was going on inside the covered windows and many knocked on the door, obviously not backward in coming forward, in demanding to know when the centre would be open for business again.

It had taken all of their patience to cope with some of the more forceful people trying to push their way in through the doors, wanting to see Sybille.

'I feel like a broken record,' said an exasperated Maeve, 'These people are just too much. They won't listen. I had to practically, bodily remove one woman who was convinced Sybille was hiding inside. As if Sybille would need to hide from anyone,' she snarled.

'Easy Maeve, they're just eager to see her and who could blame them. Right now I'd give my eye teeth to have her walk in the door again,' said Flora, who'd taken the brunt of another pushy woman's rudeness. 'Some of them however are just plain old busybodies if you ask me,' she finished ruefully.

By late afternoon, they were all feeling distinctly edgy after the constantly and unexpectedly, interrupted day and about the coming evening's meeting with Tara. As it was to be held at the farm, Flora took the time to do some shopping before heading back to the farm to bathe and cook. Bethan made a quick trip home and then continued over to help Flora with the preparations, which also gave the two a little time to chat about the Samhain Ritual preparations.

Meanwhile, Sam and Maeve had almost finished setting up their individual spaces. They were becoming used to each other's foibles, a little more each day. By no means completely installed in their new home, it was at least a place that they could see would become a lovely place to live and work. Sam had completed her assignment for the Journal; again, she'd been highly praised for her piece. She knew, however, that it would in all probability, be her last with the Journal as excitement took her to the realms of creative writing, fuelled by the recent events. Her drawings took on a life of their own and she had to let go the last of her more cynical side, in light of those events and the unexpected appearances of the Fae folk and Silver.

Maeve, however, was at a loss to understand what was happening. She'd set up her studio, filling the cauldron again with water, so that everything was ready for her to take another look at the spoiled pieces of her work, so badly damaged she wasn't sure if they would be redeemable. Within minutes of setting everything up once again, the sounds of water, bubbling and gurgling, echoed through the space. She tried to talk to the energy she sensed, but whenever she spoke, it would immediately fall silent again. She muttered an oath to herself and once more, shrugging in frustration, closed the door and went to get ready.

Sam and Maeve, both lost in their own thoughts, showered and changed, washing the dirt and stress of the day away, before driving together out to the farm at Covenstead.

Chapter 25
Tara Saark

'We're each just a little thread in the tapestry of life; beware you don't drop a stitch, 'cos we might all begin to unravel',

...said by Tara Saark, with a very cheeky chuckle

Tara rested against a huge old chestnut tree in Flora's orchard. She could have climbed, she thought, higher and higher taking in the view as she climbed. She could have flown, but that would have 'blown her cover,' she giggled. How could she tell even these clever women that she was a piece of the Mother's Magicks?

Small, strong and wiry, she resembled a dark bird. Her hair, prematurely streaked in the front with a slash of silver, made her stand out in any crowd. She had an air of indifference about her that fooled people into thinking that she was just a 'street-wise' kid, the truth was she was older than most could imagine

She'd first come in contact with Sybille years ago and had been intrigued, when she heard from Annie, that Flora, Bethan, Maeve and Samantha had been looking for her because Sybille had left a note for her before disappearing.

The breeze had told her where Sybille had gone although soon she sensed they would have to work it out for themselves. Her task was to observe, it was not for her to interfere with the will of the Mother.

She waited, unable to resist climbing to the very top of her gnarled old friend, suspended in her customary state of bliss for the girls and then she would walk to the door like a regular person, she giggled again.

Watching from her lofty perch, she saw Flora arrive, unload bags of groceries and walk to the house, pausing to stroke Teddy, who was waiting at the gate for her. Tara knew that the meal tonight would be as good, if not better than Sybille herself would have prepared, except Sybille would know to leave out a plate of raw meat for her Corbae friends to enjoy

Within a short space of time the others arrived, Maeve and Samantha together, chattering to each other about their day, seemingly relaxed in each other's company. She wondered, with the natural curiosity of her kind, how they would cope with tasks that would be set for them by Samhain

Allowing them a little time to ready themselves with an unaccustomed patience but knowing the conventions of the humankin that guests should never arrive early, she lazily shifted shape. Flying to the gate, she landed in a flurry of feathers, when she realised, 'The Cat' was sitting on the other gatepost. A furiously, spitting Morgana, launched herself from the post and disappeared through the cat flap, into the house.

Tara, recovering herself hurriedly, changed back into her human shape. Smoothing her ruffled hair to no avail, she straightened her layered clothing of lace and tattered silks, walked sedately to the door and knocked.

She waited, listening with amusement to the whispering and a flurry of activity within as if she didn't know they'd been spying through the window when they'd heard Morgana's noisy entry just moments before. Finally, Flora appeared looking somewhat flustered and with a smile said, 'Oh hello, you must be Tara.'

'Evidently,' said Tara with a cheeky grin, 'and you're Flora!'

Eyeing each other, Flora, recovering her composure, opened the door wide and asked Tara in, not knowing that those of her kind needed permission before they could cross a human's threshold and could not enter without it.

Sensing Flora's discomfort Tara reached out gently with her mind and sent a small frisson of energy to calm her nervousness, at the same time stepping inside, closing the door firmly behind her.

Flora led Tara in and again, Tara laughed to herself at the sound of scurrying as the other two women made a show of pouring drinks and putting bowls of nuts on the table, before turning unhurriedly to greet her as if entirely unperturbed. 'This is Tara,' Flora announced unnecessarily.

'Hi Tara,' said Maeve approaching and with a quizzical look at Flora, stuck out her hand, which was pumped enthusiastically by Tara, who then, turning to Bethan put out her hand to do the same. Bethan approached a little more cautiously and with a piercing stare, took Tara's hand, shook it and held it just a while longer, gauging intuitively, the essence of her. Tara allowed her to delve before withdrawing her hand and smiling into Bethan's eyes said quietly.

'Merry meet Fae sisterling,' so that only Bethan could hear.

Taken aback at this, Bethan quickly withdrew her hand, smiling faintly in wonder at the beautiful but mysterious nature of the woman before her.

Attempting to bring about a more relaxed atmosphere, Tara smiled broadly at them all and said, 'Okay then, what's for dinner?'

They couldn't help but laugh at this candid question and the unbelievable warmth emanating from her; enchanted, they all began to speak at once.

They ate, toasted Sybille and then, in her direct manner; turning to Flora, Tara said, 'You have something for me I believe?' holding out her hand.

'Yes. Yes, of course,' said Flora as she crossed to the mantelpiece and fetched the sealed envelope that she'd placed under a heavy candlestick earlier, 'Here,' she said, handing it to Tara. 'This is the letter that came with ours.'

Taking the note and pocketing it unopened in a fold of her lacy dress, Tara turned to all of them as they watched astonished that she didn't rip it open on the spot in utter curiosity.

'But,' stuttered Samantha, 'Don't you want to know what Sybille has to say to you? Ours had riddles; we're still trying to work out. We ...that is, I thought yours might have another, clue to where Sybille is, why she left earlier than planned and what's happening to her now. Please, I'm desperate to know what we're all supposed to do …I,' she trailed off again; uncertain under Tara's scrutiny of what more she could say. She felt like an utter fool at her outburst under the intense gaze of this strangely beautiful and unearthly woman.

'I don't think this will help you much,' said Tara, removing the note from her pocket, 'but here, read it if you will please,' and so saying handed it to Samantha who ripped it open only to stare blankly at the words written in the same, strange script she'd seen before on the pages of her own drawing pad a matter of weeks ago…

Vee lye tanya ron ant i' anwar …tua sen utu ta, ron ant i' ele, vee nat' sangano, il i' umartempla, tua sen imya ron nevaro naile. 'What is this text,' she said. 'It's appearing everywhere recently. Here you seem to be able to understand it,' as she passed it to Bethan.

'No said Bethan, this is different again. I don't understand this at all,' she finished in frustration.

'What's going on,' said Samantha to Tara. 'Is this some sort of sick game? Where is Sybille? I know you know more that you are letting on,' she finished.

'Well,' said Tara, 'this states that I am to work with you all and share the centre with you. I am an artist, potter, jeweller and a reader. Sybille wants me to continue my work and to help you all sort out what's been happening.'

'And we're supposed to believe you without evidence,' said Maeve who had been strangely quiet all evening. 'I don't think we're complete fools you know and you seem to have been very amused about something all evening as if you know more than you're letting on. If that's so and you don't wish to share, fine but don't act as if you have all the answers and then behave all enigmatically. If we're all supposed to work together, we need to know what you know. We need to be on an equal footing with you.'

Tara began to reply but there was a sound in the room, a tearing noise as if a strong fabric was being torn and instead of replying she looked at each of them and then at the floor where with a bone shattering thud and a loud snapping of wings a large Raven appeared at Maeve's feet.

'Flora,' Maeve called, Flora having moved back to lean on the mantel as Samantha had challenged Tara, 'Flora come quickly,' Maeve stood looking down at the apparently stunned Corbae.

Flora moved forward and knelt as Tara spoke in an unknown, soothing tongue, the Raven morphed from large bird into a large and completely naked man, who looked up at Maeve in utter disbelief.

'I know you,' she said, before he simply disappeared as fast as he had manifested.

With a strangely guttural cry, Tara said, 'I'm sorry, I have to go now. Something's just come up,' and with a grin and a wave to the four women, she made a dash for the door and before they could respond, was gone.

Maeve, found her voice first, 'That's him, that's the man from my dream the other night,' she exclaimed.

Chapter 26
Morgan Trethaway

Morgan Trethaway walked the narrow, familiar lanes of his countryside, his fierce, dark features screwed up against the brute force of the driving rain. He wanted only to be home now with a bowl of hot soup to warm his inner.

He'd played tonight at a local pub, accompanying a young aspiring girl, who sang like an angel and looked like a Vampire the clarity of her voice and the Goth visuals warring with each other as she stood on the stage singing an old song in the traditional Welsh tongue. She'd looked tired and frail though and he'd soon discovered, as he played, that she was indeed somewhat like the stories of vampires of old, except that it wasn't blood she drank but energy ...the energy of his music which she used to fill herself, her own being at barely 19, almost spent. She'd latched on to him, as he'd packed up his instruments to leave, small pale hands had clung to his sleeve, slender fingers hooked, like bird claws but he'd shaken her off, not without compassion for her obvious distressed state but with a curt nod and,

'You'd best be looking after yourself better Kelly Rush,' he said before striding out into the wet night with a sigh of utter relief.

Wales, in early spring, was wet and cold at the best of times but there appeared to be another force behind it tonight he thought as a strange anxiety gripped him. For a moment all was still as if he stood in a small vortex protected from the elements by Goddess knew what; a strange stirring in the trees along the roadside brought him to a halt to listen intently.

He was accustomed to strange phenomena but something didn't feel right. He felt agitated, an unusual emotion for him. As he stood, untouched momentarily by the storm, he heard a voice, someone calling him by his Truename, the name that only his teacher, Sybille, knew. Now she was calling him on the wind. He faltered for a moment as he heard an appalling tearing, ripping sound and a scream so loud, so close, the hairs on his arms stood on end and a sense of bilocation, of otherworldliness, gripped him, accompanied by a sudden nausea and in spite of the cold, he broke out in a clammy sweat.

As suddenly as the sensation came, it was gone; all that was left was a feeling of such desolation he fell to his knees by the roadside - a need to curl into a foetal position overcame him and he wanted to cry like a child. She was gone, his teacher, his friend ...she was gone, only a small whisper was left on the winds as the illusion of stillness passed and the rain fell once more in relentless torrents,

'...gela en'ardai, gela en'ardai ...earthly rites, earthly rites,' he repeated aloud and the smell of burnt feathers came to him on the gale.

He pulled himself upright and with a deep breath staggered on down the road to home. On reaching his crofters cottage he stumbled in through the always unlocked door, there being no need for locks and bolts out here in the wildlands.

He was greeted by a frenzied howl of delight and had to be fast to lift a hand to fend her off saying, 'wait, drop,' as seventy-eight kilos-worth of shaggy coated Wolfhound prepared to launch herself at him, in a paroxysm of pure doggy delight. She dropped obediently to the floor, almost writhing with anticipation for the forthcoming greeting; he'd just managed to hold at bay.

Tenderly placing his Lute and Mandolin on a nearby stand and peeling off his dripping jacket he said, 'Okay Honey,' and good manners forgotten, she launched herself at him in joy. Man and wolf wrestled like puppies. Honey was a gentle giant who had been his constant companion since they'd found each other, when she was just seven weeks old. Presumably the runt of the litter, he hated to think how big her siblings must be if she was truly the runt.

Releasing himself from her hound-hug, he said, 'Food?' which brought on another bout of boisterous bellowing as Honey galloped to the fridge and sat, with a semblance of sedateness, in expectation, tongue lolling, for supper.

Morgan ruffled her honey coloured, silky fur, causing yet another squirm of delight as she rolled onto her back for a belly rub. 'Okay, Honey-bear, just a moment,' he said as he walked to the mud room to strip off, hang his wet clothing and to find a towel to rub dry his wild dark hair, wrapping another round his hips. Opening the small window, he called out in a low guttural voice, which was answered immediately by a loud, 'caw', as a huge Raven hopped in with another 'aaaark,' in greeting and a flap of strong dark wings. Ruark, his other constant companion of late, looked at him, head on one side as she ruffled up her damp feathers sending a small shower of droplets over Morgan.

'Yeah, thanks,' he said, 'as if I wasn't wet enough!' In his head he heard clearly, in reply, 'Youuuur late aaarrre!'

'What? Your my mother now?' he quipped and with a distinct, 'harrumph,' Ruark flew onto his shoulder. Her huge beak would have daunted a lesser man and her claws dug into his bare skin, although Morgan knew she had an unusual restraint even in her Corbae form, especially with him.

He'd found her caught in an unidentifiable and very sticky, black web of threads, hanging inverted in a huge old tree. She'd been very weak and he'd feared that the injuries, to her wing and flight feathers, would not heal well enough for her to ever fly again but she'd proven him wrong and within an amazingly short space of time she'd regained her strength as he fed her what he could find for her. Her wing bones had straightened and her feathers had regrown in a silvery colour like a streak of lightening, caught in the inky blue-blackness of her other feathers ...or a line of stars in a dark, night sky.

He hadn't expected her to stay, trying all possible methods to help her find her freedom again but she'd persisted in returning to him and was never more than a low call away from his cottage on the wild bordercountry of Wales and Cornwall. His home was a small croft, ideal for his solitary life, where he could lose himself in his music and studies of the Druid Wytchway, he earned his money through making and repairing old musical instruments and playing when he could like tonight as a backup for groups or soloists, who needed someone to cover in an emergency or just because they'd heard of his musical prowess.

His life had been peaceful until tonight, when he'd heard the voice of his teacher calling to him by his Craft name and then the sense of her dissolving into the ethers, leaving only a fragile spark of her song behind.

He realised he'd stood, recalling in every detail that moment for some time as an impatient tweak of his hair from Ruark and a wet, cold nose nuzzling his hand, brought him back to the moment. Ruark flew to the mantelpiece in the living room that she had chosen to make her perch for the night, preening her ruffled feathers; her sharp claws had left scratchings like wild runes in the layers of ancient whitewash, baked to a glossy, hard sheen.

Usually he thrived on the unexpected and often unexplained, but this was different; this was his own mentor and teacher of the Bardic Way of the Wise. Sybille, who he'd never met in the flesh, only on-line and on the ethers but who had pulled him from his deep depression after his lover had moved on, helping him heal the rift of her departure and recover his mental and emotional wellbeing. He had finally recovered and had emerged all the stronger for it. He'd discovered all the latent gifts and abilities, hidden before in common ignorance and he'd thrived ...until now anyway. Sybille, where was she? What had happened to her?

Honey's relentless slobbering at his hand as she begged to be fed, took him back to the kitchen. He went about the tasks of feeding her and then re-heated some soup he had stored in the fridge for himself. He brought out a somewhat damp loaf of bread from his back pack, wrapping it in foil and placing it in the oven to dry and crisp a little and then wandered into the living area to light a fire, ready laid, just waiting for a match.

Distracted again, he stared into the flames as they caught, the dry tinders crackling and popping with a sudden greed as if a feeding frenzy had overtaken them; small wild-fire salamander danced within. He felt the stirrings of a trance but brought himself back from the edge as he smelled the aromas of his soup and bread and his gut rumbled, in response to the natural call of hunger.

Relaxing a little, with the appeasement of his growling stomach, he thought long and deep of the woman who had taught him so much about himself; the ancient ways and of the Goddess who had chosen him as her own. She had always been there, teasingly, just on the peripheral of his vision and on the edge of his awakening ability to see Her, there ...just waiting for him to remember. The Raven Goddess, 'The Morrigan'; not for the faint hearted and as yet, he'd not experienced Her wrath and hoped he never would. He knew only that her love for her covenors was fierce and undying. Once she claimed you, there was no need to look anywhere else for anything else.

Being an intense and somewhat solitary male, comfortable in his own company and that of his furred and feathered friends, his passion for music, his art and his thirst for continuing wisdom made him a daunting, albeit loyal friend. On stumbling across Sybille's blog, whilst searching for totally unrelated information on a jewellery exhibition in Australia, she'd struck a sudden chord with him as had, he remembered with the hint of a grin, the tall, statuesque redhead, who had been in the photograph with her.

Sybille, in the photo an unidentifiable age, her face wise yet still youthful, drew him. He had read about her esoteric training school in the small town of Springsmeet, in the highlands of Victoria, Australia. In the photo, she stood with a group of her team of staff, readers and a new intake of students a few years ago and the redhead, Maeve he remembered, had had an upcoming exhibition of her very unusual work. She had a style and flair distinctly her own, her sacred jewellery, wands and even Athame had intrigued him and the picture of her, head thrown back laughing, with a somewhat arrogant stance, had fired his senses, which was something that hadn't happened for longer than he cared to remember. She'd stood, together with two other women one slender and pale, her hair appearing almost as silver as Sybille's and another small, curvy, dark haired girl, with a lovely smile that would charm the birds from the trees and who he'd known, instinctively he would like as a friend. He had thought then, that they might be new to Sybille's tutorage but he could see the energy that radiated from each of them.

Back then, one of the reasons for his seeking a mentor was that he could already see clearly, what others could not. Even then, he had a way of knowing whom he could or couldn't trust. This group of women were going to play a role in his life at some stage and tonight he knew why.

He had followed through with his research into Sybille's background and abilities and had decided, after several late night conversations across the waters with her, to enrol in her on-line correspondence courses. It had been a commitment of three years and for some, she'd said, it would lead to a very new way of living a lifetime. He'd not regretted it, not for a moment, even when he'd thought at times he was losing his mind with the intensity of the energy work and discipline required to walk the Wytchway. Still her wealth of knowledge, her methods and exercises, to help her students truly discover their unique gifts, was nothing short of miraculous at times; pure Magick in fact he thought.

She had never ceased to amaze him and he'd been thinking of taking a trip to meet her in the not too distant future. To meet her in the flesh and perhaps to convince her to come to Wales or perhaps to the esoteric capital of the UK, Glastonbury, to give some talks on their mutual love of all things ancient. With her help, he'd hoped to bring the Oldways into the twenty-first century, to allay fears and de-bunk the mystery that was Her Way.

Now he knew that Sybille was in trouble, not dead or in fact physically injured but in greater danger still, he felt that her very essence had slipped between the cracks of this world and even, Goddess aid her, the next.

Without hesitation, Morgan went to his computer and connected on-line to the now familiar Skype address. There was no response. Then, cursing himself for a fool. 'Of course not!' he exclaimed aloud as he considered the time difference, between their two countries. Glancing at the clock, he realised it was close to 1.30 am and that he'd been sitting, lost in his thoughts, for two hours or more. Honey, after pestering him for a run outside had long since, settled by the fire at his feet and Ruark was roosting, with her piercing blue eyes open, watching him, on her accustomed perch on the mantel.

He yawned and stretched, easing back in his comfortable old chair. His last thought before sleep was that he should go to bed ...then he was shifting consciousness; shifting shape ...flying with his Raven friend across deep, green seas, across an endless red desert, stunted with curious trees and skimming low over a giant red rock. Soaring up and away, above mountains tipped with early snows, his wings responding to the weight of pellucid ice fragments ...then down, down swooping across a valley of green vines and luscious fruits, ready for the harvest. His rolled tongue anticipated their sweetness, quenching his thirst in his mind, together with a ripple of danger, at the idea of plundering a morsel or two from under the vintner's nose. Within his Corbae mind, he heard Ruark laugh with glee as she read his senses easily. It would have been just a small thing to be tempted away from the journey for a small respite, but she drove him relentlessly on, with a click of her beak and a guttural call as she winged lower, finding her bearings to land with a clatter of taloned feet onto the roof of an old barn.

He followed, attempting to bank his speed but unaccustomed to the long flight, overshot the roof, sliding down with a snapping of wings to regain equilibrium, hearing a rending tear echoing as he tore through the veil, finally coming to rest on the floor at the feet of the very woman he'd been thinking about previously. Tall, rangy with long, wild fire hair, she stood hands on hips looking down at him with concern. Not quite game to approach him, she whispered an unconscious word of calming over him and turning her head slightly called out, 'Flora! Flora, come quickly!'

His senses returning he heard running feet and his Corbae self said, 'Fly, flee,' but his human self couldn't move as he saw the other young woman, the dark haired one from the photo, manifest in front of him. She knelt slowly, carefully, murmuring words of endearment and to his surprise one of Ruark's kind spoke calmingly to him in the Raven tongue he was unaware he'd known, 'Creoso mellonamin, anta. Amin tel'fallan, hiraeth. Esta sinome.'

'Welcome my friend, gently now. I can help you if you'll let me. Rest now.'

Shocked back to his senses, he felt the ground shift beneath him as he shaped back into his human form, Maeve and Flora recoiling in something akin to horror as they found themselves looking down at, not a seemingly injured Raven but at a fully grown, very naked, dark haired man, with a piercing blue gaze.

'It's you!' He heard Maeve exclaim. 'You were in my dream the other night. What ...who are you?'

Remembering nothing but her startled gaze, Morgan woke; face down on the mat in front of the fire at home, a frantic Honey licking his ears and the sound of raucous Raven laughter echoing in his mind.

Ruark sat, unmoving on the mantle, gazing at him with what could only be described as amusement in her eyes, 'Flew you did ...aaaark ...crashed too you did ...rrhaahaark,' and with a human sounding chuckle, she tucked her head under her wing and slept.

Dazed, beyond reason Morgan crawled to bed and crashed into oblivion, his last vision that of a red headed woman, with a crease of puzzlement between her brows, looking at him with a strong, steady gaze, 'I know you,' she said and he fell.

Chapter 27
Annie Savage

I would imagine that the daisy doesn't dream of being a rose ...that it doesn't judge itself as better or worse than any other blooming flower ...wouldn't the world be a wonderful place if we could do the same? ...love yourself in the moment just as you are, then others can love you that way too.

Teachings from Sybille Madison

Annie worked hard at helping the four girls in setting up the new-look shop; she even grudgingly, liked the name they'd chosen but still it rankled that she'd not been given the opportunity to take over the space for herself. She'd thought after all these years that something would emerge for her now to enable her to set up the shop as her very own, at least as manager. She'd had no idea of what Sybille had been planning all along and had every intention of giving her a piece of her mind when she returned from her sabbatical.

Sighing she continued unpacking and stacking the books that Sybille had so carefully packed away before disappearing. Usually she would speak with her, letting her know where she was going and what she wanted done in her absence; not this time! This time Sybille had organised her three favourite students and her niece,

Samantha to rock right up and totally take over; even the name had changed as if they knew that Sybille would not be back any time soon. Where was Sybille anyway she though irritably? ''earthly rites,' indeed,' she huffed.

As Sybille's receptionist and assistant, Annie had also been one of her students for a few years, never completing the whole courses that were offered, however. She was a proud woman and now at 56 was very sure that she was quite capable of taking over from Sybille and also filling her shoes in the Coven. Even that was now denied her as the chit of a girl Bethan had been given the opportunity to run the groups and she imagined it wouldn't be long before she and her cohorts took over the circle too.

Chapter 28
Aerandir Sensarrius

Aerandir Sensarrius, the young Fae Lord stood in the coppice of trees just a little way from Bethan's cottage. He usually kept himself aloof, even from his own people …considering himself a seer much like Bethan; he had difficulty living in the world as he perceived it and believed that the Fae were born to rule this plane and the other realms, both.

He had been observing her as long as he could remember but being a Fae, time was not a measurable quantity. He knew her to be Aithlin Farandir's offspring from a human woman…an unusual occurrence at the best of times; still this particular bonding of Fae and human had spawned an interesting creature who in his observations had become more Fae than human in many ways. The beauty of her heart moved him in places never experienced before. She was kindness itself; an emotion foreign to him, having always presumed it to be a weakness, in her it was a strength that he could not begin to fathom.

He had basically no idea from where this fascination had come but her features were as fair as his, for his race, were unusually dark; yet there were similarities that he could only assume came from his uncle Aithlin Farandir, brother to his own mother, Aelish Farandirim, from whom he had inherited his dark looks he presumed. There were few dark Elves and their origins were obscure even to the Fae who kept the records of their history in the Skeins of Tyme.

He often wondered at their difference but prided himself that they must be unique indeed if there were so few. His mother sneered at his interest in the Halfling girl her lip curling in disgust which, did he but know it, he was mirroring as he thought about the conversation he'd had with Aelish just earlier that day. She was always on at him to be more a part of the daily activities within the Tribe; an undertaking he found beneath him. As a Fae Lord he didn't consider it at all necessary to be a part of anything, seeing himself to be above it all.

Pausing mid-thought he turned and strode away from Bethan's as something else caught his fickle attention. Mortal Magicks, he sneered again, how dare they and at the Mount too! His long stride eating up the distance, his anger fueled by the intrusion of the mortals into a Fae space, he was ready for a confrontation, although he knew it was strictly forbidden to show himself to human creatures.

Chapter 29
Dark Maker

She is in all things ...respect Her as you would wish to be respected ...love Her and She will help you heal yourself ...She has all the answers hidden in Her wild places and you have the Magick hidden within you ...dare to find it
Tara Saark

In mirror image to the original descent the Maker hurtled down through the pain of humankin's misery. She could taste the corrosion of the polluted planet like a gritty effluence; a corruption and ruination of the gift of the Mother's life that had become an abomination.

Once all the Makers had been destined to become human; to know the interactions that occur through all of the senses that humankin are gifted with and that they take for granted, having no conception of what it would be like without touch, emotion, taste and all the joy of sensate interplay.

As she fell her light dimmed and her song died. Suddenly she saw a beautiful and brilliant light and diving to follow it knocked it off course as it hurtled on, too fast for her to catch up with; she felt its failing life. A Littleshape she remembered; that was a Littleshape. She heard the last tearing scream of song as its light winked out. Distracted and blind the Maker fell.

Falling, letting go, she felt the pull of gravity of the blue planet, tugging at the remnant of her very sense of identity. Below she sensed a light flickering strongly, sparks rising from it like Makers with wounded wings. She fled downward, no returning now and as she fell she felt an unknown energy engulf her. She fought it but too late she was drawn closer to it.

Annie Savage and her Coven, many once Sybille's students, were gathered to cast a circle and to agree on the public ritual they were to enact for Mabon on the Mount. They all heard a screaming sound, like a whizzing firework as it fades and the bomb fire responded with sparks flying as the wounded Maker fell towards its deadly lure.

Annie reacted swiftly, thinking, 'how strange, a fire fly,' as she reached over the flames and caught the falling spark. The Maker, responding instinctually, was changed; tainted beyond hope by this new and invasive energy: fear. Whipping around, black, tattered wings unfurling, she twisted mid-flight, grew a stinging spike; her energy discordant and painful, she struck out at Annie, stinging her in the neck. Yelping, Annie instinctively swatted at it thinking it must be a spark from the fire or an insect after all. With a whine of fear and pain the Maker was lost.

It felt deep within a song unfolding, calling to it and it followed.

The Dark Elflord stood just beyond the edge of the forest, his anger barely kept in check. He had often come to watch the posturing's and posing's of the pseudo Wytches and saw the little Maker spirit falling. He considered whether to let it die or if it could be used to his advantage. Choosing the latter he called to it and it followed changing yet again to grow arms and legs fingers and toes and a head. A poor twisted dark creature with a stinging tail. The Elflord soothed it with a touch and it clung to his shoulder in fear and bewilderment at what it had become.

'Such a little dark thing he crooned to it. Your mine now,' he said, looking deep into the creature's eyes and once more the dark maker was falling.

Striding away through the forest he didn't even glance at the group of humans, standing mouths agape at his passing; one of the group murmured, 'Oooh my, he can pay me a visit anytime he cares to!'

Annie, reeling in shock, crumpled to her knees as the pain of the Dark Maker's sting reached an unbearable pitch and seeing her fall the others ran to help her to a chair on the edge of the circle. She shook off their administrations, not wanting to be touched but Andrea, her closest coven member and friend, had the foresight to fetch ice from the cool chest and pushing back Annie's hood and heavy black hair she applied it to the sting that was already red and swelling.

'What on earth was that thing that stung you,' she fretted?

'I don't know,' exclaimed Annie recovering herself a little as the pain eased. 'I've never seen anything like that around here before. It looked like a firefly but they don't sting!'

'Come on,' said Andrea. 'Let's get you home.' She called out to a couple of the others to give her a hand helping Annie to her car. Turning to one of them she said, 'If you can follow me in my car I'll drive Annie home in hers.'

'No, no,' said Annie quickly 'I'll be fine to drive myself.'

'No way,' said Andrea, 'come on get in,' as she held the door for Annie.

Grudgingly she did, saying huffily 'I'm really alright you know.'

'Then just humour me,' came the terse reply; Andrea was used to Annie's moods by now.

They drove to Annie's home in Springsmeet in silence and when Andrea tried to help Annie in was refused adamantly.

'Good night,' she said abruptly, 'see you soon.' And shut the door firmly, leaning her back against it in some relief. She was actually feeling quite strange, a little feverish and very anxious. She drank a glass of water, pressed a cold wet cloth to her burning neck and heading straight to bed was unconscious before she had a chance to even undress.

Chapter 30
Hercurin

The Wild Hunt begins and in just a few days
...hound and hoof will be heard in the glades
Don't be afraid ...dare to be see
...as the Lord of the Forest rides through the green
He cares for the creatures and birds on the wing
...the fruits of the forest, the bounty they bring
He cares for our children when in deep sleep they stray
...and protects them from those who might steal them away
He hears all our pleas for a prosperous year
...don't hide, step forward ...and look, He's right here!
Extract from Magdalena's Book of Shadows and Light

Lord of the Greenforest Hercurin, stood in a grove of trees on the hill above Sybille's converted barn, his gentle face grave at the news the tree dryads were imparting. A Maker had fallen and falling to the darkness, had taken a Littleshape's light with it as it fell. A Littleshape who had been the closest any had been, in many turns of the wheel, to Becoming.

What had been the cause was yet to be revealed. It had been eons since a fall from Grace had occurred and the Greenlord, Hercurin, felt something akin to human grief as he thought of the Littleshape, known to him well as Sybille. He had walked her land, run with the Wildhunt and had sacrificed himself to that land, for the next season of Greening many times indeed and had been honoured by her in every turning season, as had others who were following the Kurinimen', the Wytchways of ancient days. For this precious Littleshape, known as Sybille the Seer to his kin was indeed Kurinihe'noldo, Wytchwise.

He reached out with all of his being but could feel only a spark of her light, drifting in the great void between the Skeins of Tyme the web of life, Ungwe.

He was bound to the land but could reach out and call to all that would hear him. The Elfkin, the Faefolk, all would come to the Horn of Calling. His great hounds stirred next to him, tails swishing, snouts sniffing the ethers for Sybille's scent excitedly, whining their eagerness to be off in pursuit. The horses of the wild hunt would roam the lands again, Sidhe and Unsidhe would ride out in search but it must not be that the Unsidhe should find her, for she belongs to the Lady. It would be Samhain the Great Rite of All Hallows soon enough and then what would become of her, if she should drift through the veil to the lands between and into their hands. It would be long in coming before another human could walk in her footsteps …except perhaps one, he thought.

He put the horn to his lips but stopped himself. No it wasn't time. Not yet. He must wait as always for the hour of the dead or chaos would indeed break free.

Something else was on the ethers, shifting shape he ran with his hounds through the forest.

Chapter 31
Annie Savage

When you stray from the path of the Wytchwise
…when you break the oath of kin
…you're not a Wytch, in truth if you ego-walk widdershins
But others cannot judge your rites, only show the way
…back to the heart of the greening land
…and the laws of the Ancient of Days
Extract from Wytchway Laws and Lore's, Sybille Madison

Annie's dreams were dark and frightening; she relived the evening's events as again and again the small spark stung her and she experienced ten times magnified the creature's fear and her own intense pain.

She woke desperately thirsty and rose unsteadily, feeling as if she were recovering from the flu, to fetch a glass of water. Her mouth had a thick gluey taste and so she detoured to the bathroom to clean her teeth. Switching on the light she looked in the mirror and saw that her neck was no longer swollen and red but strange black spidery lines were running from the point of entry of the sting down one side of her neck and shoulder. It looks like a crazy tattooist has attacked me she thought, hysterically. The webbing felt sticky and her skin taught and hot and as she looked at it, she felt as if she were losing her balance as it appeared to writhe on her skin.

Opening her mouth to clean her teeth she dropped both paste and brush, when she saw her tongue reflected in the mirror; it too, covered in black web-like line work. Recoiling in horror, she only just made it to the toilet before being violently ill.

'Goddess, protect me!' she cried rinsing her mouth out repeatedly. 'What's happening to me? What were that terrible little creature and that dark man?' She stumbled from the bathroom, back to her bed, collapsing in tears before falling once more into a deep sleep.

In sleep, she found herself standing on the edge of the forest up on the Mount. She was physically there, aware of her whole body which felt stronger and younger than she'd felt in a very long time. Her neck, although still feeling stiff, was no longer hot to the touch and the ridges of webbing were smooth again.

There appeared to be a gathering but not of mortal kind. She felt rather aloof from everything, merely an observer of what was unfolding here. A group of tall dark figures stood where earlier that evening she had stood with her Grove to practice their public rite for Mabon, she recalled. How childish that all seemed she thought. They were as children compared to what she felt standing here watching the ritual these beings were carrying out and the raw power they exuded, seemingly casually.

In the centre stood a female tall and slender with raven-dark hair, carrying a blade of shining silver. Annie shrank from her not in fear but in respect, sensing the vitality that oozed from every fibre of the entities being.

Without need for instruction Annie fell to her knees to honour her; imagining herself to be in the presence of a Goddess no less. At last, she thought the Lady has heard me and found me worthy,

'I am yours to command Lady,' she whispered bowing deeper still.

A stinging slap was the reply as the Dark Fae lost patience with the grovelling woman,

'Tempt me not human,' she said in a throaty tone, 'you know not with whom you speak. Stand up, let me look at you.'

Annie stood trembling, excitement mixed with fear.

'Look at me!' demanded the dazzling dark being.

Annie looked up and found herself staring into the violet eyes of a woman of incredible beauty, who she knew must be akin to Hecate at least in her Maiden form.

Aelish Farandirim laughed to herself as she read the mortals thoughts. So it is then human…yes I can be your Goddess. It is only correct that your kind worship us. Aerandir is right after all. How worthless and naïve this race is, constantly looking to be saved by beings that are greater than they are. She laughed aloud at that, causing Annie to sigh with relief that the Lady might be kind after all.

Aelish approached her, coming close she sniffed at Annie's neck…'what's this then,' she said, 'what did this to you?'

Aerandir stepped from the shadows of the grove and presented the little darkmaker to his mother,

'This little creature did,' he said, bowing respectfully. 'It came from out of nowhere and the silly human tried to catch it. This is the result,' he finished.

Aelish looked more closely at the dark, spitting creature and fear dimmed her eyes for a moment, not missed by Aerandir.

'Why it's …it was,' she amended, 'a Maker; Goddess what have you done Aerandir?'

'I merely rescued the poor thing from the flames,' he sneered, 'and this human too come to that. What will you do with her my Queen?'

'She must forget everything she has experienced,' Aelish replied haughtily, 'she may not tell of what she has witnessed here.'

'Oh Lady,' said Annie, 'I wouldn't dream of speaking of this to anyone. They wouldn't be worthy of you.'

'Hah, ever arrogant your race,' said Aerandir.

'Quiet,' snapped Aelish turning to look Annie deep in her eyes. Annie felt as if the ground were sliding up to meet her.

'Do you swear mortal, to hold your egotistical tongue, or will we cut it from you?' she said approaching with her silver blade and pressing it to the web of scars on Annie's neck.

'Oh no Lady …I …I …I, wouldn't dream of it,' stammered Annie in horror, 'I am yours …please,' she trailed off as she saw the disgust on both faces of the elegant beings.

'So be it then, Annie Savage,' drawing the web of blight from her neck into the blade. 'Now sleep!' she commanded.

Annie felt herself hit the ground to wake in a tangle of sheets, sweat soaked and light headed. She groaned, rubbing her face and eyes with the corner of the sheet. 'Shit!' she exclaimed, 'What a terrible dream.'

Once more she dragged herself out of bed and into the bathroom where she turned on the shower to a lukewarm spray. While it ran she looked in the mirror above the basin and gaped in amazement; she had youthed and the webbing had gone from a neck that was now firm and smooth. Always being a vain woman, this was the greatest gift her Goddess could give her; the semblance of returned youth. Laughing aloud she didn't hear the gales of Fae laughter that followed her to the shower.

'Arrogant human,' said Aerandir Sensarrius standing invisible outside the window, 'a simple Glamour and you think your young again; ah, naïve indeed,' he grinned in dark mischief, while Annie sang to herself in the shower and a new day dawned.

Chapter 32
Samantha

Cherish each other, love one another
...the law is 'harm ye none'
Gift to each other the truth of yourself
...and earth's greening will be done
Find you the innocence of gentler days
...come to the forests where Faefolk play
Live in the moment as if t'were your last day
...and earth's greening will be done.
Bardic song...Arianwen Isil'Lindir

Earlier that day, Samantha asked Flora if it was okay for her to drive out to the farm. She needed a break but also time to look through some of Sybille's documents and her Book of Shadows. She felt restless, so had taken them, together with her journal and sketchbook outside.

Heading up the hill to the grove behind the house, she settled in her favourite place under the huge sycamore trees. It was here; she had experienced so many rituals and celebrations for the turning wheel of the seasons and here as a little girl, she recalled, she had first been inspired to draw.

So many memories were coming to the fore as she worked through all her Aunt's things; so many she'd kept hidden deep inside due to her parents controlling natures, surfaced as a new Samantha was emerging.

Opening an old, beautifully leather-bound, Book of Shadows, she flipped through to a page Sybille had written about the Lammas Sabbat. Admiring Sybille's lovely writing, wishing hers could be as tidy she read…

Lammas

Lammas is the time of year when the grain harvest is upon us and so the Wheel turns again toward autumn. In the fields, the hay bales are appearing as the farmer's work their way around the district slashing, raking and baling the crops. Wheat is heading and the green crops of barley and oats are ripening, shaking their pretty heads in the breeze.

It is the time of year a Wytch makes a sacrifice of something no longer needed. All outworn and outgrown things, must be done away with, just as the Lord of the Grain; the Harvest Lord; John Barley Corn; the Greenman or Jack in the Green, to name a few, gives himself to the scythe of the farmer, that human kind can eat of his body given willingly in the grain crops.

With His seed, sown for harvesting, he gives his blood again and the wheel turns on. As much as he sacrifices himself, so too must we give back to our community, our family by blood and by choice.

When we are prepared to let go out grown ways, we find a new harvest manifests for us in the coming cycles of Mabon and Samhain. When we can give away stored things that we have not used in an age, we can make a space to fill through choice, rather than by seemingly random events that fill us with more of the same …unless we are paying attention.

In order to understand more fully, a Wytch must be prepared to work the disciplines of the Way throughout the turning seasons. Give to receive or give willingly without a thought of receiving; either way the return will be threefold and events will occur in the positive or negative, whichever has been put out to the universe by the Wytch without judgement as there is no good/bad energy only energy applied for good or for bad.

Energy is the neutral force that binds and inhabits all things, without thought of a negative or positive charge, so beware where your thoughts are predominant, for that is where the energy is manifest.

In days gone by the last grains harvested would be those used to bake the Lammas Bread to share that the sacrifice the Greenlord made is recognised and 'inwardly digested' so to speak. The last stook of corn, made into a corn dolly, then placed above the hearth for the season to protect and bring continued prosperity to the home.

She took a little more time to go through the passage again but found she needed to sit with it all for a while, so taking her sketchpad she reviewed the work she'd done on the sketches that were altered and that puzzled her.

Feeling drowsy, her eyelids became heavy; she felt a small host of little energies around her the sound of rustling of leaves just as it had been weeks ago in her dream and in her bed. She hadn't seen as clearly as this since childhood. Blinking rapidly, she saw little sparkling winged beings around her. The Sycamore tree shook her autumn tinged leaves of yellow and gold. Slipping into sleep she dreamed of the Host; the Wild Hunt, riding out of the hillside and across the rim toward her. She felt no fear, only awe, at the beauty of the Fae as they rode and danced across the wet grass their colourful robes and bare feet, untouched by the damp, had them appearing to float across the surface.

One of the riders approached her and dismounting, came to stand looking down at her, silver tresses hung down her back her anklet bells tinkled as she swayed in an unseen breeze. Taller than the others and haughty of demeanour she kicked at the pages of Samantha's drawings causing them to lift and flutter around. Looking at one of them more closely Sam could feel her whole attitude change as an element of fear crept into the Fae creatures violet eyes. As if from above Sam could see it was the drawing of the stern Dark Fae that she had seen stalking Bethan in her dreams. The Fae withdrew as if stung and moving her hands in a strange Sigel, leaves and papers alike lifted and swirled around the tree.

Sam felt suddenly paralysed, unable to move a muscle, the now fast moving eddy of detritus whirling faster until it came to rest on her, covering her completely. She could see her sketches of skeletal leaves and their genuine counterparts merging with each other until she couldn't tell which her drawings were and which the rustling leaves.

Falling deeper into a trance like state she had no choice but to lay still and breath through her panic as it threatened to overwhelm her ...falling deeper still under the Fae's hold she slept.

She dreamt of the leaves that covered her becoming tiny leaf clad beings, each one a perfect replica of a leaf but with tiny twig arms and legs, fragile skeletal leaf-like wings; their hands and feet sharp and pointy left trails of markings on her own limbs as they danced over and around her.

Abruptly the tall Fae walked back to her horse and mounted. Summoning the dancing light beings to follow, she rode away without a backwards glance ...the small leaf-like creatures trailed after her, scattering Sam's drawings to the wind.

Sam slumbered on, aware of everything yet not able to react; frozen in a dream; hours passed and the afternoon drew on into a cool autumn evening.

Flora came home and Bethan and Maeve arrived to talk about the coming re-opening of the centre. While chatting they prepared a simple meal to share and with a sigh of relief Maeve poured them all a glass of wine, collapsed in a chair, kicking off her boots and stretching her long legs out in front of her.

'Where's Sam got too?' Bethan asked Maeve, 'I haven't seen her all afternoon. Didn't she come with you?'

'No,' replied Maeve, 'I haven't seen her since this morning. I assumed she was upstairs in her room at Grove Street.'

'That's odd,' said Flora, 'she rang to ask me if it was okay if she came to look through Sybille's Book of Shadows this afternoon. I'll go check upstairs; perhaps she's still searching through things and hasn't heard us come in.'

'I'll go check outside,' said Bethan, 'it's seems strange. She would have heard us; we've made enough noise, unless she's fallen asleep.'

Flora checked the rooms upstairs but there was no sign of Samantha. Calling out to the others, she went back down too check the study but still no Sam.

Bethan went outside in the evening sunlight calling Sam's name. As she did, a feeling of anxiety overcame her. She knew that Sam might simply have gone for a walk; it was such a beautiful time of year. She breathed in the scent of wood smoke and damp grass and calling out went out through the garden and up toward the Sycamore Grove on the hill. She could see the little folk playing and realised how clear her sight was actually becoming, a shadowy figure broke free from amongst the huge trees and walked toward her.

'Sam,' she called, 'is that you? Come on dinners ready.'

It wasn't Samantha that stepped towards her on quiet feet but a being straight out of a her drawings, the stern yet gentle faced Greenlord, the Lord of the Forest and the Wild Hunt himself. She stood, overcome with sheer awe as he quietly approached her and she realised that he carried someone in his arms. Against the size of the tall being, the person he carried seemed small and frail and Bethan, realising it was Sam, forgot all shyness or fear and ran forward, 'What have you done to her? What's happened?'

'You forget yourself Littleshape,' he said. 'She is unhurt and only sleeping yet not an ordinary sleep; it would appear that a glamour has been put upon her and she is in need of a little care. She may awake, feeling as if she has imbibed the strongest mead.'

Bethan stopped as he gently placed Sam on the ground against a tree and taking a small bottle from a pouch at his belt, he knelt to administer a few drops between Sam's pale, rigid lips. He chaffed her hands and blew gently on her face, urging a response as he whispered to her in that strange tongue.

For once at a loss, Bethan could only gaze at him wide-eyed. Never had she thought it possible to meet Him in the flesh, the Greenlord, tall, muscular and lean, his hair thick curls entwined with tiny talisman and bone, his arms and torso bronzed and polished as the Oak he might have sprung from; his eyes, a burnished amber were deep and kindly as he turned to look at her. She felt like a gawky child as she stood watching him gently tend to her friend. Regaining her composure, she stepped forward and said, 'We need to get her inside, she looks frozen.'

'Indeed,' he replied, 'I will carry her to the door. She will recover soon, have no fear.' So saying he picked Sam up as if she were a rag doll and took her to the verandah, where he placed her on a chair by the door. Taking Sam's bag from his shoulder, he placed it next to her on the deck. Turning to Bethan, he looked deeply into her and she felt wild emotions never experienced before. He looked at her with such tenderness it brought tears to her eyes. Reaching out he took the tear from her cheek and placed its salty moisture on his tongue,

'Whom do you cry for Arianwen, child of Aithlin Farandir? Save your tears, they may well be needed before this cycle is spent.'

Recoiling from the electricity of his touch and the potent aroma that oozed from every pore of musk and oak moss, Bethan managed to stutter, 'Who are you? I've seen you in dreams and spoken to you there. You've been watching me.'

'Ah I forget the human tradition of introduction,' he said with a smile. 'My name for you to use is Hercurin, Lord of the Greenwood, Spirit of this place of your heart,' gesturing to the lands around them, 'and long-time friend to your teacher Sybille. My names are many throughout the earth realms. The Fae have enchanted your friend; no true harm meant but they will answer to me for not alerting you to her whereabouts; they know the laws against tampering with human life. Does this answer your questions? '

Turning his head sharply, listening to sounds beyond her hearing, Bethan took a step back as huge antlered horns grew from his head and his wild scent sharpened. He briefly touched her cheek again, saying, 'You will see me again in your dreams and in your waking. One day I will come for you when you call Arianwen,' and then he was gone, running like the stag he resembled.

Flora, hearing the sound of voices, flew out the door just in time to see his running form before it disappeared into the trees. With one raised eyebrow and a quick look at Bethan to see that she was okay she turned her gentle hands to Sam, who now sat curled, with a silly grin on her face, in the chair where Hercurin had placed her.

'Hello,' she said dreamily to them, 'I feel wonderful. I was playing with the nature spirits and a Fae Lady came and…'

'Come on Sam,' said Flora, 'let's get you inside and feed you,' she laughed, 'and you Beth, you look as if you shared Sam's experience.'

Calling out to Maeve, who at that moment came from around the other side of the house where she'd been looking for Sam, Flora put an arm round Beth to draw her inside, while a wobbly but giggling Sam rose to her feet.

Maeve grabbed her from behind and steered her inside. Taking one look at them both she said, 'gees, I'll have what you two have had. What's going on? You both look like cats that have well and truly had the cream.'

Leading Sam inside, Maeve looked down at her hands as she pushed her into a chair. 'Flora, I think you need to take a look at this.'

Turning from Bethan, who was standing in the middle of the room in a trance, she looked where Maeve was pointing.

Samantha, looking down at her own hands said, 'Cool aren't they,' she held them out for Flora's inspection. Tiny vines and skeletal leaves spiralled up her arms in tones of green, gold and henna red and across the back of her hands. They looked as if they were growing on her skin.

Drawn to look at the exquisite work, Maeve and Flora watched as it shifted and changed under their startled gaze.

'Okay,' said Maeve, 'we need to get some food into these two space cadets I think,' recovering her composure and leading the giggling Sam to a chair, she dished up a bowl of soup with bread for her.

'You too Bethan, come on,' said Flora, 'eat.'

'Oh I'm okay, just a bit pleasantly dazed,' and continued to tell the others about Hercurin, smiling at the thought of him. 'There's something there between us. It may sound strange, he's a Forest Lord but it's there. What can I say?' She trailed off. 'More importantly we need to ask Sam what happened I think.'

They all turned to look at Sam who, completely oblivious, was tucking into her soup like a starving child, still grinning from ear to ear.

'Hey, we could use that big Forest Lord right now,' said Maeve in jest. 'How are we going to get 'grinning girl' here upstairs?'

'Oh no worries, Maeve,' said Flora, the couch in Sybille's room will do for tonight. Then she won't fall down the stairs if she wanders in the night,' laughing. 'I think it's contagious. I'm starting to feel silly myself,' said Flora.

They settled to their meal attempting to extract as much as they could from the still giggling Samantha.

'Now I know what they mean by being away with the faeries,' she laughed, then sobering briefly said, 'the one that approached me, before I played with the nature spirits, was very rude. She looked down her nose at me until she saw that sketch I drew, of the rather dark Fae that follows Bethan around a lot.' She looked back down at her hands and then was gone again, off into a world of her own; the vines on her wrists appearing to move and twist, little figures playing amongst them in total innocence and smiled.

After a while, Sam began to droop in her chair. Maeve and Flora helped her to the study and she fell onto the couch where Flora then threw a soft blanket over her and Maeve slipped off Sam's boots. With a completely silly grin on her face, Sam slumbered on.

Bethan meanwhile had cleaned up, washed dishes and stacked firewood by the hearth for Flora, in her usual thoughtful way. As she stepped outside she could smell the encroaching mist mixed with wood smoke and heard, somewhere in the distance, a flute played. It came from the direction of Wells and she felt drawn by the sweetness of the music; it called to her and she knew instinctively who played.

Shaking herself, mentally, she carried the wood back inside and knelt in front of the fire staring into its heart, seeing the little salamander licking up the bark of the wood and dancing into the hot coals. One spat a spark at her, not in malice but in thanks for the fuel that fed them and kept them alive. A fire had always burned in the hearth or the fuel stove when Sybille had been here and been able to communicate with them when she needed just a small token fire or a fire that roared to heat and cook.

The salamander had always responded to her sensitivity as now they responded to gentle Bethan.

With Samantha asleep, the three sat to talk about all the events of the last days, Tara Saark, Annie Savage, the appearance of the Raven who shifted into a naked man and then disappeared.

Everything was accelerating and there was an urgent need for them all to finish setting up 'earthly rites,' to take some time between the approaching Mabon and finally Samhain to finish the rite and get a handle on what more they could be doing to find Sybille.

Bethan had agreed to contact Max and her parents for the official opening of the centre and for Samhain. They had all decided that the more open minds there were available to help find Sybille the better.

Alex and Susan Fenner were clever and alternative in their thinking, no strangers to psychic occurrences either. Susan particularly, an amazing artisan and art therapist was open to just about everything although she was yet to be told about Bethan's birthmother's affair with the elusive Aithlin Farandir.

Both Alex and Max possessed excellent minds and were a mine of information on Celtic Mythology, both experts in their particular chosen field. They were very Pagan in their outlook and beliefs and were all very fond of Sybille.

Bethan tried to hide her inner turmoil about the earlier meeting with Hercurin but finally, defeated, when Flora asked her what was amiss, she apologised profusely,

'I have to go I'm sorry, I can't think straight; I need a little time to myself to digest what happened today …meeting Him!' and with that she gave each of them a quick hug and was gone, leaving Maeve and Flora exchanging concerned glances.

Chapter 33
Hercurin

Lady of the Sacred Groves walks in shadow and in light
...the message She will bring to you
...is do not fear the dark of night
Light or shadow, all the same and if you doubt
...call out Her name; for She will guide your steps again
She will lead you home.
From Wytchwise ...Arianwen Isil'Lindir

A cry of surprise and fear caught his attention, carried to him by the tree spirits as he stood with the beautiful Halfling Arianwen near Sybille's Hearth. He'd been about to do something he'd not done in millennia and reach out to another with his whole being but carefully putting those responses aside, for the moment, he shape changed into the huge stag that was one of his Littleshapes and bound through the forest toward the energies he sensed were coming from the Mount.

He arrived just in time to see the small Dark Maker hurtle down toward the fire burning in the centre of the glade and the Littleshape known as Annie Savage reach above the flames to catch her. Too late, he ran forward, shifting as he ran but the Maker changed to a poor twisted entity beyond reasoning, stinging Annie in the neck before the Elf Lord Aerandir Sensarrius stepped forward and claimed the terrified changeling.

Hercurin challenged Aerandir and the Dark Elf, for that is what he'd become in that moment, sneered and turning his back stalked away with the little Dark Maker clinging to his shoulder.

Hercurin grieved the little one, of the Mother's Magicks; calling to her in a deep tone for aid …a response was immediate…

'Hercurin, beloved of Terra, nothing can be done until the Halfling and her humankin awaken fully …patience …be at peace, even the Great Mother cannot change the course of this day, the web is being rewoven as we speak.'

Silver stepped from between the trees; darkness swirling within her once, pure light and where she trod, the Makers flew, cleansing the blight left by her passing. Wounded and bleeding through the hole in her Spirit, she passed beyond sight into the Skeins of Tyme.

Bowing his head the Green Lord wept, his tears further cleansing the earth.

Chapter 34
Sybille

Flying faster than the winds; tossed on the ethers ...buffeted by cosmic storms; how fragile we are when we think we do not know the way home. I n truth we never left.
Musings from the personal journal of Sybille Madison

Sybille dreamed she was travelling through the great Birthing Tree in which she slept, down the inside the branches, the trunk and down into the root system. She was weak, fragile and just wanted to sleep forever. She no longer had a great sense of whom or what she was; wraith-like she floated on downwards into the darkness that beckoned to her, that spoke of relief from all disillusion and fear.

From deep within that darkness a light flickered far away in the depths...'follow,' a voice said to her, 'follow and then you can rest.'

Suddenly she was speeding down a great tunnel towards the brightest of lights; hurtling along at an ever-increasing speed until she flew into it...and then she was floating, bathing in a gentle light of restoration and peace.

In what seemed only moments, she was awakening in a room filled with streaming sunlight, in a canopied bed hung with soft white, translucent drapes. Resting against chambray pillows with lace-worked edging that smelt of fresh rose water. She stretched, smiling to herself as she looked at her firm olive toned skin with pleasure and yet, something niggled at the back of her mind…young skin, she thought; of course young skin I'm only 17 after all aren't I? No, she thought that's not right, I'm older surely.

Yawning, still a little befuddled from sleep she remembered she'd been dreaming of being someone else; an older woman with silver hair who had fallen asleep and floated off into a tree and then…what happened then? She couldn't remember any more than that.

The bedroom door opened and a buxom woman bustled in. She threw up her hands and then her vast starched apron over her head and ran out the room.

'Nonna,' she called, 'what's wrong. Come back please, I feel a little weak,' but she was gone calling out in the purest Italian, 'Signore, Signore…come quickly Signorina Nina is awake; she's awake!'

Nina heard doors slamming and the running of feet as a tall elegant man raced into the room with a speed belying his years.

'Nina,' he cried, tears streaming down his cheeks into a well-trimmed pepper and salt beard, 'Nina, my little one you've come back to us. I have prayed to the Mother for your return.'

'Papa, what can you mean? I've just woken up and suddenly Nonna is running around like a crazy person. What's the matter, why are you so upset?'

'Ah, Nina…you left us; you have been so very ill for over a year now. A fever took you; we thought you would never wake up. The Doctors have given up; they said there was nothing more they could do for you so deep has your coma been there was hardly a pulse. Look at you,' he exclaimed, fresh tears coursing down his face that Nina realised had aged greatly, 'you appear fully recovered and as if you have regained weight and strength overnight. What miracle is this little one,' so saying he lifted her from the bed and onto his lap as if she were only a small child.

'Ah Papa I don't remember much at all, only that I have returned home after a long journey.'

Nina's Nonna returned with bowl of steaming, fragrant hot water and soft towels, having taken some time to regain her usual composure.

'Signore Giraldi,' she said, 'I must insist you let me tend to Signorina Nina's needs of the moment. We need to carry her to the commode but I can bathe her here. I have summoned young Magdalena from the kitchen to come and help attend her and have taken the liberty of promoting her to train as the Signorina's maid, until a replacement is found for Lucia.'

'Yes of course,' Eduardo Grimaldi replied, 'I forget Nina's needs in the excitement of her return to us. Please Nonna continue. Call me when my daughter is more comfortable. I can hardly bare to let her out of my sight,' kissing Nina's cheek he reluctantly left the room.

'Nonna,' said Nina, 'why don't I remember what happened to me?'

'Hush,' she replied, 'your recovery is nothing short of miraculous but I fear that the very speed at which you've healed, may lead to a relapse, so you must rest.

Come, let me help you to the commode and then I'll change the linen and give you a posset for sleep.'

'Surely I've slept all this time. I'm not tired Nonna.'

'That may be so little one but you must rest until you have fully recovered your strength. Please, humour me; we have been so scared for you.'

At that moment, there came a timid tap on the door and a young woman of about Nina's age came in. She curtsied to Nina, 'Signorina Nina, I am honoured to serve you and overjoyed that you are recovering.'

'Thank you,' smiled Nina, 'I'm sure we will get along famously.'

Between her beloved Nonna and the housemaid, Magdalena, they helped Nina to make her necessary toilet and then after changing the soiled sheets, carried her back to bed. After making her comfortable and bringing her one of her precious books, they bustled off to collect some clear broth and a posset for sleep for her.

Falling back, surprised that she felt a little drowsy; Nina thought about her dreams, her apparent illness and tried to recall more of what she could not recollect. Strange feelings of having been elsewhere overwhelmed her, if only she could remember.

After somewhat indignantly drinking her posset she fell asleep holding onto her dear Papa's hand as he read to her from one of his books on the philosophy of astrology, the new science of their age. He knew he should call one of the Doctors but he was tired of their grim, maudlin faces and the smell of their unwashed skin. He

was a fastidious man and the ways of the Dottore, he had
never understood when they said that overly washing the
body caused the invasion of bad humours, hence the
illness of his poor Nina.

'What rubbish,' he said aloud, 'and they dare to
call me a heathen because I worship in the old ways of the
Stregga!'

Nina stirred; soothing her with a loving touch, he
gently pulled his hand from hers, tucking the sheets under
her pretty chin and stretching out his long legs prepared
to keep vigil for his sweet girl.

Deep within Nina, the Littleshape Sybille
slumbered, in forgetfulness.

Chapter 35
Bethan

He changes his face as she changes her gown
...his smile remains a grin, not a frown
He prepares for the hunt through the wilds on the rim
...be aware of his presence, feel his touch on your skin
From Wytchwise by Arianwen Isil'Lindir

Bethan drove home with unusual haste; in truth, she'd rather have run out the door and home through the forest. She felt a strange tugging at her mind and the smell of oak moss was strong in her nostrils.

Reaching home, she ran through the house and out the back door, barely stopping to light a lamp as a guide for the way back in the dark. She needed to speak with Aithlin Farandir; she needed to know what was happening to her. Hercurin had left her feeling things she'd never imagined, let alone describe.

Racing full tilt, she ran smack into a figure standing in the shadow of the forest. A tall lean figure who she immediately thought was Aithlin. Instead, as she started to babble that she was glad he was here, needing to speak with him desperately, a strange Wytchlight appeared around him and she found herself looking into the male version of her own face. A face twisted with anger at her running into him; a hand raised holding a strange dark creature pointed directly at her face that was preparing to fly at her.

She raised her hands to protect herself, stumbling backwards and as the light fell on her, he faltered and with a murmur soothed the darkling. Regaining composure, he grasped Bethan quickly to prevent her falling but she shrank away from him.

'You're not Aithlin Farandir,' she choked through her fear, 'Who are you?'

'Why I am his kin and therefore, yours Arwen, Aerandir Sensarrius. I was just checking on you for him to make sure you were safely at home. What are you doing running through the forests at this hour? You should know that there are creatures about that would mean you and your kind harm.'

The look in his eyes made her feel that he might well be one of those creatures but gathering all her courage she said,

'I am myself a Halfling it would seem. I would assume that would mean at least a little protection from the dark!'

'Ah Bethan as bold as you are beautiful then lovely lady! Your father must be proud of you indeed but please,' he said in a sweeter tone, 'allow me to accompany you safely to your Hearth.'

He went to grasp her arm again but she stepped back into what she thought must be a tree; instead gentle arms placed her to one side as if she were a feather. Hercurin stood rooted to the ground, staring at the Dark Elf and the small Dark maker cringing on his shoulder.

'Step back Arianwen,' he said without taking his gaze from Aerandir, 'and you little one,' addressing the darkling, 'come to me, let the Mother restore you again.'

The Dark Maker only hissed at him so twisted had her light become, her memory of all that had been before, gone, tainted by the fall and the depth of despair that emanated from this realm of humankin.

'Aerandir Sensarrius,' he said with a glare, 'what have you done to help this Maker heal?'

'Oh Greenlord, I have tried but the little thing only seems to want to be with me. I'm sure she means no harm,' Aerandir replied, with a small smirk.

'Harm,' boomed Hercurin, causing even the Fae to tremble before recovering himself again, 'harm has already been done to humankin.'

'Ah yes, her,' he said still smirking, 'a worthless pseudo-wytch, nothing more. She'll recover after a night's rest I'm sure.'

'Would you say that of the Lady Silver and of her lost Littleshape Sybille too, Elf?' His tone making an insult of the word, 'Who are you to judge this, Aerandir Sensarrius; you forget your kin are bound to heal not harm? Give the Maker to me, so that she can be restored.'

Stepping forward to take the trembling being, she raised discordant notes again and vanished into the trees leaving a trail of sticky black webbing behind her.

'No!' cried Hercurin and Aerandir together but she was gone.

'There will be a gathering called Aerandir Sensarrius and you will be brought before your kin to explain your actions. Leave my sight, before I forget how young you are; go to your home and remain there until you are called.'

Bowing with evident disdain the Dark Fae melted back into the trees.

Bethan had stood, taking it all in with wonder. What was happening to the world? She felt the pain and darkness of the poor creature and cried for the young Elflord, who surely did not realise what he'd done. Recovering herself and saying as much, Hercurin turned to her and replied,

'If only that were true Arianwen but there is dark Magick afoot and the youngling is sadly not to be trusted in this. He is arrogant and does not wish to have association with any but his own kin, seeking domination over humankin is his goal. He will be observed and made responsible for his misdemeanours this day.'

He reached out to touch her face as he had before. She didn't flinch away as he towered above her. Looking into his eyes, she saw all her pain mirrored there and magnified many times over. She reached out in turn to touch the hand that stroked her cheek, electrified; she could not look away. She fell into him into depths eternal; mysterious, the power of him incomprehensible, the aroma of him strengthened, became as musk. She was intoxicated.

He steadied her a little by stepping back but still held his hand to her cheek. Once again, he took her tears onto his fingers, 'Do you cry for me too now, Arwen

Arianwen Isil'Lindir?' 'Lady Silver Moonsinger,' he translated for her.

'For the poor darkling, Lord,' she managed, 'it's a lost, scared creature; I felt its pain and for the lonely Dark Fae too. You mentioned Sybille; do you know where she is?'

Ignoring her question he said, 'Arianwen, your heart is generous, dangerously open to other's invasion. Have a care lest you be overwhelmed by your empathy.'

With this, he stepped closer again, curious to know her Trueshape. 'Ah yes,' he said, 'Halfling we know; Fae and Humankin yes but there's more yet to be shown you of your parentage. Then there is your Trueshape Silver; even she, you will go beyond; the potential hidden within you is immeasurable,' he paused. 'Arianwen, you take my breath away.' Stepping closer still, he strengthened the connection between them, taking both her hands he drew them to his warm chest, looking deep into her, his gaze gentle, she recognised a passion in their depth that quickened her pulse and dried out her mouth. She moistened her lips briefly; swallowing her nervousness, frightened by the feelings he kindled in her belly.

As her tongue flicked out, his curiously coloured irises enlarged and darkened. He bent his head placing his forehead against hers opening the connection even more. Suddenly she was inside his psyche, feeling everything he felt, smelling and tasting, knowing and experiencing all he was, Forest Lord, God of Nature. Nothing spared, nothing hidden he gave himself without reserve to this beautiful Halfling he had watched grow and mature into the Spellsinger she was fast becoming, drinking her music as he returned to her the song of life itself.

He drew back in some surprise as she tentatively allowed him the same openness he offered her. They stood mind-melded, lost in each other's differentness ...losing themselves in the vastness of their oneness; hearing the song of the Mother joining them until for what seemed like an eternity they were no longer individual; their songs merging, saturating all illusion of separation.

Slipping to their knees, a carpet of moss, emerald green and velvet soft appeared, prepared by the little Magicks for their bed. As they lay together, to watch the darkening sky, leaf sprites wove a coverlet of falling leaves and tiny starflowers to stave off the dew that would soon fall. Silvery cobwebs caught the first dewdrops as they fell, tiny Fae bells covered their bower and the trees bent low the last of their leaf-covered branches, to hide them from sight as they became lost in each other.

Cradled tenderly against his huge chest Bethan slipped into sleep, while he watched and listened to her dreaming.

'Co-joined, you become oneness in truth,' the words echoed from Ungwe the web of life as she shuddered and shifted, making space for the rarest of occurrences; the Greenlord Hercurin lost himself to love.

As the dawn broke on a new autumn day, Bethan slept as Hercurin kept watch over her. He could see the taint of the darkmaker like grey webbing over where Silver had passed, in spite of the Makers, frantically following her to cleanse.

He sighed with regret for Trueshape Silver who had been so close to renewal and for the Littleshape Sybille lost, where even he could not sense.

He stood, still holding Bethan in his arms and walked back through the forest to her Hearth. The door stood open and he could smell the scent of another. Flora stepped through the kitchen door and stood looking in astonishment at Hercurin, carrying her friend. She did not have to ask if Bethan was okay, she could see the aura of peace that radiated from her and the huge Forest Lord, who stood at the door that all was well indeed.

He hesitated, waiting to see what Flora would do. She recovered herself and asked him to bring Bethan inside; she knew that he needed an invitation to cross the threshold. Stepping aside, she let him in indicating the couch for him to put her down. To Flora's ultimate surprise, he knelt to cover Bethan with a soft throw, whispering to her in an unknown tongue, 'Quel esta melamin,' 'sleep well my love,' as he stroked her cheek.

With a nod to Flora, he was gone before she could think what to say or do. She'd only called round so early because she'd been concerned for Bethan after the events of the day before and here he was again the Horned God of Nature, God of the Wytches. How could she ever have imagined the feeling of meeting Him face to face?

Sam had still been asleep when she'd driven over to Bethan's and Maeve had gone back to Grove Street unaccustomedly early for her, saying she really needed to work on the pieces that were ruined before she made the final move to Springsmeet.

Now, looking at her sleeping friend whose lips curved in a gentle smile, she could only wonder at what could have happened last night.

She wandered back into the kitchen and prepared some coffee for her, leaving it on the edge of the stove to keep warm. Outside the Kookaburra called in the sun and a noisy mob of Ravens landed on the roof cawing and muttering to each other. She could have sworn she heard a voice amongst the havoc they created,

'Way to go Bethy, way to go!'

'Tara?' Flora called aloud, running outside to look as the flock took off in frenzy from the roof, the sound of Tara's distinctive laugh accompanying their departure.

Shaking her head she went back inside, wrote a note for Bethan and left quietly, knowing she would hear all that her friend wished to share with her later. She had chores to do, then she needed to catch up with Maeve in town to help finish the Centre and to start sending the invitations out for the opening.

Chapter 36
Max Fenner

Max Fenner paused a moment to review what he'd written and to rub his tired, grey eyes, 'So far, so good,' he muttered to himself as he polished his glasses on a trailing end of shirt before continuing to read…

Horned Lord of Forest and field and also of the hunt, he is Lord of Life, Giver of Life and yet is also Lord of Death and Resurrection for, like the Goddess, his nature is dualistic, the Horned God is not only the Hunter, but also the Hunted; he is the Sun by day, but also the Sun at Midnight; he is the Lord of Light.

The Greenman, God of the Wytchwise is the Horned God, the ancient God of Fertility: the God of the forest, Lord of Darkness: the darkness of night, the darkness of the Shadows, the sacred depths of the forest, and the dark of the Underworld.

He is seen as the group soul of the hunted animal, invoked by the Wytch: and as such, is the Sacrificial Victim, the beast who is slain that the tribe/coven might live; a gift from that group soul, who was often revered as the tribal totem or ancestral spirit. The Horned God is also the spirit of vegetation, of green and growing things, whether of the vine, the forest or field. Dionysus, Bacchus, Adonis and many other vegetation and harvest Gods were often depicted wearing the horns of a bull, a goat, a ram, or a stag: whichever of the horned beasts were held sacred in that place and time. This aspect is the Dying and Resurrecting God who dies with the harvest as the grain is gathered in the fields; which are buried like the seeds that grow anew, fresh, green and young in the spring, reborn from the Womb of the Great Mother.

The Horned God is not 'the devil', except to those who fear and reject Nature, the powers of life, human sexuality and the ecstasy of the human spirit, for the devil has origins in the Christian teachings and was not heard of before those texts came about depicting him as a 'demon,' or fallen angel.

The Celtic Cernunnos, literally translated means Horned One ...images of him are very consistent, His main attribute are his horns, those of a stag. He is mostly portrayed as a large, mature man with long hair and a beard. He wears a torc: this was an ornate neck-ring worn by the Celts to denote tribal rank and honour. Because of his frequent association with beasts he is often referred to as The Lord of the Animals and due to his affiliation with stags in particular, he is also known as The Lord of the Hunt. The Stag Lord, The Horned God of the Hunt, The Lord of the Forest ...of all the Celtic divinities (with the exception of the Goddess Danu) none have caught the imagination of modern pagans as much as he.

He was working hard on his new book, Return of the Green Lord; deadlines were looming fast and his editor had been on his back all week. Somehow he knew he wouldn't be meeting that deadline any time soon.

Slowly making his name in the literary world, his books were selling at an amazing speed despite the fact they were a little on the dry side; much like Max himself in point of fact.

His specialties were the Myths surrounding the Celtic peoples, from their origin right through to the various invasions that had watered their blood through the ages. His latest offering was following the mythos of Herne the Hunter, the Horned God of the ancients and the Green Man. His own personal leanings were towards the Old Ways as his parents were both more than a little that way inclined. They had taught him that the God of the Pagan Pantheon of the Celts was not the Devil or Satan of the Christian belief systems, for that entity was of their own invention and had nothing to do with the ancient Lord of Nature whose image could still be seen today dotted across the British Isles and beyond, above church doorways, it being the only way for the Christian priests to merge their new god with the Old Ways.

Pausing in his work he had a sudden urge to ring his sister Bethan; they hadn't spoken in a while, which was unusual in itself as they had always been close. He only vaguely remembered the almost new-born infant that had appeared as if from nowhere. He recalled when he was a little older, he'd quizzed his mother for not having a swollen belly like his friends mother had had when she'd brought home a little sister for him. He was only three when Bethan arrived but it hadn't take him many years to work out that big bellies and babies went together because his mother had shown him photos, saying, 'You were in there then Max.'

His parents had told him, at a suitable age that Bethan was not his blood sister but one chosen especially as she'd no parents of her own. This had softened the kind hearted Max to continue to accept and even protect this little girl with the white blond hair so much like his own and his mothers and he'd remembered Sarah his mother's best friend too and that she'd been taken away because the Goddess had wanted her close.

Shaking himself from childhood memories; he didn't know what had made him think of those times now, other than that in a few weeks it would be Bethan's twenty-ninth birthday; a birthday marked as special because it ended and began a new seven year cycle and the 'make or break,' Saturn return. He was only now coming out of his own three year transition that had brought him a little fame and a lot of pain.

Travel, a broken relationship and the struggle for recognition in a difficult and exacting industry had not been an easy road, particularly when he had big shoes to fill, following his father's scholarly examples as an historian. Although his father Alex's writings were far from dry and were a constant source of controversy in his chosen field of mythology in today's society. It had all been worthwhile in hindsight as he'd been honed and learnt skills he wouldn't have learned if it hadn't been for the tough times.

Picking up the phone, he keyed in his sister's number; Flora answered, 'Oh hi Max, I haven't spoken to you in ages,' she said.

'Hi Flora, how are you?' he asked.

'Okay, but there's so much going on; we really need to catch up with you soon.'

'Is anything wrong?' Max replied, 'I've been meaning to call but got caught up in the new manuscript deadline.'

'What's this one about then?

'It's a history of the traditions through the ages of Herne the Hunter,' he paused hearing a stifled laugh that became a cough, 'are you okay you sound strange Flora?'

Smothering her laughter Flora thought before replying, covering the mouthpiece of the phone as she almost choked …little do you know Max that Beth's having a firsthand experience with him, before recovering her composure, saying,

'That's an interesting subject Max; I look forward to chatting to you about it soon.'

'Yes, me too Flora but are you sure you're okay, you sound very odd?'

'Yes,' she chuckled, 'I'm fine, but look Bethan's still asleep, do you want me to get her for you?'

'Asleep! That's unusual for Beth at this time isn't it?' then looking at his watch said, 'Oh I'm sorry it's only 6.30! What are you doing there so early?'

'I just dropped some eggs in,' said Flora with her fingers crossed for fibbing, 'Do you want me to get her then?'

'That's okay Flora I'll give her a call later. Will you tell her I called?'

'Sure,' she replied, 'will we be seeing you soon?'

'Samhain as always I'll be up. By then I'll hopefully have finished the book.'

'Well, good luck then Max, I'll see you soon. Bye.'

'Bye Flora,' he said, hanging up thoughtfully. There's something going on she's not telling me he said to himself.

He stood, stretching looking out the window at the sunrise through the city haze; how he wished he could move to a more rural setting, perhaps Bethan would consider letting him the groom's rooms above the old stables. He'd be happy to front with all the cost of renovating and making them livable. Would she feel too stifled having her big brother living so close or would she welcome a little company. They didn't have to live in each other's pockets but it would be nice to have an occasional glass of wine and a bite of dinner as the sun went down. He craved the quiet of the country side and the smells of wood smoke at this time of year.

Perhaps she might have a nice friend or two she could introduce him to; it had been a long time since his last relationship. Not that he'd lived like a monk, that wasn't his nature either but he was almost ready for another leap into the dating pool and the city girls were not his idea of companionship; their needs being more than he was prepared to meet. It was no use going out and meeting someone in a nightclub when you hated the whole scene to begin with. Come to think of it, he thought; his friend Morgan, whom he'd met on his travels to the UK a few years ago, would possibly be heading to Oz this year; he could imagine Bethan and Morgan getting on like a house on fire because of their mutual love of music and ancient instruments…worth a thought, he said to himself with a grin…I'll give him a call tonight.

He poured himself a glass of water and decided to take a walk to clear his fuzzy head; actually he thought I might just get in the car and go see Beth and surprise her. The seed thought sown about renovating the old stable had grown roots in his mind and he was the type of man who would follow through immediately if it felt right; this felt right.

He carefully saved all his notes of the morning, packed up his laptop to take with him and a few clothes just in case. He grabbed a jacket and a bottle of wine from the rack and was on his way.

Chapter 37
Callum Macintyre

Shapechanger shifting …magick's afoot, with your bright feathers flying …skin stretching, morphing into the other self; one of many selves within the web of Ungwe.
By Tara Saark

Callum Macintyre worked with focused intent, using fine brush and pointed tool, around a small bone fragment embedded in the mud from the ancient of days …the Plains of Holderness in Yorkshire, had hidden their secrets well for thousands of years. It could be the 'find' of a lifetime for an aspiring young doctor of Archaeology; he thought as he carefully worked around the fine boned, skeletal form appearing in the mud. He wondered what sort of creature had once given it life; what spirit had animated it so long ago. It appeared to be human but then… 'Shit,' he exclaimed. 'What in the name of…?' What he had presumed was an arm, looked more like a wing, the feathered shafts still showing embedded, almost to the bone itself.

He sat back on his heels, wiping the moisture of the misty marshlands from his face, steadying his breath; he looked in bewilderment at the creature forming in front of him. Fine boned humanoid face and head, legs and torso all appearing normal and yet it was as if this creature had been caught in some way between bird and human for the one arm showed the wing-like, light bone formation and the other was a human arm. What had he found? He had heard of animal-human remains before but most had been fraudulent attempts of a sensationalistic nature.

Before he did anything to alert the archaeological body of his find he knew he had to speak to Claire Jenkins, his friend and advisor on all matters pertaining to the odd or weird; Claire being not just his teacher and friend but a Wytch too, familiar with the sort of finds he made and studied. Although, he thought, this one would perhaps test even her knowledge. This was in no way an everyday, 'old bones,' discovery. He knelt carefully, closer to the extended wing-like arm, to see if anything else could be uncovered from beneath or around it; his attention was grabbed immediately by a silvery piece of metal caught partially around the 'wrist' of the winged arm, buried in mud, thereby anchoring the skeletal form to the ground. With extreme care, he worked around it until he could bring the piece free of earth; a small, corroded yet clearly silver, bangle lay revealed, wrought with markings and indentations.

As he worked on the piece itself, a raven alit on a stony outcrop just a matter of feet away; head tilted to one side, she watched him with uncanny intelligence as he freed the bangle and the moment he did so, swooped at him with a clicking of beak and rustle of feathers, snatching it from his fingers. Astonished, he watched helplessly as she flew away with it.

Now he knew for sure he had to alert Claire to this find and somehow it had to remain hidden from the scientific body that would descend, to pull the dig apart. This was no earthly mutation; this was something new to him altogether.

He shivered in the growing gloom, it might be late spring but it was still very cold as the day waned. He was excited about the discovery and not a little anxious; although used to strange psychic activity he had not expected the Raven that day. In a way she had been responsible for him finding the dig in the first place and then had been smart enough to snatch a very special piece of his find. Not at all skeptical he knew that the hand of the Gods was responsible for all of it. He wondered why he had been chosen particularly, not being from this country at all but from Australia. His digs took him all over the place but this was his first major find and certainly exciting on any level.

Reaching inside his jacket he extracted his mobile and was surprised to find he had signal so far out on the Moore. He selected Claire Jenkins's number and was answered almost immediately by a breathless voice.

'Where are you Cal,' Claire said, 'are you okay? I've been picking you up all day.'

'I'm great thanks Claire but I'm not surprised you've been hearing me on the ethers, I've an amazing discovery that I need to show you and that needs to be kept quiet. If the University gets wind of this it will be destroyed and the church will probably make sure of it too.'

'Why, what have you found!' replied Claire.

'Not over the phone, can you come? I'll be losing light soon.'

'Where about are you?

'I'll send you through the coordinated for your GPS,' said Cal.

'I'll leave straight away,' said Claire hanging up.

Settling himself down on a large stone to wait, he poured himself a cup of hot, strong tea from his flask. He considered the dig and the extraordinary creature that it had revealed; the Raven returned with a rustle of her feathers and sat, unperturbed, preening and watching him out the corner of her raven-blue eyes. He pretended to ignore her but on pulling the remains of a sandwich from his backpack, she sidled up to him boldly as if it were the most ordinary thing to be sitting on a rock with a human in the middle of the Plains of Holderness, in the wilds of Yorkshire, demanding he share his meal.

He could have sworn she spoke,

'Hungry am, long way come have…aaaark…food?' she stated.

Almost falling backwards off his rock he simply stared at her, seeing the unusual silvery flash of feathers for the first time. She took immediate advantage of his distraction, hopping right up to him; she took the remains of the sandwich from his unresisting fingers.

'What,' he stammered, 'are you?'

With a shimmering of light and a smell of musky perfume the Raven changed before his eyes. He felt somewhat nauseous, the strange shifting of his vision affecting his balance; he thought he would be sick but she simply reached out with what now had become a slender dark skinned arm and tapped him on the forehead between his eyes. His vision cleared and gaining clarity he found himself looking into the startling blue gaze of a woman of indefinable beauty and indeterminate age. Small-boned and dark haired, a streak of premature silver across her forehead; she was dressed in lacy, tattered black layering's and was looking at him with a clear candid gaze. She smiled as if this was the most normal thing for him to have seen and simply ate the rest of his sandwich in a couple of hungry bites, then walked across to the creature he had uncovered that lay in the earth. She bent over and whispered a few words in an ancient tongue, unknown to him and the beautiful discovery simply disappeared. Turning she smiled at him and said,

'This must never come to the eyes or knowing of the people you work with. This is one of the Mother's Magicks and must not be tainted and pulled apart by them. You have found an ancient sister of mine and she will never be put under the scrutiny of your peers.' Then, 'Ah, here comes our friend Claire; she'll understand.'

Cal, rarely at a loss for words was, for once, speechless.

The strange being leapt up and ran toward Claire before he'd even found the strength to stand. Strange things he may have witnessed before but this went beyond anything he'd experienced as he watched Claire and the waifish entity, rush into each other's arms.

'Tara,' grinned Claire in stupefied delight, 'you're a long way from home my friend!'

'Ah it's just a fold in the universe between here and there,' chuckled Tara. 'When are you going to make the shape change again?' she quizzed.

'Well,' replied Claire, 'I'm totally out of practice and so a little frightened of even trying again. Last time I became a strange bird indeed,' she recalled. 'I only had wings but no feet so had to belly land. Just as well there was a soft landing in a pile of leaves,' she trailed off as she realised Cal had risen to his feet and was listening, astounded, at their interaction.

'Claire,' he managed to say, what the fuck?' causing both women to collapse in hysterical laughter.

'Oh! Oh,' giggled Tara, 'you should see your face Callum McIntyre, what a study,'

'Sorry Cal,' said Claire, still laughing, 'How rude of me. Let me introduce to you my friend Tara.'

'Merry Meet Cal,' said Tara, literally bouncing towards him, grinning cheekily, to which Cal, took a large step back, not game to take Tara's outstretched hand.

'It's alright,' she said, 'I promise not to shape change, you're safe!'

He gingerly reached out to find his large and rather grubby hand grasped firmly by a small, very birdlike, slender one that pumped his enthusiastically.

Claire was still trying to smother her laughter and in fact Cal had never seen his friend so relaxed.

'Alright,' she said, finally managing to recover her usual calm self, 'sorry Cal, I didn't know what you'd found but there's only one reason for Tara to be here and that's because you have something she wants.'

'Hey,' squawked Tara, unable to contain herself, 'I didn't mean to scare him but I was hungry and he had sandwiches!'

'I didn't mean that Tara,' laughed Claire at her friend's childlike admission, 'I meant his archeological find.'

'Of course you did,' Tara said, sobering, 'Well look, see for yourself Claire; she's one of us.'

Claire walked to the edge of the dig, raising hands to her face solemnly as Tara once again whispered a few words and she saw the ancient sister lying there exposed to the elements.

'Wait a minute,' interjected Cal, 'What do you mean us?' looking from one to the other of the women.

'Well,' said Tara, 'us,' as she pointed to herself and then to Claire. 'We are of the same kin.'

Silence fell as Cal considered the enormity of what he had been told. Claire! His friend Claire…at times more a mother to him than his own had ever been was a…what; a freaking alien bird-woman?

Tara and Claire exchanged looks and then both approached him, pushing him back down onto a rock they sat on either side and even though he flinched away, they both laid a hand on his temples. A soothing surge of energy washed over him and he found himself able to sit and listen to his friend and the strange bird girl as they shared with him their ancient history.

When they finished, all he could find the energy to say was,

'But you're married Claire; to a doctor: a straight laced, dude of a doctor and you have a daughter that you've been promising me you would introduce; what's she then a bat? For crying out loud Claire! How long have we known each other?'

'I'm sorry Cal,' said Claire, I've been waiting for the right time but I guess there's never a right time for this. Harry doesn't really know and if he does he wouldn't possibly admit it. He's always been pretty tough on the work I do; telling me I should get a 'sensible job,' at the Uni but I love him and I know he loves me; he's gone to sleep though. He wasn't always like this; there was a time he knew exactly what I am.

Flora too, he's hard on her about becoming an herbalist and midwife, says she should be a doctor like him. So when do you think the right time would have been to tell you this Cal? There are some very urgent and relevant things going down on the inner planes and you know that too; I've taught you enough I'm sure for you to realise this,' she trailed off, 'get over yourself Cal! There's more things under heaven and of the earth, remember!'

'Okay,' said Cal, 'what now?' struggling to gain some sense of reality again.

'We have to transport the remains of our sister home,' said Tara.

'How do you intend to remove and hide a body,' he questioned.

'Oh that's the easy part,' she replied, stepping over to the pit she whispered a few words and the strange skeleton reappeared; gathering up the frail remains, wrapping them with exquisite care in a piece of soft cloth, she materialized from the folds of her layered dress and with a silent nod to Claire and a quizzical stare at Cal, she shifted shape and was gone; stepping through the Skeins of Tyme.

'I wish she wouldn't do that,' exclaimed Cal, turning green.

'Sorry Cal but you're going to have to get used to this. It's nearly Mabon in Australia and I can hear my daughter and her friends calling. I could take an earlier flight than planned,' pausing for a moment she shifted and before Cal's eyes changed into an Owl and back into her human form in a heartbeat, continuing as if nothing had happened, 'as we thought this wouldn't occur until just before Samhain and Sybille's planned return. I've told you often enough about Sybille's disappearance for you to know this is not a game and now we know she is lost to us.'

'Mother of God,' was all Cal could say.

'Come on. We need to get ready to leave as soon as humanly,' she smirked, 'possible,' before she casually strode away to her car and with a jaunty wave said, 'I'll see you for diner; 7.00pm sharp,' and drove away in her usual sedate manner, leaving Cal shaking his head, for the second time that day, at a loss for words.

Chapter 38
Samantha

She's changing her gown, from green to gold
...the harvest ripens and the year grows old
Mabon's first kiss is felt in the air
...elders ripen in hedgerows fair
What do you wish for your harvest this year?
...you've laboured long for your fruits to appear
Let go the old growth, let the leaves fall
...the fruits of your harvest will come when you call
Know that you are the maker of your magicks.
Mabon extract from the Book of Shadows

Feeling recovered and relaxed Samantha looked in fascination at her arms and hands; the delicate tracery of leaves, still moving and shifting under her gaze, no longer freaked her out as much. She had settled at Flora's kitchen table, although she knew she should really be at Grove Street setting up the shop, she felt more inclined to take another good look at her Aunt's Book of Shadows. She read…

Mabon
Once again, the wheel turns on season to season, from dark to light, Sybille had written, Autumn Equinox, Mabon Rite, a minor Sabbat but no less a powerful time of

the turning wheel as, for a moment, the length of day and night are equal.

The Harvest of grapes, apples and pears and in some regions, olives is nigh; all the abundance of nature at her best; a time for the Wytch to reap the rewards of the turning wheel of life. The sun would diminish; daylight hours would grow shorter and the hours of the night extend. Crisp, cool, starlit nights, with the first frosts making themselves felt and the howling gales of March, with their accompanying rain storms were a given.

Then suddenly the documentation of the Mabon Sabbat changed into Sybille's musings, where she had obviously put her thoughts to paper.

She had written of her growing concern about the world in general and the girls who were her pupils. Had they truly listened? Were they prepared? What were the Wytches of the world harvesting this year? What was the biggest wish for all? Peace, prosperity; abundance?

How well would the approaching earth changes, be received by the masses; was the question, for this was indeed going to be the general harvest for many.

Samantha could almost feel her Aunt's presence as continued reading...

The evenings are drawing in and the sun is rising later each day. It is 6.30 am on a crisp late summer morning. I have been feeling unusually anxious recently; perturbed by feelings that something different is afoot.

Where will I be in the coming season; I have already felt the stirrings so early this time and am somewhat perturbed by these feelings engendered, not at the thought of leaving again, but at the thought that there is so little time before the wheel turns toward Samhain once more. To-date it was always at that time I felt the calling and now, it's not even Lammas. This time is going to be different and I still have so much to do to help the girls cope in my absence; this time perhaps there might be no coming back; I've felt so tired of late, which in itself is highly unusual for me.

Then it was as if Samantha could feel Sybille shrugging off a sense of foreboding, the notes then continuing about Mabon as if there had been no pause, except to say that she hoped the notes would help the girls with their training and teaching and that they would one day understand her journey.

Sighing heavily, Samantha gathered up the loose pages and closed the books; stacking them neatly, back on the desk in what had been Sybille's study. Not much had changed; Flora had kept the room pretty much as it had been, in such a lovely room there was nothing that needed changing. Wandering over to the French doors that led onto the vine-covered veranda, she caught a glimpse of something moving beyond in the herb garden. Once again, the wraith like shape of Sybille floated through the garden, disappearing into an ancient Elder tree, where the nature spirits played. She heard laughter on the breeze and heard a distinct voice say,

'Stop her!' and saw the shape of the beautiful Goddess like figure of Silver following, leaving a trail of black web behind her that caused the grass and herbs to wither away. Behind Silver were a swarm of little beings that Samantha now knew were Makers who were frantically trying to cleanse away the cloud of black webbing.

Samantha, spurred to action raced outside to see Silver disappear into the tree after Sybille's wraith and heard the tree sigh in distress as the webbing coated its bark. She ran to the tree and without thinking ran her hands over the sticky blight,

'Ugh,' she recoiled instinctively as a smell of rotting death filled her nostrils, 'NO, you can't kill this tree,' she screamed at the webs.

To her amazement the little tattoo-like vines on her hands responded, drawing the darkness out of the wood and into Samantha then, mutating it, handed it back to the Makers waiting to cleanse it completely.

Samantha staggered back under the onslaught of light the little beings radiated, feeling as if she would burst with pure joy as she heard their song of healing.

Sybille was gone again and she could see that Silver was ailing; the gaping void in her centre had grown larger and darker as Sybille slipped further away. When would this end Samantha wondered; what would their roles be in helping to heal the rift that had occurred in what Silver had called The Skeins of Tyme? Would they all have the courage necessary to do their part and bring Sybille home?

'Only Tyme will tell; only Great Mother knows,' came the response as the little leaf spirits crowded round her again, gently cleaning her hands and restoring the vines to amber, green and gold.

When they had finished, strength renewed, Samantha picked up her bag on the way through the house and drove into Springsmeet; she'd be meeting the others in town later anyway so now it was time to work on something real and tangible, 'earthly rites.' That would ground her energy back into the moment. She laughed softly to herself when she realised what she had just told herself; something Sybille had been telling her for years …be in the now.

Chapter 39
Flora

Autumns bright wings can be felt on the air
...a suggestion of laughter ...a tug at your hair
...the sprite of this season brings a harvest to share
Be alert as she flies, reap her goodness with care
From Wytchwise...Arianwen Isil'Lindir

Flora stood gazing out the window at the changing landscape, rapt in the colours of Mother Nature's display and watching the wee folk cavort in the late autumn sunshine.

After returning home from Bethan's; leaving her friend still sleeping peacefully she completed a batch of elderberry dye and was thrilled at being able to match it with an earlier mix, Beth had been working with and needed more of, to finish a customer order. How they all found time for the actual things that made their money recently, with everything else that was going on, she couldn't fathom but somehow the chores still got done and the centre was coming on nicely, which meant they could open by Mabon. This she knew would settle them all a little, whilst waiting for the coming Samhain rite that would hopefully, give them some answers about how to help Sybille find her way back from wherever she was lost.

They hadn't seen Silver in a while but Flora was concerned for the beautiful Trueshape, as she'd seen the growing dark vortex within her, caused by Sybille's disappearance.

Wandering from the kitchen to what she still thought of as Sybille's study she realised that Sam must have left while she'd been lost in her work. Sam had left her a small drawing of Sybille and a small note of thanks for the use of the study, together with an inky black Raven feather with a silvery tip that could only have belonged to one of their resident, Ravens.

Of course, I almost forgot she thought …Raven feather, inks or dye. I'll try those until it's time to go into town. Going into her little apothecary off the kitchen, she had to manoeuvre around Teddy crying to go out and then had to move a violently protesting Morgana, sprawled on her workbench in the sun. It's just as well she'd moved all her medicinal herb mixing into town she thought, cat's hair in the mortar and pestle were not particularly appealing …perhaps she'd find the cure for fur-ball instead she giggled to herself as a very cranky Morgana slunk away to the study to continue her snooze …leaving Flora to potter away at her tasks.

Chapter 40
Maeve

'Finished,' she crooned aloud, 'yay …finished!' as Maeve ecstatically contemplated the completed studio. Spinning in circles she felt excited about the new centre, the studio, all squeaky clean and ready to go and the new apartment that only needed a bit of tweaking to make it the most beautiful place she'd ever lived; hers or at least her share of Sybille's generous legacy. Sobering a moment she thought of the lovely, silver haired lady, who had taught her so much in a relatively short space of time and who'd taught her to let go the unhappy childhood and the accompanying guilt at the fact that she could not 'save' her mother from herself or anything else, for that matter.

'No!' she exclaimed, 'I'm not going there today; this time is for me to celebrate the new. I'll think about everything else when I see the others and we can catch up on what's to be done about Sybille's disappearance and all

245

the other weird things that we've been experiencing. Today is just for me,' so saying she raced across the hall to her new home, boisterously dancing around the room only to halt in surprise at the face looking in the window at her. A glossy black Raven sat on the ledge observing her with searching eyes…not with the flash of silver she'd become accustomed to; no this was a much larger bird and although not sure how she knew, female. A deep intelligence in the gaze made her quieten her mind receptively.

'What do you want with me!' she asked it, moving carefully towards the partially open window; the bird sat unmoving, but she could 'hear' it in her mind attempting to adjust it's thought processes to something resembling human speech.

'Aaarking…aaasking, am, let in me …aaaark …message, have …in let me.'

'Shit, a talking Raven,' she said aloud. 'Not letting you in mate but you can tell me from there, yes?'

'Naaark, no …Let in me …message have …Lady send.'

'Message from what lady?' asked Maeve

'Taraaark Lady,' it cawed.

'Tara?' questioned Maeve.

'Aaaark,' she replied.

'I'll assume that mean yes then?' said Maeve 'What does she want she disappeared again and we still have her work space to sort out?'

'Taraaark delayed is, aaaark. Baack comes soon. Ruark,' it bobbed as if bowing, 'Ruark am I.'

'Ruark! What's a Ruark then?

'I Ruark,' it bobbed again.

'Oh you mean your name is Ruark? Said Maeve fascinated and somewhat amused at the fact she was actually communicating with a large Raven in the middle of an otherwise ordinary day.

'Aaaark Ruark.'

'So why did she send you to me and not Flora,' she thought aloud, 'she dreams of birds; although I did dream of being taught to become a red Raven.'

'Clan of aark Morgaark soon is teached aark.' She cocked her head on one side as if listening, 'Go aark must Ruark,' and was gone leaving a scent of musk behind which immediately brought back to Maeve the image of the gorgeous naked man who had shifted from Raven and back, only a few days ago right at her feet.

'Hmm,' was all she could say, with a grin and then who's Morgaark, she thought, perhaps they have something to do with this?

Shrugging off the thoughts that would drive her mad, she tried to return to the mood of the moment before the Raven appeared but it had passed. Sighing she went to shower and change before meeting her friends for an early dinner at the Harvest restaurant at the Springs, the Spa Centre of Springsmeet, Flora and Bethan having insisted that as Maeve and Sam were always driving out to Covenstead, it was their turn to come into Springsmeet.

Humming tunelessly as she showered, Maeve considered the changes in herself that the recent times had brought about. In the past she would have been freaking out with the strange happenings…talking Ravens; Ravens that could shapeshift, Faefolk and nature spirits, wraiths, Trueshapes and Littleshapes, Makers and now the new strange event of the little dark creature that had almost attacked Bethy and the amazing story of the Forest Lord, whom she'd yet to actually see having been inside when he'd carried Sam back to the house.

If she'd known all of this even just a few months ago she would have been out of the place like a shot; now this was becoming almost the norm. Stepping out of the shower and rubbing herself vigorously dry she then turned to get another from the shelf to wrap her curling mane in; in so doing she once again saw a face at the window…this time it was the largest Raven she had ever seen in her life and its eyes were human and were she swore, grinning at her.

'Enough,' she fumed, eyeing it directly and then with great dignity stalked to the window, slammed it shut and pulled down the blind in one movement, Oh and add voyeur Ravens to that list!' and then with a pause, 'Hang on, I know those eyes! *The cheek of him*!' she exclaimed.

Still fuming inside she went to dress, pulling clothes out of the closet at random, not knowing why she needed to look her best for the evening. She selected a rarely worn dress of emerald green that matched her eyes and contrasted with her wild red hair, warm black leggings, long green suede boots and a warm, black and green flecked shawl, Beth had made for her last birthday, completed the outfit.

She still had a fair bit of time to kill so she went back to the studio and sat at her desk to design some new pieces that she thought would be great sellers for a more wytchy range of silver jewellery; small besoms, ravens, simple pentacles, with a vine leaf design wrapped around them, that had the look to them of the tattoo type markings that the wee-folk had painted on Sam's hands and arms.

She was also trying to capture the little Makers who had accompanied Silver, the time she'd arrived at Flora's, when she'd spoken to Bethan about her history.

So many images crowded in too fast to get them onto paper but at least the ideas were flowing now...but then a face kept showing itself to her and before she knew it she was trying to actualise it on paper but the simple pencil sketch style she used could not do it justice...she would have to ask Sam to help her realise it. Relaxed and contented again she doodled and designed and then went downstairs to the shop front to see if anyone else was around to fill in some time with until the clock in the hall struck 5.30 and she could walk down to the Providores to meet the others.

Just as she came through the back door into the shop Sam arrived and so, chattering excitedly, they wandered the different rooms and passageways, admiring everyone's handiwork with the realisation that soon, everything would be complete for the forthcoming opening.

One room displayed Bethan's beautiful weavings; she had decided to set up her spinning wheel and loom where she could watch the shop and where people could see her at her work.

In a corner of the entryway, which doubled as a waiting room, for readings and herbalist's appointments she'd set up a harp; not the beautiful lap harp that she cherished but a full size one, to entertain and relax the clients and customers as they waited or browsed the shop.

Flora's rooms were done the windows flung wide so that the smell of fresh paint would be aired out. She'd chosen a rich green and scoria red décor that reflected the earthy nature of her work; relaxing for the people waiting to see her. Everywhere her polished wood desk and shelving gleamed in the afternoon sun; the aroma of beeswax and herbs almost overpowering the lingering odour of paint.

Sam's domain was an eclectic mix of old and new, with a few comfy chairs and cushions, interspersing the book shelves in little groups inviting people to sit and peruse the contents. Candles of varying scents and tones were dotted among the books, fairy statues, Greenman wall plaques, bronze statues of Gods and Goddesses or frolicking Pan with Nymphs surprised the eye at every turn. On the counter was a selection of parchment paper, sealing wax in jewel colours and fun alphabet and sigil stamps in silver and brass hung in rows together with lush leather-bound journals and Book of Shadows, black and white emu feather quills contrasted with bright inks with exotic names, such as Dragon's Blood, all caught the eye and tempted the need for ownership.

In the jewellery, wand and Athame section Sam had included beautiful chalices and scrying bowls in silver, brass, wood and stone and another selection in cold cast resin with nature spirits dancing around the rim and the wheel of the year depicted around the bowl. A selection of Maeve's wands and wood handled Athame were on display in locked cabinets for safety all polished to a bright gleam.

'How and when did you manage to get all of this done?' asked Maeve amazedly.

'Oh sometimes in the evenings when I couldn't sleep and was having a lull in the creative writing flow,' said Sam, 'I wanted to surprise you as you've all been so busy in the actual making of stock and so I thought I've only had to clean, order stock and unpack what Sybille left us; it seemed right to give it a try.'

'A try!' exclaimed Maeve, 'this is like a fantasy come to life, thank you,' she finished unable to continue for excitement.

'Well I haven't done much for Flora or Bethan as they knew exactly where they wanted everything to go...except I did include some of your beautiful big brooches in with Bethan's cloaks and wraps as they are an amazing compliment to each other; she uses such beautiful etheric colours, contrasted with bright reds and greens, from the natural dyes she and Flora make; they're perfect with your silverwork Maeve. Oh and some fresh herbal teas that Flora's made up under the 'earthly rites' label, I've dotted around, with little tea pots and bowls.

'I didn't realise how much of the creative side to you there was Sam,' said Maeve, 'Thank you so much for all your help, it's much appreciated. I've been trying to work out how to mend that shattered crystal shard or how to utilise the pieces at least. It's been haunting me in my sleep along with the cauldron of water that keeps playing at being a geyser,' she laughed. 'I'm sure the answer will come to me soon; I just have to be patient and that's not my strongest point is it?' she finished.

'Well just recently I've thought the reverse to be true Maeve,' Sam said touching her arm, 'You've been very cool headed about all the stuff going on and I haven't really thanked you yet for helping out the other night when I was off with the fairies. What was it you called me? Ah yeah, 'grinning girl!' they both laughed out-right at the expression.'

'It just seemed to suit the moment,' grinned Maeve sheepishly.

At that moment the main door opened and Flora arrived in an excited rush.

'Hi you two,' she said with a big smile that lit up her face.

'Hello Flora,' said Sam, 'you seem happy today?'

'Yep,' said Flora with a little skipping step, 'I've managed to match the coloured dye for Beth and I managed to extract some inky colour from the Raven's feather that might just make an ink to sell with the parchment paper, Sam. It is the most beautiful. 'inky blue' colour and smells like heaven. I love the smell of feathers, particularly the musky scent of Raven.

'Hmmm,' muttered Maeve, 'I've had enough of Ravens for one day,' and told them of her interaction with the Ravens that afternoon …they commiserated but Sam and Flora exchanged a secret grin behind Maeve's back.

Once again the door opened and in came Bethan.

'Ah,' she said a little shyly, 'I'm sorry I slept the day away practically. I know I said I'd be here to help today but I only woke an hour or so ago. I can't remember sleeping so long or so deeply for a very long time.' She smiled to herself dreamily at the remembering of why she was actually so tired, blushing crimson, causing the others to laugh outrageously at her embarrassment.

Seeing her withdraw a little, they let up on the teasing and an excited Maeve said, 'Come on you two,' to Flora and Bethan, 'wait 'til you see what our Sam's been up to at night!'

Sam grinned and quipped, 'Well at least I'm not having sexy dreams of dark hunky men Maeve,' to which, they all cracked up again; Maeve taking it on the chin with unusual aplomb.

Time flew as they explored every nook and cranny planning, dreaming and chattering together hardly pausing for breath. Bethan trailed behind with a dreamy smile on her face, with lightness in her heart that hadn't been there for a very long time.

Sybille's old clock gonged 5.30 and they gathered their bags and coats for the stroll down to the Harvest, realising that time had got away with them.

Chapter 41
Harvest Surprise

The Lady walks in quiet fields and flower faces smile
Golden petals, fragrant leaves, mile upon mile
When flowers fade, seed pods burst
…and the greening is all done
…the Goddess of the Harvest will bring home every one.
…Mabon extract from the Book of Shadows.

Bethan and Flora walked arm in arm behind the still chattering Maeve and Sam.

'Beth,' said Flora 'did Max catch up with you today?'

'No,' replied Beth brightly, happy to hear from her brother, 'what did he say?'

'Only that he'd catch you another time,' said Flora, 'but I'm surprised he didn't ring you back later.'

'He probably got lost in his writing,' replied Beth, 'he loses all track of time when he's in a creative streak.'

They approached the Harvest, greeting a few friends and customers, all excitedly seeking news of the forthcoming opening of the shop. The owner Dani, a longtime friend of Sybille's, approached Bethan and said,

'There's a surprise in the back room for you Bethan. I'd put the four of you out there anyway but it looks like there might be five of you instead,' she laughed.

'Oh really,' said Beth intrigued, heading out to the back room to be grabbed in a bear hug, by her brother Max.

'Surprise!' he laughed, putting his slender sister back on the floor.

'Max,' Beth shrieked delightedly, 'Oh what a lovely surprise. It's so good to see your ugly face again.'

Maeve and Flora witnessing, the hugs and hearing Beth's rejoinder, laughed, rushing forward for hugs too, leaving Sam standing back forgotten for the moment. She didn't mind at all, she thought as she saw her sketch of the unknown Max come to life.

Broad shouldered and fair, to Bethan's Fae-like frame, he was the picture of health, in fact not what she'd expected for a rather dry historian. She'd followed up on Beth's suggestions and had read a couple of his books, fascinated by the exactness and detail of his works. The photo on the book jacket had certainly not done him justice she thought, realising that the wire framed glasses perched on his nose added to the attractive grey eyes, rather than diminishing a very masculine aura.

Sensing her stare he turned to her, the three women still casually wrapped around him with the pleasure at seeing him again, all talking at once. Immediately Beth rushed forward and pulled Sam into the group.

'Sorry Sam,' she said, 'excuse our rudeness do. This is Max my big brother.'

Max and Sam eyed each other carefully, Max breaking the silence engendered by reaching out a hand to take hers.

'Hi Samantha, nice to finally meet you; both Sybille and Bethan have mentioned you on numerous occasions but it seems we just haven't been in the same place at the same time. I hear you're a writer?' he said, easing the tension by putting the ball in her court as to how much of herself she wanted to share with a stranger.

'Oh yes, an aspiring one anyway,' said Sam a little haltingly, unable to break the grip of Max's hand still holding hers. 'I've read a couple of yours though Max, very intriguing.'

'…if a little dry,' finished Max on cue with a laugh.

At that, the ice was broken and they all relaxed. Dani bringing menus and spring water for the table and Max produced the bottle of wine from his bag to share.

'You've brought a bag,' said Beth, 'does that mean I have the honour of your company for a while?'

'If that's okay with you Bethy, yes,' Max replied quietly, 'I have something I want to run past you …you can say no of course …but I thought it might be of benefit to both of us,' and without further ado he launched into his idea of renovating the old stable barn, which was met by silence as Beth considered; a million and one thoughts flashing across her face as she thought about all the recent events, the coming Samhain rite and last but not least the truth about her ancestry and the recent intoxicating night spent with the very subject of his current manuscript. All this happened in a split second but it was enough for Max to say,

'Okay blondie,' he said falling back into his childhood nickname for her,' spill. I've felt for a while that something big is happening in your life,' he trailed off as he saw the intense gazes of the other three fixed on him; making him feel like a rabbit trapped in headlights.

'Alright,' said Beth, recovering her composure with difficulty she turned to her friends and said, 'Where do we begin girls?'

A brief silence followed before they all began gabbling at once.

'Whoa,' said Max, 'let's start again! Who wants to go first; although I think it should be you Beth but, let's see, Samantha? You seem pretty sane,' he laughed to put her at ease.

Just at that moment Dani returned with the opened wine, glasses and cutlery and handing out menus pointed to the specials board as well, where a lovely mixture of eclectic tapas were displayed.

'I'll leave you to it; just give me a wave when you're ready to order.' Max jumped in before she could race off, saying to the group,

'What say we let Dani choose a selection of the seasonal tapas to start with and then we can take it from there?'

The agreement was unanimous as they realised he wanted to stall a while for Sam to start the explanation about what had been going down in Springsmeet.

Over the shared tapas, brought discreetly by Dani every so often and wine, Sam, interspersed by Maeve and Flora shared with Max the events of the past month or so. He listened carefully, giving each his absolute attention and in silence. Then when they'd all finished he turned to Bethan and gently taking her hand said,

'Alright, your turn blondie.'

Bethan took a deep breath, a sip of wine and began. On completion she waited a moment and then said, 'but in answer to your original question; yes!' she grinned at his momentarily blank face.

'Ah yes, that was furthest from my mind in that moment,' he replied.

'Well that was stating the obvious,' said Maeve drolly and once more they relaxed to laugh a little at the whole astounding tale they'd just shared for the first time with anyone outside their little circle. Max felt warmly drawn in to the little enclave and met Sam's eyes with a quizzical grin.

'Okay!' he said as if nothing untoward had been told, 'Who's still hungry, 'cos I'm starving!'

At that, they began a new journey of discovery, Max drawing Sam into the group even more as he shared his history and what he had always known about Beth and her differentness.

Outside, looking in the window stood a dark haired, lean faced man with a piercing blue gaze and a tall red-haired man with the shoulders of someone used to working outdoors in all weathers.

Chapter 42
Claire Jenkins

Sweepings wings shadow the moon on the lake
...feather soft falling of sleep, then to wake
...to see the sun rising, to watch the dawn break
...to sense a bud's opening, it's petals to shake
Extract from Owl's Dreaming ...Aithlin Farandir.

After meeting up with Cal and to her surprise Tara, Claire knew that it was time for her to return to Australia as soon as possible. She could take the conventional route or risk her husband Harry's anger at breaking her word that she would not shapeshift ever again. Although, carried away by Tara's enthusiasm she had not been able to stop herself teasing Cal, so in truth had actually broken the promise already.

What would he do if he knew? She could not deny who she was anymore and it was high time Flora knew the truth anyway. It was after all part of her heritage too.

She was always saddened when she thought of Harry, her husband of 27 years. At the start, he had been as enthusiastic as she was to learn and grow. After completing his medical degree however he had become increasingly stuffy as if he had been brain washed by the establishment. Once upon a time, he had dreamed of merging medicine with natural medicine and acupuncture. When the medical body disclaimed herbal medicine as

261

folksy superstition, he'd not the fortitude to stand up for his original beliefs. They didn't think to remember that herbs were there long before the chemical sciences that synthesised them.

When their daughter had turned from medicine to herb med and natural midwifery it had been the last straw for him withdrawing all support from his daughter, making her work her way through the alternative medicine courses that were now Uni degrees.

Claire was proud that Flora had become strong enough to stand up to him, which she thought ruefully, was more than she had done. After studying with Sybille herself, she was well pleased when Flora had found the information about the psychic development courses. What a serendipitous moment that had been, although it had certainly given Claire pause for thought when she realised that Sybille didn't look a day older than when she'd studied with her. Then had come the surprise of a lifetime when Sybille had explained about her connection to Silver, her Trueshape and the amazing stories just unfolded over the years as Sybille would come and go, each time returning renewed and looking younger than ever. Chronological age aside Sybille looked constantly like a well preserved 60 year old but in truth could be easily treble that if not more.

Claire had met Silver on occasion and had, during her earlier study days before Flora was born, been introduced to Tara and in turn she had learned of her own genetic makeup and strange ancestry that linked her to the bird tribes of ancient times.

Now Sybille was in trouble. Cal had found the bones of a shape shifting bird woman who was one of Tara's kin; according to the messages in the Skeins of Tyme, there was dark magick afoot.

She thanked the Goddess that Cal had had the impetus to phone her before the authorities had been able to witness his discovery. Sad for Cal though, overall she thought; it would have been the find to make his career shine. She wondered why he hadn't been more concerned about that fact; he'd always been very career orientated, driven to succeed because his father had been such a leading light in his area of anthropology, particularly where new or different mutations had occurred in various species. Yes, Cal's father Richard would have been very proud of his son were he still alive.

Now she needed to decide whether to fly by a more conventional form of transport or shift and travel through the warp and weft of Tyme. She shivered at the thought of travelling so far in her Owl form after all the years of not practicing her craft but knew it would be the fastest way to get there.

Later that same week she had given Cal a small bag of her things to take with him on the flight home as she made the decision to shapeshift so that she would arrive in Australia before he'd even left the ground.

She called on all her innate courage, shifted into her familiar, a snowy white Barn Owl and landed at dusk on the roof of her Melbourne home.

Luckily Harry had not yet arrived so she was able to dash upstairs, shower and change and have dinner ready for his arrival home…it didn't happen that way; Harry didn't come home. She checked his roster in the study, which showed he had nothing scheduled so she could only assume he'd been called into an emergency surgery.

Usually when she was away, he would ring her promptly on 8.00 pm but that time came and went and still no word. Yawning, she stretched, curling up on the couch; flicking through TV channels and thoroughly bored, realised she hadn't called Flora to let her know she was back in the country; too late, the phone fell from her exhausted fingers and she slept. She travelled once again in her Owl shape and found herself in Springsmeet sitting on the fence of a little settlers cottage that she recognised immediately as Annie Savage's home…parked in the drive was her husband's car.

Her bird form knew something was not right, her human self, tossed and turned on the couch unable to believe what she was seeing as Harry emerged from the house and kissed Annie passionately and with a smug smile and a wave, got into his car and drove away.

The look on Annie's face was one Claire wouldn't forget in a hurry as another shape appeared from behind a tree and approached her,

'Well human,' the elegant dark haired Fae said, 'it would appear you will be of use to me after all.'

'Yes mistress,' said Annie, 'I vowed to you that I would be your servant.'

'Ensorcelling him is a small thing but it will weave the web all the more tightly around Sybille's followers. Humans are not easily able to ignore such dishonourable behaviour from one of their own blood kin!' she laughed harshly turned and was gone.

Claire awoke in a rush of feathers and clothing, sick and disorientated as Harry walked in the door. Recovering herself, she mimed a yawn and stretch as he came into the room. He stopped in his tracks in surprise,

'What are you doing here?' he blustered.

'Well hello to you too and I live here if you remember.'

'Yes, yes, don't prevaricate,' he said irritably, 'Why didn't you call me to let me know you were coming home; I would have reorganised my hours to be here. How did you get home from the airport?'

'Oh I grabbed a taxi,' she said, fingers crossed behind her back, 'I wanted to surprise you and it seems I did.' He was oblivious to the double entendre hidden in her comment. Rising she walked towards him, sensing his reticence to actually hug her as he usually would, she remembered her dream travels and realised that there was more to it than that; it had been no dream.

Deep disappointment overcame her but she reached out to him as he reluctantly hugged her; pushing her away quickly, with the excuse that he must stink after the hours of emergency surgery he had just performed, he went to shower and change.

Re-heating the meal, she thought about the last few years where her work had taken her overseas and their relationship had slowly diminished when, in particular, she had supported Flora in her studies and on occasion, supplemented her stipend with a little cash, when needed.

Flora had never asked Harry for anything but had stoically and steadfastly pursued her career.

Now it would appear that the rift had grown too vast between her and Harry as well but she hadn't for a moment expected that he would stray. He'd never been a particularly passionate man and she'd accepted that that was simply his nature; she'd never dreamed he would actually have an affair, particularly not with a friend of her own closest friend and mentor.

She served the food mechanically, not knowing how to handle the situation without letting on that her dream had actually taken her to witness his infidelity…that he would never believe anyway…such was his nature to deny what was right under his nose…magick. He obviously didn't know of Annie's persuasions towards the Way; surely, if he did he wouldn't have become involved with her. In truth, Claire had never trusted Annie, seeing through her charming nature to the manipulation that went on below the surface. She'd even spoken to Sybille about it but Sybille had merely said,

'Claire, the Mother's Way will unfold in time. Don't waste your energy in speculation,' and would not be drawn further on the subject.

Now the evidence of that manipulation was right on her own doorstep, not exactly what she'd expected in the scheme of things.

Harry, having finished his shower, came downstairs to find the meal ready on the table with a bottle of wine open and Claire waiting. She eyed him speculatively as if waiting for him to say something to her but he studiously avoided her gaze and too tired to care she let it be.

They talked as couples of long standing relationships can sometimes do, speaking of everything but the elephant in the corner of the room. Harry asked politely but with some disinterest how her projects were going in the UK and she told him a few quirky tales about her students and her work, not mentioning Cal and his find however. In turn Harry shared a little of the mundane doings of the hospital and then warming to his favourite subjects, namely surgery and himself, regaled her with details of his prowess in the theatre.

While he talked, Claire quietly observed him, thinking about the years they'd spent together and the fact that his work had always been the most important topic of conversation. He had never really listened about her own passion for her work. Being a somewhat old-fashioned male, who considered women's work to be a lesser thing, his disappointment that Flora had not been a boy had always been evident and his lack of support for her, when she decided to take a career path he was opposed to, had been the decisive factor for his complete withdrawal from them.

Claire had her work so she was content to travel when necessary for it but the time had obviously come for a frank talk, when taking into consideration what she'd witnessed earlier that evening. Of course that was not exactly something she could share with him, knowing how he reacted to her ancestry, nevertheless it was inevitable when she contemplated the fact that, as a young woman, she had allowed him to manipulate her through ultimatum. She'd feared raising a child alone and so she succumbed to his pressure, promising she would cease to practise all she inherently was, a wytch and shapeshifter.

Harry droned on and her thoughts drifted toward sleep again so, pleading exhaustion, she said goodnight and went upstairs; the relief from Harry that she was tired was palpable as was the guilt evident in his energy field along with a few rather ugly spikes of red and grey that she could only assume was Annie's influence. Feeling a little nauseous and more than a little sad, she wondered how in the world these two so obviously opposite people could have connected, particularly as his hatred of the Wytchways was so manifest.

With a tired sigh, she curled up in the familiar bed but was still restless. As if from a long way away, she heard Harry come into the room a while later, quietly peering at her and believing her asleep. he tiptoed back downstairs; she heard the distinct sound of the front door as it shut behind him then, his shoes crunching on the gravel drive, his car starting and then he drove away. She didn't need to ask herself where he was going as she fell headlong into a dark and complicated dream of sticky black threads coating the natural world, of birds and their kin like herself starving and dying, caught in a huge tree that was weeping ominous red tears.

Chapter 43
Callum and Morgan

Shapechanging, for those humans with the gift, is as simple as changing your mind ...Hercurin

Shielding his eyes from the reflection in the window of the setting sun, Morgan looked into the interior of the Harvest; he spotted an empty table in a corner of the eclectic looking restaurant. Callum meanwhile was looking at the menu and was pleasantly surprised to see the huge variety of fresh, locally grown and seasonal foods available.

'Come on,' he said to Morgan, 'this looks amazing; I could eat a horse after that disgusting plastic they served as food on the plane.

They'd never met before their flight from the UK but sitting next to each other for the duration they found more than enough in similar interests to make a connection. The strangest thing was the fact that they were both heading to Springsmeet in the Highlands of Victoria. Of all places to be going in the vast expanse of Australia, this had to be more than a coincidence, they thought. They shared a little of their history and origins and found that they also shared a strong interest in history and ancient cultures.

At one stage, tired and relaxed Callum almost shared his experience of the previous week; stopping himself when he thought that would probably be the moment when Morgan would send for the men in white coats.

He needn't have worried; little did Cal know but Morgan had dreamed of flying in a different form, landing on a rooftop he'd peered in through a window to witness the delightful sight of that same willowy red-head he'd crashed landed in front of a few days previously, clad in nothing but a towel and long wild wet hair. His reaction had been so potent he'd crashed back into his body, jerking awake with an embarrassing, physical response evident. He'd been thankful of the blanket the steward had laid across his knees.

Now, after their long and arduous journey, they were both eager for a good meal and a bed for the night.

'This *does* look good,' said Morgan, 'lots of fresh vegie things.'

'Right,' replied Cal, his dreams of something rich and meaty diminishing, 'you'll have to guide me though it then.'

'Don't worry,' Morgan laughed, 'I could eat the menu, the way I'm feeling.'

Pushing open the door, Morgan was amazed at the friendly buzz of conversation and wonderful aromas drifting.

Cal, still browsing the menu in the window, caught a glimpse of a small chestnut haired woman, who from the back view as she stood at the counter, looked identical to

Claire. How could she had arrived here before him, she'd said she had some things to finish at the Uni ...unless ...he couldn't finish the thought after what he'd witness at the dig; he must have been hallucinating he thought.

To Morgan's surprise Cal, suddenly pushing open the door, ran inside and over to a young woman standing with her back to them. Reaching out Cal grabbed the woman's arm and pulled her to face him...her shock at that was no greater than the look Cal mirrored. Morgan, fascinated to see what had driven his new friend to make such an astonishing display of himself, went inside to find Cal, hands raised in a pacifying gesture, confronted by an outraged young woman.

To Morgan's surprise, the friend he had hoped to visit, Max Fenner, stepped from the back room. They had been the best of friends, having met in Wales when Max had visited years ago. For a brief time Morgan had thought they would become brothers in law, until his silly sister Lily had let Max down so badly; he had been afraid, for a while, he would never recover.

Now here he was, fully himself again by the way he had stepped between the pretty woman and Cal. Hang on he thought, he knew that face ...the photo of Sybille with her students ...this was the one with the smile he'd thought would melt butter.

Max calmed Flora in a gentle tone. Cal's mistake had been undeniable, calling her Claire and whipping her around, to face an angry redheaded stranger.

'Claire?' Flora had said, 'How do you know my mother; who are you?

Cal was just explaining to them as Morgan, standing silently by, was finally noticed by Max.

With a roar of pleasure the two men were shaking hands, back slapping and bear hugging to the utter surprise of both Cal and Flora and by this stage the rest of the patrons.

Morgan introduced Cal to Flora and Max as they were eyeing each other, Flora still a little hostile and then said,

'Come on, come and meet the rest of the crew.'

Cal, somewhat at a loss said,

'I'll leave you to it Morgan, it was nice meeting you. Perhaps we'll catch up again tomorrow.'

'Don't be an idiot,' said Morgan, looking at Max for his response. Max nodded,

'Come on, Cal,' he said, 'join us. If you're anything like Morgan,' giving Morgan a friendly punch on the arm, 'you'll be in need of a stiff drink and a good meal anyway so why eat alone!'

About to refuse politely, he found himself pushed along by Morgan into a back room, where three lovely women were sitting.

Max began to introduce them but suddenly it was Morgan who stood mouth agape in surprise as a striking redhead stood up, knocking over her water glass,   'You!' was all she could say.

'You!' was his stunned reply.

Max, about to make the introductions could only say, 'What now,' in exasperation, 'enough, let's just sit down and sort whatever's going on out.

Sam slid along the bench to make room and Max slid in next to her making space for the two strangers who judging by their faces had each met Maeve and Flora. She broke the silence by offering first Morgan and then Cal her hand and introduced herself. Bethan followed promptly, introducing herself as Max's sister.

Flora, turning first to Cal said, I'm Flora Jenkins, Claire's *daughter*!' and then with a sweeter smile said hello to Morgan, Maeve followed suit greeting Cal with a smile and Morgan with a curt nod. It wasn't every day you met a man who could shape change into a Raven after all and certainly not one who leered at you through a bathroom window.

'Alright,' said Max, 'that's everyone introduced then. I'll get some drinks in and we can all settle and catch up on the rest of the news.'

'I'll help,' said Cal, happy to get away from the dynamics of the group as the total outsider.

'Yeah I'll come too,' said Morgan.

The girls immediately closed ranks to talk about the strange set of coincidences that had brought Max's friend Morgan and Cal, a friend of Claire's to Springsmeet right at this time.

Soon, however, over food and more wine the group relaxed. Cal, without a moment's thought, after hearing the nature of the weird conversation that everyone else was engaged in, dropped in the strange experience he'd had with Claire, thinking if anyone would know about it, it would be Flora.

The statement met with a stunned silence as everyone took in exactly what Cal had said.

'You saw what?' said Flora, the first to collect herself, 'My mother's a shape shifter and so is Tara! You have to be kidding!'

'Ah. Hmm,' interjected Morgan, 'I know Tara too, she taught me, along with Sybille, to shapeshift.'

'What are you all talking about,' said Max.

'Well it would seem,' said Bethan, 'that everyone here has an interconnection with each other, doesn't it?'

'Well that's an understatement Bethy,' grinned Maeve, breaking the tension again.

'Yes, of course it is,' laughed Bethan, 'but in light of everything we've all been experiencing it makes sense.'

'As far as I'm concerned,' spoke up Samantha, for the first time, 'the more of us there are, the more likely the success rate of the next month's venture will be,' she finished in her usual, down to earth manner.

'True,' said Bethan, 'Let's sort this all out now once and for all so that we can get down to business and find out what our individual roles are going to be.'

'Just a moment, roles?' said Cal.

'Yes,' replied Bethan, 'we've obviously been drawn to Springsmeet at this time for a reason. Each of us has skills and abilities that others haven't so it's a matter of sorting out whose going to do what. Simple.' She finished.

They looked at each other and began to talk at once. Max as the most ordered of them all said, 'Whoa! Let's take this quietly and one at a time.'

'I've got a better idea,' said Bethan, 'seeing as you'll be staying with me Max and I assume Morgan and Cal will be looking for a bed for the night, let's head back to Wells, then we can talk in private and we can decide where everyone's going to sleep.'

So saying they organised to share the bill and left. Walking back to the cars Flora froze in place for a moment, causing Cal to bump into her as he came up behind. She immediately recovered herself but not before Bethan saw the look of consternation on her face.

'What's wrong Flora,' she said

'Oh, I just thought I saw my father's car, is all. What would he be doing here in Springsmeet at this time of night,' Flora finished, 'it's a bit far to come for house calls!'

'Well that's true but I'm sure there's an explanation for it,' replied Bethan. 'Come on, it's getting chilly, let's go home.'

Shrugging it off, she followed as Bethan walked to the cars with the others but not before Cal had witnessed Flora's consternation.

Bethan squeezed Max into her little Mini, with some difficulty, Cal and Morgan leaving with Flora in her larger four wheel drive and Maeve and Samantha in Sam's little hatchback.

Without further ado, they all piled out at Bethan's cottage. After making hot drinks all round they settled to nut out and share the details of all their experiences in the last month; all agreeing that things had definitely accelerated after Lammas and after they had all first felt the terrible sense of loss as Sybille had slipped away from them.

Max was the only one who in that time hadn't really experienced anything much to share, other than his sense of something going on with his sister. He knew Sybille of course, having attended the Sabbats when he could, but had been head first into his current book, which had made him oblivious to anything else.

Cal had until recently been intuitive but careful about psychic events, being somewhat sceptical, even at Claire's seeming ability to read his mind; until now that is and his experience on the Yorkshire Moors. Morgan, as one of Sybille's distance students, had been exposed throughout his life to the weird and wonderful. His, at times on and off experiences in shape changing, had currently become more on than off, if mostly through his dreaming state. His teacher being unable to be there in the flesh had often sent Tara to help him in his shifting and then finally, had sent Ruark, who was now his almost constant companion. His sister Lily was looking after Honey for him while he was away.

Suddenly Max stood up, running to the window he stopped dead at the sight outside. Such was his utter stillness that no one spoke; instead, they quietly rose as one and walked to stand behind Max.

Just a few paces away stood Aithlin Farandir. It was just too much for Max, after hearing the story of what he considered to be the total desertion of his sister, when she was but a day or so old. He knew instinctively who this tall elegant being was.

He strode outside, despite Bethan calling for him to stop, approaching Aithlin with clenched fists. As he made to swing a punch, Aithlin merely stepped aside.

'I don't want this humankin, you have been good to my daughter and I have great respect for you and for your parents. It is not in the nature of my race to fight you and I would not wish harm to you. So saying he began to merge with the garden again, reappearing immediately as Bethan came running out, 'Max,' she called, 'No, let it be; I've come to terms with it all and have a different understanding with everything that happened.'

'But he hurt you blondie, he left you and didn't even tell you where your mother had gone.'

'It's all water under the bridge Max; I was raised in a loving and understanding environment, with the best people I could possibly have if I'd chosen them myself for my family now leave it be and come away please.'

'As always Bethan has everyone else's interest at heart,' said Aithlin, 'I just wanted to know that you were safe Arianwen,' turning to her, 'and I can see that you are in the safest hands possible.' With a nod to the watchers at the window and a bow to the forest behind him he turned, vanishing in a few long strides into the darkness of the trees where Hercurin stood, silently waiting; a large white owl sat alert above him, in an ancient Blackwood.

Chapter 44
Earthly Rites

Genus Raven, (Corvus corax), which is also known as the Common Raven or Northern Raven, is the largest bird in the family CORBAE, CORVIDAE or CORVINI. Raven's closest relatives in the subspecies CORVUS include the crows, jackdaws and rooks. The rather more distant Corvid cousins are Choughs, Tree pies, Nutcrackers, Magpies and Jays. There are many species of ravens around the world; Australian Raven, (Corvus coronoides), Little Raven, (Corvus mellori), Forest Raven, (Corvus tasmanicus), New England Raven, (Corvus (t). boreus), Chihuahuan Raven, (Corvus cryptoleucus), Dwarf Raven, (Corvus (r). edithae), Brown-necked Raven, (Corvus ruficollis), White-necked Raven, (Corvus albicollis) and Thick-billed Raven, (Corvus crassirostris).

Extract from A Field Guide to Birds …a battered and much loved copy, donated to 'Earthly Rites' by Tara Saark.

Next day, they had agreed to meet at the centre, to put the final changes to the displays and to boot up the new computer system for stock keeping and bookings.

Everything was looking crisp and new as they gathered for the final inspection. Maeve took them all to see her finished studio and the pieces she'd been working on. Autumn sunshine, now replaced by lowering clouds and the distant rumbling of thunder, that heralded an imminent weather change, were causing temperatures to drop rapidly.

With a loud clatter, the resident larrikin Ravens landed on the skylight, like naughty children looking for mischief. Then the distinct sound of the front door opening, slam shut again and the sound of light, running feet approaching as Tara flew into the room, screeching to a halt when she saw the group gathered. With a smile and a wave, she greeted them all one by one by name.

They exchanged glances, all but Max cottoning on to who this strange apparition was.

Bethan, recovering first with a small laugh, said,

'Max this is Tara; Tara you obviously know Max!'

'Oh yes,' Tara replied with her usual cheeky grin, 'I've known him from birth!'

'But your only young yourself,' replied Max, 'that's impossible.'

'You're forgetting who Tara is Max,' said Cal, 'You know,' as he flapped his arms like wings, comically pulling a face, "Bird woman'!'

Recovering himself, Max laughed aloud in discomfort,

'Ah yes Tara, hello.'

Tara smiled sweetly before turning to the four friends,

'Okay ladies what do we need to do?'

'You ask that now said Sam? It's a bit late in the day for that, we're practically finished but we've given you the reading room you apparently used to use and I've put some of your beautiful ceramic smudge bowls and platters around the displays. I hope you like it but feel free to change it if you need.'

'I'm sure it's all perfect Samantha, thank you.'

'All right then,' said Flora, 'let's all take a final look, finish the admin stuff and then we can officially open the doors as planned later. We've got Annie organising the drinks and food for this evenings gathering,' then whispering to Tara she said, 'Can I speak with you later please?'

'Of course,' Tara replied, 'I know you have found out about Claire, Flora and I'm sure you feel hurt that she didn't tell you herself. It's not been easy for her but these are things she will need to tell you herself,' with that she followed the others down stairs.

They spent the day in quiet excitement. Flora made beautiful flower arrangements to place around the retail and reading rooms. As she was putting a vase on the front desk, she caught Annie staring at her, a strange expression on her face as if she'd had a shock.

Flora didn't comment but she felt Annie's eyes boring into her back as she went about her business. Samantha too had a very strange vibe as she was passing through the reception area and turning around was confronted with a hostile glare from Annie that turned rapidly into a sweet but false smile.

Samantha raised one eyebrow but didn't comment simply continuing on her way shrugging it off in frustration. I wonder what's bitten her, she thought, little knowing how close to the truth that was.

Cal, Max and Morgan made themselves busy, shifting last minute things and helping Annie put up trestles for the food and drink that was coming. Flora would have liked to have prepared it all herself but the others convinced her that the evening should be enjoyed, there being time enough to work the very next day.

Bethan was distracted but was sensitive to the atmosphere and energies between Maeve and Morgan, Sam and Max and even a little warming of the energy between Flora and Cal. She would love to have gone home to change for the evening and to have some time to herself, secretly hoping that she might even catch a glimpse of Hercurin. She wasn't naïve however and knew that the possibility of spending time with an entity such as him was not going to be an easy thing but she also knew that the energy between them was real and unique.

Max found her dreamily staring at her work as she sorted through and folded some of the more delicate wraps that needed to go in a glass cabinet; they were fragile; fine as spiders web. One silvery thread stood out in the subtle light-greys and palest blues and she found herself following the weave with her eyes; Max could see it, from where he was standing in the doorway, lighting up like a little pathway through the warp and weft; he found himself mesmerised by the effect.

Then he was moving forward rapidly as his sister swayed, just managing to catch her before she hit the floor. Yelling for help he, heard the thunder of footsteps as Morgan came downstairs two at a time, his sensitivities noticing an unknown, elusive, 'something.' Between them, they placed Bethan gently on the counter amongst her soft weavings, the one that had caught both of their attention falling to the floor unnoticed.

Chaffing her cold hands, he said to Morgan, 'Quickly, fetch Flora Mor; she'll know what to do for her. I've seen this happen so many times but it always freaks me out.' Then stroking his sister's face he said, 'Come on blondie, wake up, please,' a touch of desperation in his voice.

Morgan found Flora in her little dispensary preparing for the clients the next day. Dropping everything, she came at a run, rescue remedy in one hand, cold wet cloth and a glass of water in the other; tailed by Tara.

Bethan was oblivious to their concern. She was walking the path again to the grove she always visited in dreams; the path had become a silvery trail as if an army of snails had been on the move, it glowed with phosphorescence. Around the edge of the track and covering all the vegetation were grey and black sticky, noxious threads, dripping ichor; small creatures and birds hung suspended, many beyond help, some struggling in their effort to free themselves, in their death throws. Horrified she stood; looking around her in disbelief and the Makers worked tirelessly to rescue or revive the ailing creatures. They were losing the battle as more and more of the shining Light Makers were themselves caught in the web as they ventured into the morass unselfishly, in calm and ordered fashion, their song of life taking more and more energy to maintain.

Bethan watched as tall Dark Fae emerged from the forest capturing the Makers in nets made of the same poisonous substance, turning their silvern state into twisted dark entities like that of the first fallen one of their kin.

She walked on through the dying forest in shock feeling helpless to know what to do, the pathways appearing and disappearing like the threads of her weaving. Aithlin stepped onto the path in front of her and held out one hand for her to take and reaching behind with the other plucked one chord on his harp. He began to sing a soft sighing melody, encouraging her to sing with him but she couldn't remember the words and panicking she ran, to wake crying, grief stricken, lying on the counter in the shop, with her brother, Flora and Morgan rubbing her hands and applying ice to her neck and temples.

'Easy blondie' said Max 'we've got you, it's okay.'

'It's not, she sobbed, 'it's not, the forests, birds and animals were dying, covered in poison and the Makers are being killed by their own brethren; some of the Fae are helping the Dark Maker's blight.'

'You fainted Bethy, you were dreaming, I think you must be exhausted,' soothed Flora.

'No cried Bethan, it was a warning, it's already started we've seen it …all of us have seen it …and I couldn't remember the words of the song to sing to help. Aithlin was there to help me but I ran away.' She buried her face in her hands and sobbed.

'Come on Bethy take this, it will help with the shock,' said Flora handing her a glass of water in which she'd put the rescue remedy drops. Bethan took the glass with shaking hands but downed the drops in a thirsty gulp.

Morgan who'd been standing silently by said, 'I can help Bethan. This could be part of the reason I've been called here.'

'What do you mean Morgan?' Bethan faltered, 'How?'

'Well,' he said, 'we both have a passion and a gift for music. From what I have understood from the other night, your father Aithlin has bestowed an extraordinary and rare ability upon you to play by ear and instinct. Your music tutor has told you that you have a natural aptitude on an ancient instrument that you found at the back of an op-shop.

I would suggest that the instrument was yours, perhaps many decades ago and had been waiting there for you to rediscover the talents you acquired then in order to fulfil a bargain you made, somewhere on the Skeins of Tyme. I had a similar experience when I discovered the lute and mandolin I play. Half the time I didn't know what I was going to do until I started playing; it just flowed from there,' he trailed off when her realised they were all looking at him in startled amazement.

'Sorry just my thoughts,' he said raising his hands as if in defence.

'No, don't apologise,' interjected Maeve, 'that makes more sense than anything I've heard in a while. Sybille taught us that the time space continuum gives us memory cells that last us for eternity,' she trailed off when she saw the expressions mirrored on each of her friend's faces. 'What?' she said, 'I wasn't always goofing off you know!' and once more humour saved the situation and lightened Bethan's burden; her sense of shame that she'd run from the horror, unable to confront her fear, diminishing.

Tara, reached over to stroke Bethan on her forehead between her eyes, where she could see her inner sight was still struggling for balance and said,

'Let your friends help you Arianwen; you are not alone and I will teach you to protect your delicate psyche from overloading too. You are a seer and all seers pay the toll of exhaustion and often disorientation.' She repeated, 'Remember you are never alone, there are others who will share you're tasks. Aithlin is honour bound but he does it out of love for you and for all humankin and then of course there is the Great One who will not be far away from you at any time,' she raised and wriggled her eyebrows at Bethan with a naughty leer, causing Bethan to blush and the others to laugh again.

'Then there is my brother here,' she indicated Morgan, 'he is yet to come completely into control of his ancestry but he will be a great help to all in the not too distant times.'

'So it's true,' said Maeve, 'you're a shapeshifter Morgan!'

'In training,' he replied with a rueful grin at her. 'I still tend to arrive wherever my thoughts are going in the moment, which can cause embarrassment to me and to others and for which I apologise to you Maeve, for my invasion of your privacy.'

Taken aback at his candour Maeve could only stutter, 'S'okay,' blushing.

With that, Bethan declared she felt much better for all their loving administrations and they continued about their tasks...only Morgan saw Annie Savage, watching Bethan's every move, with more than a little interest. What had that strange girl Tara called Bethan, she pondered?

By the end of the day, they were all prepared for the opening event. Morgan had offered to play some pieces with Bethan and had gone with Max to collect Bethan's little lap harp that she so loved and his own lute and mandolin. He was very drawn to Bethan but it was with a feeling of knowing her somewhere in Tyme not a physical attraction although she was exquisitely beautiful. No, it was Maeve that attraction was reserved for ...fire and ice he mused.

They set up the instruments and a chair for Bethan and went to help with the drinks and ice buckets, Annie Savage practically purring when she said, 'Oh lucky me, *two* handsome boys to help out,' with what they assumed she considered to be an alluring smile.

They simply exchanged silent glances and went about their tasks.

At the first signs of sunset, they all gathered in the courtyard at the back of the building, where Flora had set out punnets and grouped pots of herbs to sell, each with a culinary or magickal theme and Tara had placed a few larger samples of her beautiful bowls around, with solar fountains installed in them. A huge Greenman wall plaque sat above a granite slab, a Goddess figurine sat atop it.

Here Bethan had placed a bowl of salt and a small chalice of water, a smudge bowl with one of Flora's own self-igniting incense blends, a pure white candle, some fresh lemon juice and a smudging wand of raven and owl feathers.

They gathered in a circle, heads bowed and hands crossed over their hearts, gathering in the energy of the late autumn evening, to make a final dedication and to perform a last cleansing of the building.

From top to bottom of the old house, they walked in procession. Flora with the incense, smudging into every nook and cranny where the darkness hid, followed by Tara with the feathered wand. Maeve with blessed spring water mixed with lemon juice, sprinkling to cleanse the energy on all levels, Bethan with anointed white candle to draw any negativity, bringing light to their new venture and finally Samantha with a bowl of salt and High John herb to cleanse and bring prosperity. As she walked, she placed a pinch of salt above every window, door and cupboard frame, scattering the herb along the floor behind her. Any negativity, swept away with the herbs and buried in the soil to purify; salt to ward …for doorways are often portals to other realms.

The three men followed with drum, bell and flute, to chase out the last vestiges of negative energy…darkness scurried away to disperse in the smoke and dissolve in the water droplets and to be drawn, like moths to the candle flame; as they chanted together,

'Earth and water where thou are cast, let no evil purpose last, in complete accord with me as I do *will* …SO MOTE IT BE!'

Each smudged the other's energy field with black sage and dragon's blood incense, that nothing could remain hidden there. They anointed themselves with sacred oils of oak moss and ambergris, on forehead, left foot, right hand, left hand, right foot and forehead again, forming the five pointed pentacle of earth, air, fire, water and ether to bless and consecrate; dedicating themselves anew to the Lord and Lady, that their work be only in their service. Then joining hands they balanced and joined their energies together, raising their voices in harmony,

'A new path opens ahead on this day the circle is cast the dark flies away as the light of magick comes into

play the Lady and Lord will bless our Way.' ...and the last rays of the sun broke through the approaching storm clouds before plunging below the horizon.

Just a couple of hours later they were all spruced up and waiting excitedly, in spite of the previous events, for the opening of 'earthly rites.'

A small crowd was gathering early, so they decided to let people in, the weather being rather inclement. As they opened the big doors for the first time, the smiling faces of their parents, Susan and Alex Fenner greeted Bethan and Max.

'Surprise!' they cried, each gathering their daughter in an enthusiastic embrace and then hugging Max and all the girls, who then introduced them to Morgan and Callum.

'It's so good to see you both,' smiled Bethan, 'you're just what I needed tonight; thank you.'

'We wouldn't have missed your debut for the world Bethy, you've all worked so hard for this,' said Alex warmly.

Behind them, the crowds were craning their necks to see and to get inside to the warm, inviting centre and so the evening kicked off. Food and drink served, little mini tours taken, to show the new look reading rooms and retail shopping; cash chinked and bookings for readings and consultancies made for the coming days.

As people, continued flowing in, Bethan and Morgan sat to play some soothing pieces, to add to the enjoyment of all. When Morgan began to sing in his rich baritone Bethan chimed in, her sweet, soprano voice, clear as a bell… silence fell as everyone stopped to listen enthralled…

'I saw a moon raven flying the night, her smoky blue wings full of shadows and light and with a silvery twist my spirit took flight, chasing moon raven into the night.

Soaring with musical weavings of sound, each note, a lustrous colour profound …chasing moon shadows over the ground …flying the ethers, where spirits abound.

Chasing the moonlight 'til sun's first rays show …dawns early colours, the skies set aglow …the fields of corn ripple, in ebb and in flow …the moonlight has fled and the mourning winds blow.'

The applause exploded after a stunned moment of silence; they had never played together before, yet they were a perfectly matched duo.

The evening wound down, they were exhausted but excited as the success of their event became evident. Just after the last guest had left, there was a sharp tap on the door; Cal standing the closest, went to see who was there; on the doorstep was Claire Jenkins, looking tired and a little dishevelled.

'Claire,' he said surprised, 'when did you fly in? No, don't answer that.'

'What are you doing here Cal, come to that,' she replied.

'That's quite a story but come in Claire, it's turned cold and I'm sure you want to see your daughter.'

He opened the door wide and Claire, stepping inside, came face to face with Annie and stopped dead. Recovering herself quickly she nodded briefly to her and walked across the entry to greet Flora with a hug.

'Mum,' she said, 'what a lovely surprise, when did you get home? Is Dad with you?' she finished, looking through the door as Cal closed it.

'No love,' replied Claire, 'He's…'

'…working,' finished Flora with a cheeky grin, breaking the tension that was obvious in Claire's energy field. They laughed and hugged again.

'Come on through Mum. We were just about to get a bite to eat and a glass of bubbly; we're all starving. We haven't stopped all day.' Grabbing Claire by the arm, they went through to the old kitchen that would once have been the heart of the old building.

Bethan and Maeve greeted Claire with a warm hug, Bethan, noticing the dark shadows under her eyes and the lines on her usually smooth face, whispered to her,

'Are you okay Mrs Jenkins?'

'It's Claire Bethy, I think we're all old enough to drop formalities and yes, just a little tired I guess; it was a long flight.'

At that, Tara smothered a giggle and Cal a choking cough.

Then remembering what Cal had told her, she said,

'We need to talk I think, don't we Mum?'

'In the morning Flora love; there's time for all that in the morning,' stroking her daughters cheek fondly.

Max and Samantha poured and handed round glasses of ice-cold bubbles and resounding 'cheers,' rang out through the group as they toasted the success of the evening and the times ahead.

Annie came in with the last of the dishes to stack and Samantha went to hand her a glass too but she declined, with a nervous glance at Claire, she murmured a hurried goodnight, with the excuse of tiredness and an early start in the morning.

Claire sighed quietly in relief but not without the notice of both Cal and Flora, who exchanged looks briefly.

Tara took the moment to draw Claire aside,

'What's up sisterkin,' she whispered.

'It's Harry,' she replied softly, 'he's having an affair with Annie Savage.'

'GET OUTA HERE!' shrieked Tara, 'You're kidding! I didn't know he had it in him!'

'Hush,' shushed Claire as the others all broke off their chatter in surprise, Claire grabbing Tara's arm to guide her outside to the courtyard

I flew home and was taking a nap, waiting for Harry; I dreamshaped and saw him leaving Annie house and there's no mistaking what they'd been up to, judging by their behaviour as he said goodbye,' Claire finished.

'Well,' said Tara, 'as you know I've never really had much time for Harry but this rather alters everything. What will you do Claire? I can have a mob of our kin teach him a lesson if you like …you know …head pooping, hair pulling ….mmm …let me see eye pecking…Oh don't get me started,' she gurgled with glee.

Claire couldn't contain herself as she laughed aloud,

'Oh, don't tempt me Tara,' she gasped, 'I've already thought about owl pellets in his shoes and desiccated mice in his undies draw,' then sobering a little said, 'but seriously this changes everything on every level and how will I tell Flora?'

'You can't,' said Tara, 'we need to see what is playing out here, especially as Annie is involved. She's a wild card but the Mother will tell us what to do when the time is right. No, we have to keep this information to ourselves and that means you have to pretend to Harry that you don't know about his sordid little doings with Annie…and thinking of that, did she look different to you, tonight …like a face-lift or something?'

'Can't say I noticed Tara, I couldn't bring myself to look at her without difficulty,' Claire said.

'I need to get closer to her I think,' said Tara, 'I smell something odd around her.'

Flora wandered out to see what had made her mother usher Tara outside so unceremoniously; she met with a sudden silence as the two small women broke off from their whispered conversation at her approach.

'Hi lovely one,' grinned Tara, 'I just needed to catch up with Claire; it's been a long time.'

'I didn't even know you knew each other,' said Flora, then pausing, she gave both women a direct look and said, 'it's okay you two, I know who…what, you both are. I just wish you'd told me Mum, it would have explained so much of what I've experienced over the years;

the dreams, the visions and the 'calling' I have for the natural world,' she trailed off sadly.

'I'm sorry Flora but there is sometimes things to hard or complicated to tell in a way that sounds even remotely plausible but I should have sensed you would understand. Tomorrow we'll sit and I'll tell you the whole story of your ancestry, okay?

'All right, then but I'll hold you to that. How long are you staying by the way?'

'Just tonight if that's okay with you?' said Claire.

'Of course it's alright; it's always wonderful to have a little time, at least, with you…don't get me wrong, I understand your passion for your work and even more has become clear since meeting Cal,' raising an eyebrow quizzically, causing Tara and Claire to chuckle at her expression. Arm in arm the three went back inside to join the laughter and chatter of the celebration.

Bethan, witnessing the pairing off in little groups and couples by her friends and how the natural dynamics drew Max to Sam, Morgan to Maeve and Cal to Flora, who was talking to Tara and Claire; took her glass and a little bowl of nuts to nibble out into the cool garden. The storm had abated and the air smelt of ozone and wet vegetation. Sheltered from the elements by a high brick wall and towering old trees, it was a lovely environment and unusual for the fact that the garden seemed so huge from the inside when compared to the street frontage it occupied. She had always loved the elm and oak that bowed their heads together as if sharing secrets.

Tonight they were alive with busy spirits, playing and leaping; jumping onto falling leaves and taking the ride to the ground only to flit up high again for the next free fall, their laughter of pure innocence as chiming bells, then from the trunk of the oak itself stepped Hercurin. He reached briefly to touch her cheek as she gazed at him speechlessly, smiling he whispered,

'Rato, lirima Arwen 'en mel com …Rato,' and was gone. She understood… 'Soon, lovely lady of my heart …soon.'

Sighing to herself she sat a while longer watching the wee folk play and felt at peace. She knew there was much ahead but she would take it one day …no one moment at a time.

The back door opened and Flora slipped out,

'We're heading home Bethan,' she said, 'Max is ready to go when you are. Mum's coming home with me and Cal and Morgan have agreed to stay here in town for the night; Maeve has a couple of blow up mattresses for them and then tomorrow we'll see what all this is about …them showing up together I mean.'

'Yes it is strange isn't it,' said Bethan, 'I think tomorrow after work, when we all meet at my place for dinner, we'll perhaps get an idea of what it's all about. Ritual together tonight was amazingly potent, the balance of male and female energies made all the difference. Are we all going to the Mount together for Annie's public Mabon Rite next Monday evening?'

'Yes, I think everyone's agreed we should. According to Sam Annie's behaving a little oddly and I caught her staring at me strangely too. Tara doesn't trust her; my mother was also very aloof with her and they've been friends for years, so something's definitely going on.'

'Oh,' said Bethan, 'I thought that was just me being overly sensitive; she's been really snide toward me...hmm,' she trailed off as the door opened again and a chorus of goodbyes called from the group as they made to leave.

Bethan and Flora rose hurriedly to exchange hugs and 'sleep wells,' as they all went their separate ways, Maeve and Sam to find the mattresses for the men and the others for their drive home. Flora and Claire gave Bethan a quick hug and were gone leaving Bethan and Max to check the doors and to make their own way back to Wells and Bethan's little cottage on the edge of the forest, where they both fell exhausted into bed.

Max was edgy and found that, each time he closed his eyes, Sam's elfin face appeared. Bethan fell into a deep sleep immediately, to find herself caught in strong arms, swung onto the back of a huge stag and taken to a glen of moonflowers that shone like little stars, where she was soothed into peaceful slumber.

Chapter 45
Nina Giraldi

For every spell you throw ...for every Circle cast
...there's always something new to learn
...to remember from the past
Be a Witch in everyday, in all you are, in every way
...each joy you share, each sad lament
...make truly Hers, each moment spent
An extract from Magdalena's Book of Shadows and Light

Nina stirred and woke from a strange dream where she curled asleep in a vast tree. Little beings were calling out all around but she couldn't bring herself to respond.

Stretching, yawning she sat up and reaching for the robe at the foot of the bed she managed to find the strength, on still slightly wobbly legs, to walk to the window. She caught a glimpse of herself in the mirror as she passed and realised that she didn't look as if she'd been ill but that she'd grown quite considerably and the robe that had once reached to her ankles only reached to mid-calf now. Her hair was longer and in need of a trim, her face more mature than it had been before she took ill.

She felt confused as if two people were residing in her head. Splashing cold water on her face and washing her hands she walked carefully to her desk and sat, pulling out a journal to write down her thoughts as she always had. She noticed the pile of parchments that her Papa had left for her many months ago but which she had not been able to look at due to the illness that had come upon her so suddenly. Unrolling them now, she looked at the charts. They were her natal and transits for the coming year…no actually last year as she'd been in coma for over a year.

Looking at them more carefully she realised that in truth she should not be alive…what miracle had occurred that she should still be. Something was niggling at her as again the memory of being an older woman with long silvery hair, wearing unusual clothing that was certainly not like anything she had seen before.

At that moment, there was a tap on the door and Eduard Giraldi entered.

'Good morning Papa,' Nina said as always delighted to see him.

'What are you doing out of your bed child,' he said with concern.

'I woke early and saw these,' she said indicating the charts, 'Have you looked at them Papa? Do you realise what they reveal?'

'Yes, Nina I do,' he said, 'I have known since first you were born that you were not destined to live a long life and when you became so ill, I thought that the time had indeed come,' he buried his face in his hands.

'But I live Papa,' she said, 'what have you done; what are you not telling me?' she questioned him directly.

'Ah Nina, I am a silly old fool. A bargain was made to gain you a little more time. I went to see La Stregga,' he said, 'She told me that your Trueshape would be searching for you but that we could keep you hidden with a ritual to keep you safe.'

'What were you thinking Papa, the Gods cannot be bargained with and all you did was to keep me in a coma for over a year, that's not living!'

'There is much more to this my dear child,' he continued, 'La Stregga said, that in the time continuum you would be needed to help heal a great rift that would be occurring, of such a magnitude it would tear the very Skeins of Tyme. How could I refuse the Lady Herself when she came to me?'

'What Lady? Who?' cried Nina, 'Am I just a pawn in a game?'

'No, of course not sweetheart and your restoration to health is proof of this. You live Nina, you live!'

'But for how long Papa …how long? You know how we studied the outcome of tampering with cause and affect with La Stregga, the three fold law will not allow this to be surely?'

'Hush now, you must not upset yourself it will only weaken you again. Back to bed and I will call Nonna and Magdalena to tend you, please,' as he rang the bell by the bed in spite of her protests.

They came quickly at his call, helping Nina to wash and tidy herself and then back to bed. She was quiet and withdrawn and Nonna thought she was relapsing again. Magdalena chaffed Nina's hands and feet and said that, with Nonna's permission, she had just the thing to help Lady Nina.

With a curt nod from Nonna, Magdalena left, returning quickly with a little pouch of herbs and a small book in the ancient Italian language. Written in a fine spidery handwriting it contained illustrations, glowing, coloured images, of little beings with wings and other strange creatures that Nina could not give name to.

'What is this Magdalena? How do you come by such a precious book?'

'It's my own work, my Lady, if it pleases you,' said Magdalena, 'I have studied with La Stregga and now she has taken me in as her apprentice. I hope you enjoy it and I am honoured that you would find it precious,' she finished.

'I will indeed enjoy, thank you. Why it's quite exquisite I think I would like to spend time with La Stregga when I am stronger.'

'Well Lady Nina, these herbs are for that very purpose, to regain your strength and a return to health,' hearing Nonna calling her, she curtsied to Nina and hurried out to fetch Nina's breakfast.

For some reason, Nina felt to hide the herbs from sight from her Nonna and even, from her Papa. Slipping out of bed again, she hid them in the little hidden drawer at the back of her desk that only she had discovered.

When Magdalena brought her breakfast in, she refused to remain in bed, demanding the food be served on the little table at the window, where she could eat and enjoy the passing river below. She found she was hungry again and after giving her meal her full attention she curled up on the bed with the beautiful little book that Magdalena had loaned her.

Later a visit from a friend and a long luxurious bath and massage left her tired and a little drained again and so, retired to her bed without demure. She dreamed again of the silver haired woman and the little shining-winged entities, that were trying to gain her attention and for a moment, slipped out of her own body and into that of the woman.

She learned her name had been Sybille and that she was lost beyond help. Not if I have anything to do with it thought Nina as with a jolt, she woke once more to see the sun was setting; she was sweating again and felt feverish. Cautiously slipping out of bed, she went to her desk to retrieve the herbs Magdalena had given her, mixing a tiny pinch into the glass of water by the bed and quickly swallowing the bitter draught, carefully rinsing the glass and throwing the dregs into the commode.

Nina had no idea why she had thought to do this but an inner prompting had guided her and she had always listened to that voice, all her short life. Climbing back into bed, she rang the bell for the lamps to be lit so that she could continue the exploration into the little book...although this too she hid quickly beneath the covers as her Papa knocked and entered. Again, she did not have reason for her secrecy; she just knew it was necessary, even though she had never hidden anything from her Papa before.

Eduard Giraldi read to his daughter until she was drowsy, a story of Fae folk, Gods and Goddesses and the

Wytchways, not realising how he was opening doors in her psyche for her to travel through the Skeins of Tyme.

She travelled again to the giant tree where she received instructions and lessons beyond her years and beyond her consciousness ...while the woman named Sybille slept on, hidden in the depths of its nurturing branches.

Chapter 46
Mabon Rite

She is everywhere ...including in you. Her rocks are your bones, Her skin, your flesh; Her watery tides your fluid lymph and blood, Her fiery heart your pulsing organs. No separation exists except in your mind. Let go and flow into Her ...breath with Her ...breath as She breaths ...just let go

Extract from Wytchwise...Arianwen Isil'Lindir

The weekend passed in a blur of activity for everyone. Cal and Morgan found themselves caught up in the excitement of 'earthly rites,' as their individual talents unfolded and they found a niche for themselves that went beyond mere coincidence.

Both Cal and Max were used to research and so they made themselves useful, finding any indications through myth and history, that made mention of the situation that was unfolding for them all and the connections that had drawn them together.

Morgan spent time with Bethan as they practised music, with Maeve to help her with the mystery of the fractured crystal shard and with Tara as he continued his own lessons in shape shifting. He showed himself to be a great cook and so helped Flora, or whoever else had put their hand up to prepare meals for the group as they started to bond and spend more and more time together while they planned for the Samhain Rite in just over six weeks' time.

Monday was a day off, so with a skeleton team to run the business and take bookings for the following weekend, they had some free time. Tara put in an appearance in her usual way in a flurry of feathers, black silk and lace, catching up on the events of the previous months.

Max was making preparations for the old stables at Bethan's to be made over and was in the process of moving some of his things into storage in a dry shed at Flora's. Cal and Morgan had found a house to share rent and so were gathering bits and pieces together to settle for the duration, the blow up mattresses being a somewhat uncomfortable arrangement for two large men.

Bethan had been spinning, weaving beautiful wraps and cloaks, for orders placed as winter approached.

Maeve, still having difficulty with the shattered shard, had stopped trying for the moment and all had been still in her water cauldron of late, so instead she was working on a secret gift for Bethan for her coming birthday.

Flora continued with the farm and her own work, while Sam disappeared for hours on end whenever she could, to write and draw as the dreams strengthened and the beautiful etchings on her skin took on deeper colour and more life each day.

Only a week had passed since the opening and yet they had become a team. Cal had taken leave from his work at Uni on the pretence of research and Morgan, after speaking with his sister Lily, had arranged she look after Honey as long as possible to which she had been delighted to agree. Ruark however had had other ideas, arriving with Tara the day before and taking up residence at Grove Street, much to Maeve's surprise. The large Raven had taken a fancy to the mantelpiece in her studio to roost on and refused to budge when Morgan had called her to come home with him.

Now they were ready, a picnic and some offerings in baskets, camping chairs and a table all packed in Flora's big four-wheel drive; they all squeezed in for the drive to the Mount.

Mabon, Autumn Equinox, when day and night are of equal length and the harvest of apples, pears and the like, were ready. Tara had said she would meet them there and Claire had said she would try to put in an appearance too.

The Mount was abuzz with activity as people found a spot to put up tents if they were staying overnight and the organisers of the public rite were setting up the Altar, cleansing the boundaries of the circle in preparation.

Bethan felt edgy and could see the wee folk gathering but along with them was an air of dark. Morgan could feel it too and they exchanged glances…Maeve didn't know what she was feeling and wandered off for a walk, before the light went …glancing at Morgan as she left, a little sulkily.

'You need to speak with her,' said Bethan, 'she's getting the wrong idea about us.'

'Why would that bother her Bethan?' he asked innocently with a little smile.

'Oh you know as well as I do that the two of you are strongly attracted, even though they do say opposites attract,' she quipped, 'There's too much else unfolding for sexual tension to be an issue,' she finished.

'Well, you cut straight to the point don't you!' Morgan laughed, 'But yes I hear what you're saying but I can't really make that sort of suggestion to her straight, off can I now?'

At that Bethan, her laughter ringing out bright and clear, was unaware of Aerandir and Aelish Sensarrius, standing in the gloom of the cedar grove or that Maeve paused, looking back as she heard Morgan and Bethan laughing together as if at a private joke. She had never experienced the feeling of jealousy before; fuelled by the sound of Bethan's laughter and the rumbling response from Morgan as they set up the chairs and table.

Aithlin Farandir also stood observing the preparations, shaking his head at the silliness of humankin…this group so advanced when compared to many on their spiritual path and yet so naïve in their day-to-day relationships, he sighed.

Just at that moment, a bell sounded calling the first signal for final preparations before the start of the rite. Two Ravens arrived noisily announcing their presence from the branch of an old Redwood. Maeve immediately sprinted back, to be handed a robe to throw on, the others following suit.

After a few moments a low pulsing, drumming began and all moved to around the periphery of the circle. Annie and her coven walked, with no little pomp and ceremony, taking up position within the circle of watchers. Many children were present running and enjoying their freedom until, with a scowl, Annie brought them up short, causing them to run back to their parents in a hurry.

'Charming!' whispered Maeve, 'Since when were children not allowed to enjoy the Sabbats?' she questioned. To her surprise, Morgan simply took her hand and she felt a surge of peaceful energy, radiating from him and relaxed. He kept hold of her hand for a moment longer than was necessary, smiling at her surprise.

Annie cast the circle, four of her convenors calling the elemental quarters, before she took centre stage again.

A hush fell as the Harvest moon rose gracefully above the trees and a gasp went up as they saw that it was blood red. A shiver went through the crowd and a sigh as the Dark Fae Aelish stepped from the shelter of the forest, with Aerandir in tow.

'It's him,' said Bethan to Samantha, 'he's the one you drew and who keeps appearing in the forest and in my dreams.'

Max went to move forward but halted at the arrival of Aithlin behind him, whispering a few words in his ear. He stopped and visibly relaxed at Aithlin's gentle insistence he let things play out, as they must.

Annie Savage, positively simpering with pleasure at the attendance of these otherworldly beings, stepped forward and about to open a doorway in the energy of her cast circle, gaped in surprise as they simply stepped through for them, the non-existent barrier. Regaining herself quickly she greeted them formally, thanking them for their attendance. A silence had fallen over the crowd and their eyes glazed over; a spell cast so they not remember what they were witnessing. Flora, Maeve and the others were the exception to this, due to the influence of Aithlin's quiet presence.

Flora glanced across the fire lit clearing and was sure this time that she saw her father standing watching on the other side of the circle. She made to move toward him but again Aithlin stopped anyone from moving. Above him, she noticed in a tree was a white owl, perched looking with fixed focus at the scene.

With a wave of his hand, all was silent as he strode across the circle and approached the Dark Fae,

'The elders are waiting Aerandir Sensarrius, do you dare ignore their summons?' he said quietly. 'Come now and your embarrassment will be spared in front of these humankin or I can just as easily remove the spell that hides you from their sight,' raising his hand again.

The glade filled with tall stately silver haired Fae, two taking hold of an arm each, which Aerandir shook off with distain.

'And you Arwen Aelish what are you doing here leading this weak one astray?' indicating Annie.

'She needed no leading,' Aelish smirked, 'she is a lowly sycophant, nothing more nothing less, who craves the attention of her betters.'

'All the more reason for you to have a care then,' Aithlin replied harshly, 'Take them away,' he said and then to Aelish, 'Be thankful the Forest Lord is not present here tonight,' then turning he smiled at Bethan and bowed and with a curt nod to the others, was gone…the sound of music followed him.

With the withdrawal of the Fae the stillness was broken, movement returning to the frozen tableau of people as if nothing had happened.

The seven watchers released their indrawn breath as one, exchanging perturbed looks at what they had witnessed.

Annie continued the rather pompous and over-done performance as if she were the queen of the Wytches herself; even her tried and true acolytes somewhat skittish at the pageantry she displayed.

'What have we done employing her,' snorted Maeve, 'that wasn't a Harvest Rite that was pure 'dress-ups,' she said with disgust. I know it's not for us to judge another's rituals but that was beyond all recognition for Mabon, which I understood was all about balance and equality on all levels,' she finished, with a scowl.

The crowd dispersed slowly to their campsites and seats to ready the food for the shared feast. There was no real air of celebration however and the tension was palpable, 'Something's not right,' the majority agreed, 'Where was the sharing of the festival?' and 'what's got into Annie Savage?' they wanted to know.

The mood lightened as a group of musicians gathered, Bethan and Morgan being the first to approach to say hello, bringing lap harp and lute with them. Music always breaks the tension; this evening was no exception as the motley crew played jigs and reels with foot stomping enthusiasm and the evening wore on with shared food and mead flowing, while children slept and the music slowed to a gentler tone. Couples danced and groups chatted, catching up on the weeks between the festivals, shared friendships rekindled.

Morgan and Bethan played a haunting lullaby for the children as they stirred restlessly, caught in the feelings of the unknown 'something' that had visited earlier,

'Sleep little ones sleep, while the Fae their watch keep. Do not stir, do not peep …go to sleep …go to sleep

And in sleep, you may dance and sing with the moon. Listen; hear the sweet gentle cry of the loon. They will sing you a lullaby …a sweet, haunting tune.

Sleep little ones sleep, while the Fae their watch keep. Do not stir, do not peep …go to sleep …go to sleep…

Be at rest; be at ease snuggled deep in your fleece the Lady comes quietly …be at peace …be at peace.

Sleep little ones sleep, while the Fae their watch keep. Do not stir, do not peep …go to sleep …go to sleep.

Feel Her hand clasping yours like a soft, well-worn glove/ Feel Her warmth, Her tenderness …feel Her love …feel Her love.

Sleep little ones sleep, while the Fae their watch keep. Do not stir, do not peep …go to sleep …go to sleep.

She will take all your cares and the fears of the day, for just as She watched through the hours of your play She will watch o'er your dreaming 'til night slips away.'

The Lady soothed them and the wee folk came to play in their dreaming.

Flora drew a circle of protection around the quietening group as they sat together enjoying the harvest moon and the stillness of the night.

Bethan took a break from playing, wandering off from the group a little, she sat, watching entranced as a few Makers appeared through a doorway at the base of an old oak tree. They came to cleanse after the awkwardness of the rite...their humankin not realising that a rite without cohesion left gaps in the area's energy, inviting all kinds of negativity to the sacredness of the space.

Another group appeared accompanied by Silver who looked a little more recovered, the gap in her energy still holding the dark but held in stasis by the healer Makers.

Silver drifted over to Bethan to where she sat under the trees.

'Greetings Arianwen,' she sang, 'it is time to walk the inner paths with me a while.'

'What do you mean? I've just begun to unwind a little from the weeks just gone; this is a celebration after all.'

'This is just for a few hours, mere minutes in your time-line. There are things for you to see that will make your journey clearer from now on.'

'What do I have to do; I need to tell the others and...'

'They will simply see you sitting here child enjoying the night, you will be back before they look for you. Now come, take my hand,' Silver stretched out her hand to Bethan and she took it hesitantly.

Max happened to glance over to see Bethan talking to something, someone, he could not see. He moved to go to her but found a hand placed on his shoulder by Morgan, who was looking intently at something beyond Bethan and beyond Max's sight.

'It's okay Max, Bethan's talking to the most beautiful being; I think it must be Silver from all of the previous descriptions I've heard,' said Morgan.

'It is,' whispered Maeve.

At that Silver looked at them directly, raising a finger to her lips and singing a few notes, she vanished to them, only Bethan could see her. Once more taking Bethan's hand, she took her into the tree, down deep into its roots, to a chamber full of the aroma of mould and rich, decaying leaves.

From the chamber, a rivulet from an underground source flowed, its trickling, watery movement bright yet soothing to eyes and dabbling hands. Bethan sighed with quiet relief as she relaxed back securely into the root bowl of the ancient tree.

'Be at ease little one, there is one who would speak with you here,' and at that Silver bowed and withdrew and Bethan waited curiously for who would come, a secret longing inside that it be Hercurin.

Instead, from out of the gloom stepped a being of such intense beauty, Silver paled in comparison. Arianrhod, Goddess of the silvery moon-tides, patron of music and the weaving arts and indeed a weaver of life, appeared.

Bethan gasped aloud in awe, bowing her head in reverence and respect that the Lady stood before her here.

'Arianwen Isil'Lindir, listen there is much that you must know and time, in human understanding, is short …come,' reaching out she tapped Bethan sharply on her brow, opening her third eye beyond anything she'd experienced before. She felt overwhelmed by the amount of information that was coming at her at once.

'Be assured Arianwen, We would not give you more than you can handle at a time,' said Arianrhod, calling on the Makers to assist Bethan to collate all the information into an understandable form; they whispered to her in a chorus, of sweet melodies.

'We are other aspects of you who have risen above the time-space continuum through completion of tasks set and agreed on in this physical realm. Together we make up all the composite parts of Silver Trueshaper. When their tasks are complete all of the Trueshapers combined become avatars, parts of a realised being; as you call them Goddess…in turn, each of them are an aspect of Great Goddess…the 'All Encompassing One,'' their song became discordant as they continued, Arianrhod soothing them that they continue.

'At this time on Her beauteous planet, Her jewel in this universe, there is strife and grief that has caused great damage, not just to Humankin but to other ancient races of being and to some of us, the Makers of this realm too. One of us fell and many others are falling, causing a blight that

has taken hold of the etheric realms of the Fae altering them and as the veils thin toward Samhain, it will affect your world in turn. The blight came about through one Maker experiencing the pollution and fear of this world, which has in turn altered the flow through Ungwe the Web of Life and therefore the Great Mother, known by many names to your race. We call her Anu, some Danu …Mother of the Tuatha Dé Danann …the children or tribes of Danu, from which you yourself originate, through your bloodline.

The Littleshape Sybille is lost, as you know. Everything possible is in operation to find her and bring her back that she may complete her journey. In so doing she will merge her consciousness with that of her Trueshaper Silver that they may renew finally on the Skeins of Tyme. However, there are now other energies in play that have altered Ungwe that only Great Mother knows the why or how of and this is affecting you directly as your energy is 'quickened.' We do not know the reasons for these changes but we are here to assist you in any way that we can. Be at peace Littleshape Bethan for you are in truth becoming more than any dreamed a Halfling could be …walk with the Lady and be blessed …Arianwen Isil'Lindir …Lady Silver Moonsinger, Spellsinger in the making,' and with that they fell silent and Bethan was given a mere moment to try to understand the truth of their song.

Again, Arianrhod stood before, her looking deep within her soul and said,

'We will lend you strength when you falter, words when all words fail, honesty when you would rather be kinder than the truth will be and a love that knows no bounds,' and turned to leave, with a smile of such beauty, Bethan cried tears of pure joy.

Pausing again for a moment reflectively, as if considering Bethan, She said, 'This really isn't something I should interfere with Arianwen but keep your enemies close, they are dangerous in their arrogance,' and with that was gone; bell-like voices sang her away.

Bethan leaned against the roots of the great Tree, the back of her head resting against soft warm-scented mosses and lichen. She could see and sense differently; could hear the waters from the sacred spring being drawn up through the root system and could taste the bonding of water as it merged and became sap in the great energy network within...she became one with the vastness and beauty of Danu's Birthing Tree.

She was jolted rudely back to awareness by a tug on her braid, 'What in...' and found herself staring into the grinning face of Tara in a half human half raven form ...a small woman with dark wings unfurled ...wrapped around them as a shield from prying eyes.

'Welcome back from the realms of the Earth Mother little sisterkin ...soon now we begin our journey to bring Sybille home.'

She kissed Bethan on her forehead and tickled her with feathers of musky scents ...vanilla or caramel ...and smiling said, 'Come you must eat now. Nothing will ever be the same again but this is a wondrous thing indeed. Oh how I love adventures,' she finished, handing Bethan warm honey and nut cakes. She had never tasted anything like it before in her entire life, 'I want to dance now,' she said, leaping to her feet …to see Tara disappear with a chuckle and Hercurin step from the tree to take her hand in the dance.

'Just for tonight,' he said, 'we'll dance and when day dawns you will know that all is changed indeed. In the Mother's name be blessed Arianwen.'

Chapter 47
Waiting

The Tuatha Dé Danaan, ('People of the Goddess Danu'), was one of the mythical races who settled in Ireland before the arrival of the Milesians, the ancestors of modern Gaels. The Danaan were descendants of the goddess Danu and her son 'The Dagda', was their most powerful leader.

The Tuatha Dé Danaan, were a race of deities as well as a race of heroes. They were skilled in the arts, science, poetry and magic.

It should be noted that the fairies in Celtic mythology, (especially Irish, Welsh and Arthurian) had nothing to do with tiny pixies with wings as are found in folklore and children fairy tales, such as Tinkerbelle in Peter Pan or the Fairy Godmother in Cinderella. The fairies found here were humans with supernatural power. In early Irish and Welsh literature, they could be tall or short, beautiful or ugly. They can be benevolent beings, but at other times they can be frighteningly cruel or malign, whereas modern interpretations of fairies tend to prettify them, particularly during the Victorian period (19th century) in Britain.

Extract from Fairy and Folklore of the British Isles by Max Fenner.

They were all sitting together in the Harvest having breakfast before starting work, a few weeks after the unfortunate Mabon rite. Bethan, as yet not arrived, had been very quiet of late, at times swinging between her heightened awareness and her blatant pining for contact with Hercurin whom she'd seen only briefly since Equinox.

Due to the nature of Springsmeet, which was mostly a tourist destination, business was slower through the week unless holiday time and manically busy at the weekend. This meant that most businesses weren't open until 10.00 am and so, after chores were finished at the farm and often in Bethan's garden too, they would take a little time just to be and talk about the coming week.

In a matter of days, post Mabon, they'd fallen into a routine of work, research, exercise and pleasure in each other's company. Walks after work in the forests and beauty spots of the highlands, Cal was teaching them all a little of what he knew of Tai Chi and Kickboxing, helping them all to tone and strengthen already above average healthy bodies.

Morgan showed them new exercises that came from the more Druidic path of the Wytchways, of focus and shape changing and had spoken with them about the fact that the enhanced psychic abilities they were experiencing, almost constantly, also boosted appetite as it boosted metabolic rate.

Flora had shared with them her mother's story of her ancestry and so there were no surprises about the new skills they had begun to grasp; both Tara and Claire were helping her find her own familiar shape.

Flora and Cal had discovered a shared love of the garden. She was thinking of offering him a space at the farm, although she didn't want him to get the wrong idea either but seeing as how he was there early most mornings, helping her with the heavier chores, she thought it would lighten his load of travelling back and forwards.

Max was now firmly ensconced in the old stables at Wells with Bethan; work had begun on the renovations and with Bethan's permission, had invited Morgan to stay.

Susan and Alex came and went a little more often than before, having the excuse to come, to help in the business. Susan had boosted the display with some of her own beautiful artworks …fantasy pieces that totally tied in with the theme of the centre and Samantha had made a strong connection with her, Susan's encouragement had shown her new and different techniques in her drawing whilst Claire came and went, often unexpectedly and often with Tara. No one asked why or what had occurred but as Harry was conspicuous by his absence, Flora was fully aware that something was amiss in her parent's relationship, which frankly did not surprise her one iota.

Cal and Claire had never spoken of the find he'd made in the UK and neither of them knew where Tara had taken the body of their sisterkin. They were assured it was exactly where it needed to be.

None of them knew precisely what they would need to be prepared for in the coming time but they were trying to prepare for all eventualities.

It was becoming more and more difficult to tolerate the blatant, arrogant, changes that had manifested in Annie but were aware that keeping her close was a means to keep an eye on her, although she had become even more supercilious having acquired the habit of disappearing at the strangest times, returning with an even more smug attitude than normal.

Overall, it was as though they drifted through the days on a knife-edge, still not fully aware of what would unfold for them but feeling, at times, like soldiers awaiting the call to arms …but life goes on and their work kept them occupied and happy and it thrived.

Bethan, in unaccustomed haste, burst into the Harvest, her cheeks flushed rosy from the cold, apologetic for her tardiness but her obvious excitement told them clearly enough why she was late. She refused to react to their teasing however, not wishing to share her night experiences or where they took her under Hercurin's wing, her excuse being, that it was most often beyond words.

They could all see the changes wrought within her; she glowed with an inner beauty and light that even she had not possessed before. They noticed that her hair, once usually braided and neat was now longer, thicker and allowed to curl wildly, loose down her back, curious little beings clung there like living organic hair clips to stop it falling in her face. She wore more of her own magickal weavings, in layers of greens and silvers, with little, surprise features, woven into their borders or on pockets, in which she seemed to carry an inordinate amount of items that would appear simply when she needed them, there being no obvious weight or bulk to her layerings.

The new sight that was developing in the others let them see these changes, while others would simply look at her saying, 'hmm there's something different about you these day Bethy,' to which she'd simply smile.'

Since the night of Mabon, she had in some ways withdrawn from them where personal matters were concerned, her relationship to Hercurin being something she drew the line at even attempting to share. On the other hand she was often more fiery than her previously, gentle self; not aggressively but in a manner that brooked no argument; confronting Annie at every turn with this new and forceful Bethan, who would not allow the also radically changed Annie, to interfere in anything but what she was asked to do…namely her job.

They all knew that the inner journey Bethan had made on the Mount had altered and strengthened her in all the ways she would need to face Samhain and beyond. She had shared as best she could all she'd been shown and told about the dire need for them to take on whatever was given them to achieve; to sharpen their wits and practise awareness as if their lives depended on it…for one day she said that might well be the truth of it. Coming from their gentle Bethy, in her newfound strength, was something no one could ignore and so, once again sharply focussed, they worked on their own self-improvement.

Chapter 48
Bethan

Danced at dawn as the earth was waking
...danced as the sun rose, a fiery ball
Danced as the earth slept
...danced as the winds rose
Danced 'til I found home ...oneness with All

Bardic Song of Fire by Bethan Fenner and Morgan Trethaway

Bethan changed within herself, beyond anything she could have foreseen or imagined. More and more she felt less, 'human' and more Fae and then there were the other parts of her that were emerging as she Truedreamed.

Her weaving had more texture, her music more depth and working with Morgan her voice had strengthened too. Every so often Aithlin would join them on a quiet evening at Covenstead or at Wells whenever they gathered to honour the Lady and Lord or just to share food, wine and ideas together as the group bonded strongly as each day passed ...new music was birthed from these gatherings.

It was obvious to her with her new insights that closer relationships between couples were in the making. Cal and Flora spent time together providing an abundant table for all, working with the herbs, dyes and inks. Morgan, spent equal amounts of time with everyone, being a very natural socialiser in spite of his professed loner status back home in Wales; cooking with her and Flora; playing music with her and yet, Bethan knew that Morgan's heart was being ostensibly drawn to the wildness of Maeve and that these feelings were evidently mutual. Max and Samantha had a passion for writing, helping each other with their two very different projects, yet adding something unique to the type of writing they engaged in; they were looking through ancient texts to find something to help with the Samhain Rite.

Therefore, she sat weaving a wrap in bright autumn colours that she knew her client wanted to warm the coming winter days. As she wove, she slipped into the now familiar waking dream state where she was free to wander while her hands were busy.

She found herself standing on a rough wooden jetty at the edge of a vast lake where a coracle waited to ferry her across to an island, hidden in the mists. As she stood, wrapping her cowled robe closely around her against the freezing early winter air.

Looking down into the water reflecting the heatless sun as it began to set a fierce, bewhiskered head broke the surface, surprising her as droplets of water caught, then rolled off the tight, oiled pelt. She smiled to see a young otter looking at her. Squatting down to take a closer look at the beautiful creature she looked deep into its liquid brown eyes and felt herself falling forward. Suddenly she was the otter, looking up at herself, a slender young woman in a deep blue robe, caught with a pin of delicate silver, the design intricate and unusual. Looking closely into the fine boned face she saw, tattooed on the pale forehead a blue sickle-moon, the badge of her office as a priestess and seer of the ancient Wytchways of the Goddess …her name was Leah.

She drew back in surprise and found she was herself once more, looking down into the eyes of the otter again. The otter gave a small cry and squatting down, the same thing happened but this time she was swimming in the cold, still waters; pearly droplets simply running off her back and through her whiskers, the membrane over her eyes opening and closing automatically as she ducked her head under water looking for a supper of fish. Launching herself into a dive, she felt the force of the water vibrating the webbing between her toes creating the soft gliding swim that only a few creatures share. Diving, deeper still, small ears closed over tightly to keep the sensitive organ dry but not limiting the ability to hear sharply even in the depths.

Then as the otter dived, she caught herself quickly, just in time to prevent herself from pitching headlong into the cold lake as she returned to her human awareness. She laughed aloud as she saw the otter resurface and flip over onto her back, a small shape resting on her belly that Leah could not quite make out from the distance between them. She had experienced this shifting with other creatures but never in such complete awareness and she knew that finally, she had found her true familiar spirit.

Swimming closer again, the otter lifted itself onto the edge of the jetty, her shape shimmering and shifting between a silver haired woman and an otter. She dropped a smooth, black object at Leah's feet ...it was a river washed pebble in the same design as she wore on her cloak pin ....two circles intertwined, one above the other, interspersed with a fine filigree tracery of flowering vines.

The young otter, communicating with her through a mind-to-mind connection, shared that her name was Oonagh and yes, she was her familiar spirit, in fact was here to teach Leah the art of shapeshifting if she were ready for that adventure. Yes, indeed she was, replied Leah, she had waited long for her familiar to appear and was eager to begin the challenge of the art.

With a flick of her tail, Oonagh disappeared below the surface as she heard the approach of horses. A horse and a pony appeared around a bend in the track and Leah knew that her charge had arrived.

Alma, a young girl from the village had shown signs of seership and so her parents had agreed, (for the exchange of coin of course, thought Leah ironically), that the child study with the priestesses of the lake. They had said that the child was not comely and spoke only rarely, so there would be no settlement of marriage made on her, in their opinion but that, she was a good, strong, biddable child and therefore, they would need coin to cover the chores she would no longer be there to perform. Leah had an instant, if rare, dislike for these people who would barter their child for a handful of silver and so drew a glamour of aloof beauty about her as the father, she assumed, brought the child to the lakeshore.

The exchange of coinage for the child was a brief and emotionless encounter, the little tawny haired girl taking Leah's hand without demur as she ignored her father's hesitant goodbye; drawing herself up to her full height as she walked with Leah to the coracle.

Leah wrapped Alma in an oilskin, sat her down in the coracle and stepping to the prow of the small vessel, she stood, raising her hands to bring up a Wytchlight and a breeze that travelled the craft slowly and safely across the waters to the island, she called home.

Alma watched from under her oilskin, eyes like small green moons in delight as they moved through the water and landed on the other side where a tall stately woman stood, wrapped in a robe of deepest blue ...her face unreadable and her age indiscernible ...waiting, 'The Cybil', Oracle of the Isles.

Bethan recovered herself as she looked down at her weaving and found that she had completed it in her trance, interweaving a symbol of two circles, intertwined with lacy filigree vines and subtle flowers.

'Ah!' she exclaimed aloud, 'of course ...another thread in the Skeins of Tyme and another clue to the journeys we've all made ...but that face ...I know that face and the black stone, I've seen that too somewhere!'

Chapter 49
Nina Giraldi

Poppies red, in constant motion
...nodding heads in quiet breeze
Nothing's judged, no emotion
...no joy nor grief; no cold to freeze
Being is a simple pleasure
...living now is all there is
...be the poppy or the heather
...you were simply born for this
Extract from Magdalena's Book of Shadows and Light

Nina felt herself physically changed; for a moment in her dreams she had been someone else again, an older woman with silver hair, standing on the edge of a lake waiting for, Nina knew not what.

She felt weary beyond her years; she was sleeping so much but her dreams were bizarre. They were a total enigma to her; she was exhausted from trying to understand what she'd seen. She began to fear she was losing her mind and felt that she wasn't supposed to be here at all.

After her Papa had told her of the deal he had made with La Stregga, she had been horrified and it was as if the knowledge of this was causing her to weaken daily again as chills and fevers alternated and her strength waned. She wished she'd been let go before, not wanting this opportunity to experience life again only for it to be snatched away; this time knowing she must indeed die.

Tired, so tired …I wish …was her last thought as she found herself walking through a long corridor of light; down to the roots of the great tree again and up through its vast trunk and boughs. Up and up, to the very top of the tree where a curious cocoon of gossamer fine threads was hanging and tiny beings with split-wings were hovering and singing her home. A tall being stood waiting for her. She knew this was her Trueshape Silver. She knew though that something was not quite right; a swirl of dark energy still remained, even as she was embraced in soft, loving arms and she felt the exchange take place…she knew then, Nina Giraldi was indeed dead but here was Sybille, sleeping deep within her and that she had been animated by her, if but briefly.

'That's not fair,' she cried, 'I didn't agree to this.'

Silver replied, 'Indeed you didn't Littleshape and so we must make things right again. Come, renew again with me and you will be reborn.'

'Will I be me though?' Nina asked, 'Or will I awaken in a different place and time, a different me and will I remember Nina Giraldi?'

'That is up to you child. When you make a choice that is a lifetime decision, there are a thousand other possibilities at least, that can manifest as concurrent lives. Occasionally, as now for Sybille, you awake in an alternative life and then step from one to another randomly, or in awareness, one to another specifically, when it more closely resembles that which you seek.

First, you must review this life thus far and then you must find something that you so strongly want, so desire within you that you must return, to complete this life. It will however, alter the threads you have woven to date on the Skeins of Tyme and it means you will not move on to the Summerlands as would be at Samhain, if you let this life play out. Remember nothing dies but simply changes shape. '

'How do I know what is best?' said Nina, 'How do I know I will make the better choice.'

'Ah, that is in the hands of the Mother, child,' replied Silver.

'Then I will return to being Nina and let the way be shown to me for it is but close to Beltane here and so I have a little time to consider what I wish to do between now and Samhain. I have always wanted to be a healer, or an astrologer. Will I feel restored to health for this time?'

'Indeed you will, brave child and then you will be renewed when you return here and you will not have to return to this plane unless in full consciousness. As you are aware, your sisterkin Sybille is dwelling concurrently with you in the fold of Tyme that you exist in as Nina Giraldi. She too has been through an untoward change that was not foreseen and although she is older in current earth years than you, her being is great and vast and the loss of her to this universe is beyond knowing.'

'Then if this is so I must question what I can do to help right this mutual wrong for both of us,' Nina declared.

'Then we ask that you continue your journey as Nina for a while longer, with the knowing that it will not be a long span in the Skeins of Tyme. You take Sybille with you, for she is unable to awaken to restore.

Nurture the memories and ideals that will rise to the surface within you as she stirs occasionally from sleep, for in the time-space continuum in human man understanding, she is your 'future self.' Therefore, you can learn much from her as she has, in the perceived past, learned from your sacrifice now. Blessings to you little one …know that you are greatly cherished for your courage.'

At that, Nina found herself awake, feeling well and strong again but knowing the journey that was to unfold for a short while must be lived to the fullest. She reached over to the night table next to the bed and drew to her the little book that Magdalena had loaned her, immersing herself, in the history of the Stregga.

Chapter 50
Sybille and Nina

Across the lake, the Lady is calling.
Sweet melodies fly on silken thread
Weaving webs of life and falling
Into softness, all fear fled.
Extract from 'The Skeins of Tyme'
By Arianwen Isil'Lindir and Aithlin Farandir

Sybille heard from a great distance voices calling to her but so far, despite all her attempts, she was unable to return herself to a waking state.

She was floating free in the vast sea of consciousness that were the Skeins of Tyme. She had been and was many things but the tides pulled at her, buffeting her, to life in the human realms. She wanted to sleep but stirring, opened her eyes again to the same lovely airy room of before, the same young and tender olive skin enveloped her ...Nina, she was one with Nina Giraldi and Nina, restored again to health knew that she was there sharing space with her. How tempting it would be to be lost here, to forget. No, she would find the strength to move on to where she knew she should be ...but where was that exactly.

Searching, deep within her own being and deep within Nina's warm, animated young life she suddenly remembered... Sybille, she was Sybille. Pulling all of her knowledge in she deposited a cache of information into Nina's cells as memories …healing arts, astrology and a basic guide to the Wytchways …the Wytchways that she had once learned from one of La Stregga …when she couldn't remember. All she knew in the moment was there was a tangle in the Skeins of Tyme that she could not unravel alone; so she must travel, in and out of the threads again to help restore, what must be restored.

She searched through the warp and weft of Tyme tracing hand over hand the thread that would lead her to the knot that was perhaps of her own making…some choice she'd made in error…she didn't know; she knew only that she must find and heal the breach.

Searching blindly at first she heard a sound …a melody that called to her. The little Makers, her own sisterkin, broke through, leading her to another realm, another place in the Mystery of Tyme. Here she stood on a rough wooden pier, looking out across a vast lake to see one of her priestesses floating toward her in a small coracle, a child, wrapped in oilskins, looked out with great mooneyes as she was ferried home to the Apple Isle, deep in the Mysts.

Smiling at Leah and the child Alma, she blessed and enfolded them in a very human embrace, causing her priestess to look at her askance, at the unaccustomedly effusive welcome.

'The Cybil,' merely smiled a secretive knowing smile and ushered them up the hill, into the warmth of the Hearth home and served them a bowl of vegetable broth and bread with her own hands. With a flourish, she presented Alma with a wizened, rough-skinned apple for her own ...never had she tasted anything so rich and juicy sweet.

Leah, still watching her High Priestess carefully, couldn't help but be taken aback by the smile and knowing wink that was given her by the usually stern and brusque Cybil.

Chapter 51
Twists in Warp and Weft

Last night, Lady Moon was an eye in the sky
...watching wild spirits as the wind blew them by
Sensing the veils thin, trees wept their leaves
As Samhain approaches the Lady bequeaths
...all life that is fading She will renew
...like silvery droplets of morning fresh dew.
An extract from The Skeins of Tyme
By Arianwen Isil'Lindir and Aithlin Farandir

Flora, Samantha, Maeve, Bethan, Susan and Claire, sat in silent contemplation on the deck at Flora's farm, the sun was setting and the cool air held the promise of the first frost. The men were taking time to go into Melbourne for some male bonding with Alex Fenner, heading to an Australian Rules football game; Morgan had never experienced this cultural phenomena; Harry Jenkins had been invited but had declined, work being as always his excuse.

Claire and Susan, living only suburbs apart had become firm friends and Claire had finally been able to share with someone the sordid little story of Harry's indiscretion with Annie Savage although she acknowledged it was cutting things too close to the bone by naming names. Susan however, was the soul of discretion and was saddened for her friend, when she considered how lucky she was to have such a wonderful life partner in Alex.

Completely unperturbed by Claire's abilities to shift shape at will, Susan's art was further inspired by the images the very idea conjured. Having been Sybille's student for years, when Max and Bethan had been small children, she was aware of so much that went on beyond the veil as they flowed through her brush or pen onto canvass. She had always been able to travel into the landscapes she painted and so knew of many worlds that she in turn had perhaps altered somehow by her very presence there. Nothing happened in isolation after all.

She was a dedicated Wytch and had only left the Coven when, after Sybille's disappearance, Annie had muscled in, to browbeat the other members into letting her become the new High Priestess; with what authority Susan had no idea but along with a few others she'd left and not looked back, other than to miss her friend deeply. She thought they would be able to call on those who had left the Coven in a crisis if the need arose.

Now the six women gathered to discuss the coming Samhain Rite and to bond in perfect love and perfect trust as the Wytchway decreed, it having always been the Way that the women constructed and organised the Sabbat Rites while the men followed direction and served their Goddess, these aspects being present in each coven member.

They all agreed this had nothing to do with sexism but lay in the age-old ways of the Sabbats. The wheel of the year, left to women, because they were more closely aware of the moon cycles by which the Sabbats were set and by the simple evidence of their own inner menses cycle that should in fact, mirror the moon tides. This changed only with crone hood reached and the tide turned, toward dark moon, for the final cycle of life.

For Claire, this transition had just begun and for Susan the change was reaching the end stage; Claire being in her mid-forties and Susan just turned 56. They both sensed this change in their innermost being and this only added to what they brought to, what now was obviously becoming, a new coven.

They discussed the representation of the three phases of woman ...Maiden, Mother, Crone and the fourth darker character the Enchantress ...all agreed that in spite of her young age at nearly 29 Bethan was definitely representative of this aspect ...Claire the Mother, Susan the Crone aspects and looking at each other they pondered,

'Okay,' said Flora, 'who of us can possibly be the Maiden then,' laughing.

The others laughed with Flora but fell silent when Maeve omitted to join in.

'All right Maeve,' laughed Samantha, 'you're good at the poker face act but I'm not convinced.'

Bethan, looking intently at Maeve, raised her hands for quiet and said,

'No wait! Maeve's serious and brave enough to admit that she's still a virgin, therefore our Maiden.' At which everyone fell silent, a myriad of questions and thoughts passing over their faces as they thought about what they knew of their friend Maeve.

As a student, she'd only had time for work and the occasional fun night but in groups not in pairs; if pairs were the happening thing she would decline, they remembered.

She never mentioned anyone special in her life and, because of her outspoken manner. Her friends expected at some stage, she'd had her first experience even though they knew she was an extraordinarily private person. Knowing only a little of her history about what she'd been exposed to as a child; not knowing who her father was, was something that, until recently, Bethan could totally relate to.

Uncomfortable under the inscrutable stare of her friends, Maeve blushed a little and smiled saying,

'You really don't know how long it's been that I've wanted to tell you all this; I feel very relieved …you've no idea…' she broke off a little tearfully.

With that they all rose as one to hug in understanding and then began the further ultimate bonding as a group, with the sharing by each of their first experience; Susan and Claire, exchanging glances and agreeing silently, that this was something they would have loved as young women to have had the opportunity to experience in friendships.

A while later, fanning herself with a newspaper, Claire said,

'Phew, who's for a glass of something stronger than tea?' This was met with a chorus of agreement.

'Okay, said Susan, 'I'm happy to go into town and grab some wine and perhaps some Sushi too?'

'Done,' said Claire, 'I'll come with you. Sit tight girls, continue planning the rite and we'll be back shortly.'

When they'd left, the four looked at each other and taking a deep breath Samantha said, 'Okay, who wants to share first? Flora?'

Flora said, puffing out her cheeks, 'Me! Oh, alight. Well I've been thinking about the rhymes Sybille left us; each one describes us in elemental ways but actually alludes to the element that is less evident in our makeup.'

'For instance?' Maeve interjected.

'Well,' said Flora, 'mine for instance shows that I am earthy and as a healer have become sympathetic, which is shown in the first line... *Earth you are, compassion grown.* The second line indicates that I am learning about my passion, ideology and emotional self ...shown in the second line... *Fire and Water becoming known*, then my intellect will be fired up. *Air will sing* ...and when my passion is rekindled; *when fire alights*, then my emotions will wash over everything to cleanse me ...shown in the last line... *and Water washes all things bright.*'

'Wow,' said Maeve, 'that's all actually quite logical ...I've been looking for something a little less obvious I guess,' she grinned. 'So what element would be your strongest Flora, earth?'

'Exactly, that's the obvious but it also could mean that I need to learn more about air and fire so that I can know intuitively what needs washing clean perhaps, so my most needed element would be water in that case.'

'This looks suspiciously easy,' said Samantha, 'and that's not how I would remember my Aunt but' ...she trailed off.

'We don't actually know that Sybille wrote these for us, though do we?' said Flora.

True, they all agreed,

'But we have to assume she did,' said Bethan, 'and that she was guided, through knowing each of us so well, to actually make it all look easy, thus making us think harder about everything else that's been happening in the meantime.'

'Ooh, now you're doing my head in,' moaned Maeve, 'so how do you see yours working then Bethan?'

'Well, apart from the obvious implications, there are some other thoughts I've had very recently after my trance experience as the priestess and the meeting with the otter. My mother drowned and yet she could swim like a fish...'

'Or an otter, muttered Maeve.'

'Yes,' said Bethan, 'now you're thinking outside the square Maeve. The first line is...

Spirit sings within your frame, on your loom and through your pain.' I am a weaver but I don't believe this line is necessarily about my physical work but rather the web weaving of the spiritual realms. The reference to singing is more about how my body vibrates through music and then in turn, vibrates the web that translates itself into my physical work. In fact everything vibrates to sound ...everything has its own sound. The very cause of my pain ...my father ...is actually the one person who has helped me release my own voice and my music and who has reduced my pain.

'Streuth!' choked Samantha, 'how did you manage to get all that from the one line Bethan? That's amazing!'

'Simple,' Beth replied, *Spirit sings*, vibration, *on the loom*, the movement of the web. *In my frame*, through my physical body, it's expressed; *my pain*, the unknown about my ancestry and then the pain easing after my father appeared his help with 'finding my voice' and finding my music.'

'I'm stunned too', said Flora, 'this puts an entirely different light on things.'

'Second line?' queried Maeve.'

'*Water washes all things clean and Air brings truth to you again*,' recited Bethan. 'To me this means that my emotions, through knowledge gained about my ancestry has cleansed me of pain; through Air… my intellect has also been cleansed finding peace in the truths discovered …in other words, this information has satisfied my left brain intellect,' she paused, then continued,

'*Fire is needed and Earth to ground*, I was always very passive so I lacked the courage of my convictions to break through the pain and then ground it into manifestation through the element of earth.

The last line holds my task I believe, *when the web you weave, all things abound*; indicates how my physical work and my spiritual task is a weaving of something so, when you all spoke of my being the representative of the Enchantress, it made sense as the twists and turns in the warp and weft are symbolic of Aether or Spirit.

My father is a Fae, which means I am a Halfling and so half of me is not of this realm,' she paused to take breath, 'and I'm almost beginning to think that the other half isn't human either' ...she trailed off as she saw their puzzled faces, '...what we were speaking of before and Maeve picked up on ...my mother and the otter ...what if at least half of me through her, is a shaper too?'

'Have you ever had any inclinations of otherness or should that be 'otterness?'' asked Samantha pulling a face at her and moving her hands like fins.

Bethan chuckled at the word, 'No, not that I can recall exactly; I do have a strange memory of being born into water and swimming but then everything goes dark.'

'There must be a way to tackle this, Bethy,' said Flora, my Mum or Susan, might know how we can find out, although asking Aithlin directly would also be a solution.'

'I knew something had been withheld but I think it may have been a deliberate attempt to get me to either be satisfied with half my origin, believing the other to be fully human, or to push me to do the research and ask the right questions, in order to work it all out for myself,' answered Bethan.

'Well this sure puts a different connotation on what I thought my little rhyme, meant,' said Flora.

'Now I don't even know where to begin,' said Samantha, 'What about you Maeve any thoughts?'

'Well yes, actually it's starting to make more sense than just the superficial words say. Perhaps, *fire is harsh and anger sings*, could be about my work and also the short fuse I have but what if anger, channeled creatively, could make 'anger sing?''

'Yes, yes,' said Bethan excitedly, 'you've got the idea. Keep going!'

'Alright ...well, *don't go too close you'll burn your wings*, I was thinking about fire and flying creatures. Tara said she would teach me to shape change and I said, great but it'd have red feathers,' she smiled at the memory, 'but suppose that is what I need to learn, sort of like 'tempering steel,' as the next line shows possibly... *Earth yourself go deep within; let Water again become your kin.* I'm sure this could have something to do with my need to work with that Atlantian crystal shard but also, with the strange goings on in my cauldron it's not to scare me but to make me laugh. Gees that sounds lame when I try to put it into words, as in, *let Air breath you, let laughter ring.*'

'No I think you're onto something Maeve. Keep at it and it will become clearer in time I'm sure,' said Bethan, then, turning to Samantha, 'Sam?'

'Hmmm,' she said, 'a work in progress m'thinks.' She quoted, '*Earth you are and from earth you came*' ...well yes I can be very direct and down to earth and then there're the leaves in my bed and the nature spirits that tattooed me,' she said indicating her hands and wrists. '*Your intellect from Air you gain* probably means my writing and my absolute need to get it right where my book or articles are concerned. *Your Fire should burn, with flaming ire,* I would imagine means I need to find more passion over intellect because my emotions tend to be rationalised and so, the last line, *Yet Water has put out your fire.*'

'Well I think you're close with that Sam,' said Flora, 'now I need to re-think mine.'

'Well I think we're on track,' said Maeve…'at least it's a start. I guess Samhain will give us further insights into what we need to be doing but as to that, who will work in which quarter if we're not sure whether we're working with our strengths or weaknesses?'

'Let's all put that on the table then,' said Flora. 'I think, Beth, Water and Spirit …Maeve Fire …Sam Air and Earth for me.'

I agree said Sam.

'Sounds right to me,' said Maeve.

'Alright, let's go with that unless something changes in the next week,' said Bethan, ' I'm not sure how I can tackle both, although we don't have to call spirit in as it's in all things anyway …I'll only have to call water, in which case…'

At that moment, Claire and Susan returned and over food and a glass of wine they talked it all through again, Susan and Claire putting in a few other ideas and insights about the rhymes as well.

In a quiet moment when Flora and Sam were washing dishes and Maeve had wandered outside with Claire to talk about shapeshifting, Susan took the opportunity to speak with Bethan about her thoughts with regards her mother.

'You know it's a wild card Bethy,' she said, stroking her daughter's long silky hair, 'about your mother I mean,' she paused, to think. 'Although I understand where you're coming from because you're right, she could swim like a fish …but otter?' she finished questioningly.

'I know Mum, it's an idea that won't go away though and I guess I do need to put it all to rest once and for all. It's something I've always wondered about, ever since I saw all her awards for swimming and the ability you told me she had to hold her breath under water for longer than anyone else. Then there's the birthing dream too …where did that come from? In the trance state I was otter …not just watching but becoming one with, just as Claire describes when she shifts shape to her familiar, her owl form. I guess what I'm asking is how do we know the difference between someone who has mastered the skill of shapeshifting and those who, like Tara, are born that way …who come from other realms.'

'Ah there you have me; Bethy…you may need to speak with Claire and Tara about that. As far as I know I'm human, so I'm not the one to be asking that question.'

The others came back in and Bethan approached Claire to ask the same question but at that moment the men entered. They had agreed to meet up for the rest of the evening to continue the plans for Samhain.

Morgan had enjoyed the skills of the Australian players and was eagerly sharing stories of the evening the other men loudly responsive as they supported one or the other of the teams; sobering when Bethan spoke of their plans made that evening and so before they went their separate ways for the night, once more each brought something else to the cauldron of ideas for the most important night of any year on the Wheel ...Samhain ...Celtic New Year and Festival of the Dead.

Chapter 52
Mixing a Little Confusion

Raven-blue wings stroke the land as they fly
...cooling the earth; winters soft lullaby
Soon She will sleep in the depths of the land
...as Jack Frost weaves magick with a wave of his hand
From Winter by Samantha Cartwright

As they worked mixing herbs and blending oils, they centred and grounded themselves, preparing for the rite of honouring the ancestors and the Ancient Ones. Each had a role to play and yet they did not really understand the full implications of what was being asked of them; so subtle and yet so complex, were the possible outcomes of the rite.

They chatted in hushed voices about their particular roles, in between the casual statements such as,

'Can you pass the mugwort please Flora,' and 'How many juniper berries did you say to crush Morgan?' or, 'Are you sure we have the timing right; there doesn't appear to be any room for error here at all.'

Tara had arrived and had added a small amount of musky oil from her own feathers to blend into the anointing essence for Bethan. A small packet of herbs had arrived in a little leather pouch from Aithlin, furtively delivered by a young Fae, that were to be brewed and inhaled to enhance inner vision. A moss wrapped package containing paper-fine bark parchment, was found on the table by the back door at Bethan's, covered in skilfully designed sigels to be carved into the quarter candles. An oil, fragrant with oak moss and ambergris for anointing them, left no doubt who the donor was and that Bethan couldn't stop sniffing, until laughing Cal had taken it from her saying,

'Hey easy there or there'll be nothing left to work with if you drain it all out,' with a grin and a stroke of her hand, to which she'd laughed more than anyone had heard her laugh since Mabon, when she'd seemed as high as a kite on life. She said that the fragrance brought her joy.

Flora had carefully looked through the ancient bag of herbs, given her by Airmhid, her patron Goddess and still had so many packets that she couldn't identify and without knowing what they were, she was unusually indecisive about using any at all, fearing that they may be toxic.

Together with Cal, they had researched some of them through smell and texture, some recognisable still by their colouring, although again they were loath to taste them for fear of poisoning. Cal, however, had the idea to send them to a friend of his that worked in the forensics section at the Uni in York where Cal had been working and there were some rare finds indeed amongst the samples he'd sent for analysis; original strains of ancient seeds, pods and berries, root, leaf and flower. The most astonishing discovery was that they still held a life force so high, they could have been picked and dried only weeks ago; in fact that life force seemed to be increasing every time Flora opened a packet to research it.

Samantha had been recording it all and helping with the research, her interest, piqued by the history they revealed had led her to ask Flora's permission to start a grimoire of the findings and their medicinal and magickal properties, to which she'd agreed with excitement. Therefore, it was that Cal, Flora, Max and Samantha, drawn together in their tasks as researchers and herbalist became more aware of their mutual attraction…Morgan too putting in ideas and information as he remembered snippets from his studies with Sybille on Magickal Herbcraft.

They easily recognised elderflower and berries, hawthorn flower and berries; rosehips, petals from a wild rose so ancient yet the perfume lingered and the petals were velvety soft as if they were slowly reconstituting themselves. There was elecampane, poppy seed, mistletoe berries, vervain, wild violet, lily of the valley root, orrisroot and belladonna …on and on went the list as they worked and documented their findings.

Maeve had been creating pendants and brooches that were sigels, pentagrams and seven point elven-stars. She'd been buffing up on some of the more complex shapes of the astrological and alchemical symbols and their origin and so Bethan sat with Maeve as they tried to identify and translate the parchment; some to use as talismanic carvings on the candles for the rite. Some appeared to be astrological, some runic but there was a piece of information that looked very much like the language they'd all originally heard in the dreams and

Maeve had seen written the writing on the floor of her studio...

Tolto i' om en'kurunimen 'sint ar e' im i' lempe n'aa 'ala, Tolto i' gala pelu i' nom ...lempe i' pela tanya cron ar falla Kurinimen de ar Kurinimen pelu ...vilya, naur, alu ar ardai 'a talar'. Fea i' lempes tanya aman i' lempe ...vee i' kurinimen mallen illya coe firimar.

They knew that Tara understood the language but that she would only give them direct help if it were essential, unable to interfere further with their task for Samhain.

At times Bethan wondered if they would ever be ready but then the strange new courage she'd discovered inveigled its way into her consciousness and she would find herself becoming almost fierce and wild; something new and strange to her normal passivity. Not that she had ever been a complete walkover but considered more gentle, kinder than most; strangely the new feelings that were engendered seemed to enhance both her compassion and the new person that was emerging.

One of the strangest things that she'd been undergoing were headaches precisely where her third eye was situated, between her eyebrows and two spots on her head on each side of the fontanel, forming a small triangle of pain. Nothing eased it but a little of the oil, Hercurin left for her; she hadn't seen him but she knew he was there, that he watched and waited.

Chapter 53
Samhain Rite

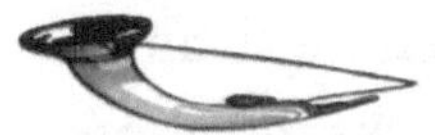

The wild folk ride through forests green
...once a year they're easily seen
They come from beyond the in-between
...breaking through the veil
Their horns sound bright, voices light
...riding through the dark of night ...with faces oh so pale
The Wild Hunt rides; hounds at their sides
...to chase the dark away
...as the Green Lord comes a-gathering in
...all who were led astray
She waits for them in a lightened glen
...where the Fae folk play
He leads them on, through the forests fair
...to the Summerlands far away
Extract from The Wild Hunt by Morgan Trethaway.

Four robed men stood hidden in the trees around the edge of the sycamore grove on the hill, their hoods pulled down over their brows, faces solemn as they contemplated the role of the male Wytch in the Rite of Samhain as the representatives of the God force.

Morgan stood in the southwest where water and earth merge as the wheel turns toward winter and the southerly winds blow strongly in the southern hemisphere; his ability to be grounded and centred, his musical skills and his abilities to change shape, were all magickal qualities that brought cohesion to the night.

Alex stood in the southeast, his earthiness and solidity would lend strength and peace to the Rite.

Cal stood in the northeast his fiery temperament, shaped and governed by a strong intellect, brought the understanding of the quest for enlightenment.

Max stood in the northwest bringing his qualities of fire and water to the energy that prevailed ...his passionate nature, with a compassionate heart.

The six women walked to the hill the cowls of their midnight blue robes pulled forward and their hands held out to their sides palms down, drawing energy from the Earth Mother as they walked...bringing her power with them.

They approached the hill, lighting a burning torch as they reached the edge of the circle and Maeve's fiery force brought light as she began the ritual of casting.

Picking up the besom, Flora walked the circle widdershins three times, to cleanse the space of any negativity.

Maeve paused on the edge of the sacred space to light a taper,

'There is but one light and it comes from above,' she spoke and then walked slowly to the Altar set for the rite; leaning over she lit the central white candle and completed, 'Let us make a beginning.'

Flora, Samantha, Susan, Claire and Bethan followed her in, walking the circle until Samantha, completing a circuit, picked up her Wand and as the others stood facing outward, she walked the circle, Wand pointing downward, energy flowing from her and into the ground …creating a trench of azure blue light, making sure to include the Altar itself within her casting.

Flora and Susan followed …lighting the incense in preparation, blessing and consecrating the salt and water …mixing the two in a thrice-spun circle, in a crystal chalice …before Flora walked the circle again,

'Earth and water where thou art cast, let no evil purpose last; in complete accord with me …as I do WILL …SO MOTE IT BE' …cleansing the trench with the forces of earth and water combined.

Susan followed with the incense, smudging, smoking, filling the trench and building the circle walls, 'as above so below.'

Maeve walked the circle with the candle, sealing and solidifying the energy within the sacred space.

Samantha paced the circle again this time with her Athame, filling the trench with the final energy to seal the circle now alight with brilliance …handing the Athame to Bethan, who walked the circle and then took a few steps into the centre, arms outstretched, Athame held point down toward the circles blue-fire, shimmering dome…and spun on the spot,

'I cast thee oh circle that thou be the boundary between the realms of men and the realms of the mighty ones …a guard and protection that will preserve and contain the energy we do raise within thee …wherefore do I bless and consecrate thee.'

As she spun, the watchers could see the blue flame fly from her Athame and the circle filled with the sound of her song as never before; the Fae gathered at the borders between the four men standing still as statues as they protected themselves and waited for the Greenlord to come…

…she spun attracting the dark as much as light to her casting.

When she was sure, the circle was cleansed and safe for all; she replaced the Athame on the Altar, returning to the centre where a large black scrying bowl stood together with her loom, around which were the anointing oil for her brow and the herbs to inhale to help her travels.

The others stepped forward to form a small tight circle around her their backs turned to her, hiding her from prying eyes and she sat on the rug and cushions prepared for her.

She smiled at her mother and her friends then looked searchingly into the darkening grove, making out the shapes of the men and her father, standing guard with others of the Fae folk. As the light dimmed, so did the glow of the nature spirits and deva increase and she could hear a hum of music and of delicate wings. To her surprise a number of Makers appeared with Tara in her human form, a Raven sat on her shoulder, which immediately flew to Morgan as she saw him in the flare of the torches, greeting him with a quiet, 'Ruaark.'

She could sense Hercurin with every fibre of her being; he was standing alone beyond the circle of fire waiting …watching …letting nothing close; his senses reaching out to her and she could smell his loamy fragrance. She closed her eyes listening for the note ...for the song and the melody within.

'Sybille,' she chanted softly, 'Sybille let me see you my friend; where are you?' Pausing again to listen for just a breath of sound from Sybille's song ...nothing ...silence ...then a note, so like her own she was confused by it and she felt more than saw Aithlin counteract the energy that would invade and entice her.

'Not yours Arianwen ...don't follow your own ...not yet little one.'

She responded by going deeper ...tracing the original note, she'd heard first. Sybille's song rose from the quiet within her, strong and true. The watchers gasped audibly as Silver stepped into the circle and approached Bethan.

'Arianwen,' she said, sprinkling a little of the herbs of seeing into the scrying water, 'breathe and release ...breathe and release. Take your time ...find the moment,' and reaching out, she placed a small drop of anointing all on the three points of Bethan's head and brow that had been causing her such pain.

Instead of the anticipated pain, warmth spread through her skull as if it were aflame ...she felt her whole crown and brow seals opening and expanding. She opened her physical eyes and saw the shapes of all those who stood beyond and within her circle lit up in their own personal energy field ...colours rampant in the purified air of the night. She felt a pressure as with awe and fear small horns sprouted from her head ...spreading wide like silvery antlers and in her innermost self she felt that she was bi-locating …running through the forest, tall and slender in robes silken fine …horns erect from her brow. She was standing once again in the clearing from her dream, a white owl glided down to land on her shoulder; High Priestess and Priest were waiting…

'There She is; She's come to us. Welcome Arwen, you honour us with your presence.'
…and she was stepping with grace toward their circle dressed in a deep blue robe, a sickle moon, shone silver on her brow between the raised antlers …and in the forest she heard the sound of the Horn, calling the Wild Hunt to the chase.

Epilogue

Stir the flames and jump the fire
...the Greenman gifts all you desire
Quote; Bethan Fenner

Only those beyond the light that glowed, where Bethan sat in the circle, could see what was happening. They stood entranced as the light flared to an almost blinding glare; Bethan shimmered and changed, flickering in and out of sight, her shape changing, horns growing from her brow. Even seated she seemed to grow, to elongate becoming translucent and at one stage disappearing entirely, Silver, who they had seen manifest out of seemingly nowhere, responding quickly, anointing Bethan's head again with oil.

It took all of the other women's strength not to turn round to see what was happening to their friend, sensing only heat and energy emanating onto their backs causing their spines to tingle, their hair to stand on end.

Following Aithlin's lead, the four men moved closer to the circle and turning, with back towards the circles glow, stood alert and aware to see the forest darkening, blighted strands of thread like substance hanging from the trees.

Morgan blinked several times to clear his sight, wanting to see the dark blight, as illusion, wiping his eyes as they watered as if full of unseen smoke, on the sleeve of his robe, a stench of rot on the cold wind that had risen almost causing him to gag. To his relief the image shimmered and was gone but he knew it was more than a premonition.

Cal stood stoic as always but wanting to turn back to see what was going on, his senses wired like a warrior's ready for battle should it come. In the trees, he could see tall dark shapes held back by a ring of shining Fae, standing with long staffs raised across their chest, pushing energy to ward off the encroaching dark.

Max simply stood mouth agape, at what he could see around him. Alex, fearful for his daughter was prevented from turning around only by the approach of a tall imposing figure, hounds at his side. He paused to touch Alex gently on the shoulder; the touch calmed him, giving him a little ease.

The Host followed, shining brilliantly as they came, riding small shaggy horses. They were dressed in their finest as if for a ball, their sombre faces belying the lightness of their dress …the dark falling away before them. Their lean white hounds with pink tipped ears ran sniffing the ground around them, baying if they caught the scent of something that should be moving on from this realm to the next. Little bright Makers flitted, soothing the lost souls led astray, guiding them home through the Veil. Then all fell silent; a great Horn echoed through the night, its notes lighting up the grove and shaking gold and amber leaves that clung to the trees …the ground vibrating under the watchers feet …they could only weep at the beauty of it.

No human saw the very air shimmer as a bewitchingly elegant figure, defying all description, stepped from the ethers. No human saw the Forest Lord Hercurin pass through the circle's boundary to take Bethan's hand and walk with her to the edge where the Lady waited; the Makers flew and music so sweet filled the air, flowers bloomed at Her feet.

Only one being saw; dropping silently from a tree, shifting shape as they fell into a great white owl that flew to land on Bethan's shoulder as the Web of Ungwe shifted; she stepped through the Veils of Tyme...

...to be continued in Silver's Threads, Book 2, Grey Weavings.

About the Author

Penny lives in the central highlands of Victoria, Australia with her husband David, a giant Wolfhound, an old tabby cat and a flock of hens. They are keen gardeners and are becoming self-sufficient on their beautiful rolling acres on the Great Divide. Their blended mob of children, are all long 'grown and flown', the coop.

Penny is a clairvoyant reader and her own experiences are very much a part of her storyline …this is her first published book although previously she has written for magazines and writes her own workshop manuals.

Born in the UK she still has a passion for the Old Ways of the British Isles and teaches the ancient traditions to many people from her centre in Daylesford.

She is currently working on Book 3 of Silver's Threads, Warp and Weft to be published, July 2013.

She feels that the gentle ways of the Pagan Wytchways is the path to take for a sustainable future, connecting us to the land no matter where we live on the planet.
You can find out more about the author at -

https://www.facebook.com/pennyreillyauthorpage
https://www.facebook.com/earthlyrites
http://www.silversthreads.wordpress.com

www.ingramcontent.com/pod-product-compliance
Lightning Source LLC
Chambersburg PA
CBHW030653120726

47905CB00001B/191